HOP SCOT

HOP SCOT

Catriona McPherson

**SEVERN
HOUSE**

First world edition published in Great Britain and the USA in 2023
by Severn House, an imprint of Canongate Books Ltd,
14 High Street, Edinburgh EH1 1TE.

severnhouse.com

British Library Cataloguing-in-Publication Data
A CIP catalogue record for this title is available from the British Library.

ISBN-13: 978-1-4483-0769-2 (cased)
ISBN-13: 978-1-4483-0786-9 (e-book)

All Severn House titles are printed on acid-free paper.

Typeset by Palimpsest Book Production Ltd.,
Falkirk, Stirlingshire, Scotland.
Printed and bound in Great Britain by
TJ Books, Padstow, Cornwall.

Praise for the Last Ditch mysteries

"An engaging plot, eccentric characters, plenty of humor"
Booklist on *Scot in a Trap*

"Darkly amusing . . . McPherson keeps the laughs and
the action rolling along"
Publishers Weekly on *Scot in a Trap*

"Wildly funny"
Kirkus Reviews on *Scot in a Trap*

"Clever turns of phrase and witty observations
fuel this fast and funny novel"
Publishers Weekly on *Scot Mist*

"Plenty of suspects and mordant humor against
a background of pandemic paranoia"
Kirkus Reviews on *Scot Mist*

"The banter among the various characters will draw
Janet Evanovich fans to this engaging,
not-quite-a-locked-room mystery"
Booklist on *Scot Mist*

About the author

Born and raised in West Lothian, **Catriona McPherson** left Edinburgh University with a PhD in Linguistics and worked in academia, as well as banking and public libraries, before taking up full-time writing in 2001. For the last ten years she has lived in Northern California with frequent visits home. Among numerous prizes, she has won two of Left Coast Crime's coveted Humorous Lefty Awards for the Last Ditch comedies.

www.catrionamcpherson.com

This book is for my friend Kathy Boone Reel,
for Phil Reel and Ashley Reel Benthall,
and in memory of Kevin Van Huddleston Reel,
with love.

THE DITCHERS

Leagsaidh 'Lexy' Campbell: 37, licensed marriage and family therapist, recent immigrant to the US, lives on a houseboat moored in the Last Ditch Slough behind the motel of the same name, in Cuento, California.

Taylor Aaronovitch: 29, Lexy's fiancé, ornithologist at a wetlands bird reserve, with a second job in a phone shop to make ends meet; only son (adopted) of Amaranth Aaronovitch.

Todd Kroger né Mendez: 39, Lexy's best friend, anaesthetist on long-term sick leave because of chronic kleptoparasitosis, lives at the Last Ditch because it is sufficiently bug-free (see Kathi Muntz) to let him relax. Works as a makeover queen (his term).

Roger Kroger: 43, Todd's husband, consultant paediatrician at a children's hospital in Sacramento.

Kathi Muntz née Poggio: 36, Lexy's other best friend, co-owner of the Last Ditch and manager of the attached Skweeky-Kleen Laundromat, lifelong germaphobe, gets illegal but effective cleaning products and insecticide from her cousin in Costa Rica, making the motel safe and clean enough for her and Todd.

Noleen Muntz: 48, Kathi's wife and co-owner of the motel.

Della Muelenbelt née Salinas: 28, Lexy's third and final best friend, receptionist at a day spa, long-time motel resident, formerly undocumented but now a citizen via marriage to . . .

Devin (briefly Dylan but it didn't take) Muelenbelt: 24, newly graduated from UCC with a master's degree in computer science.

Moved into the motel to escape dorm bullies but stayed to woo Della.

Diego Muelenbelt né Salinas: 8, son of Della and stepson of Devin. Big brother to . . .

Chihiro Muelenbelt: 2, daughter of Della and Devin.

PROLOGUE

The sacks of sand and cement were heavier than the corpse and felt even more dead, settled over a shoulder as they were, their bulk held still with both hands. The bricks scraped at tender skin and poked bruises into inner arms while they were being stacked and hefted, load by back-breaking load.

There was no running water nearby, so brimming buckets had to be carried ever so carefully along the stone passage. There was no light, so, by a guttering candle, the mortar was mixed on the flat upper panel of an old wooden door, the moulding working nicely to stop rivers of grey milk trickling out beyond the powdery berm. It brought memories of baking – only dungeon-cold instead of kitchen-warm; memories of childhood days at the beach – only dungeon-dark instead of sunshine; memories of earthing up potatoes in the spring – only dungeon-dank instead of rich and living.

Still, it had to be done. Course by course, brick by brick, the wall rose. Quicker all the time as a rhythm settled in, bricks knocked into halves to fit, thinner pieces as the arch narrowed, until near the top it was just one slice, like a biscuit. Next, a plug of mortar mixed with chips and tiny crumbs would do.

Now was the last chance before the seal was complete. On tiptoe, candle high, flame wavering, just one look. The eyes were still open, staring back, and a sharp gasp snuffed the candle out, a spiral of unseen smoke and that reek of warm wax and cold stone that would live in dreams forever.

ONE

Christmas stinks.

That is not my entry in the Grinch-off. It's a statement of plain fact about life in California. Hear me out.

The first year I lived here, I truly believed that if I made it through Halloween and Thanksgiving, things would get better. I learned a hard lesson. But then I forgot. So the next year, I relived the whole nightmare as if for the first time. The *third* year, I thought I was tough enough to take it. I learned again. This year – year four – I know it's going to hit me like norovirus and a shingles shot combined, I know I can't prepare, I know there's no escape. I just need to breathe through my mouth and try not to hit anyone.

It's the cinnamon. It's the ubiquitous, month-long, totally artificial cinnamon 'fragrance' (stench) and 'flavour' (emetic) that drenches the entire state and, for all I know, the entire country in waves so thick that if you squint, you can see them. Époisses de Bourgogne, that stinky French cheese that's banned on planes? I would hold a chunk of it to my nose like a scented hanky to survive a trip through Costco in December. The 1980s? When every woman bathed in Poison, spritzed with Opium and held her big hair in place with Elnett Extra? Like a walk through a meadow in springtime compared with Pier Nine from now till the new year.

And, as well as revolting, it's really annoying too. The stomach-churning stench/emetic of Halloween and Thanksgiving – aka pumpkin spice – is rightly condemned by all. It's no more revered than the piney-sweet naturalness of a Magic Tree in your Uber. And then they strip out the nutmeg, cloves, ginger and – I maintain – goat butthole scrapings, leaving only the cinnamon itself, revealed as the culprit of all the migraines, stomach upsets and marital discord . . . and everyone says, 'Yummy. Sprinkle some on my latte, please, so it reminds me of my holiday bathroom.'

Yes, latte. Yes, bathroom. There are cinnamon-'scented' (I say 'possessed') cakes, biscuits, scones, chocolates, coffee, tea for the love of God, plug-in air 'fresheners', fake trees, wreaths, door mats (I'm not kidding. Google 'Williams Sonoma'. But not if you've just eaten), candles (of course), deely boppers, broomsticks, soap, lotion, sanitizer these days, dental floss, drawer liners, fabric softener sheets, baskets (fruit and otherwise), heat pads for if you're ill (presumably to make you iller), binbags for if your rubbish doesn't smell bad enough already, logs because no stink is truly stunk till it's burning, tealights, pine cones, teddy bears, those bloody bottles of oil with sticks in them that only exist because they're more expensive than incense.

And all of those things, all over again, for dogs.

'You finished?' Todd asked me, when I reminded him of this one day in early December, after he had opened another door in his cinnamon-scented advent calendar and revealed a cinnamon-and-maple-bacon-flavoured white-chocolate-truffle donkey. 'Why, what does Christmas smell like in perfect-precious Scotland?'

'Sprouts,' I said. 'And the water they've been boiled in.'

'Why have I never thought of dabbing *that* behind my ears?'

'I don't get it,' I said. 'You've got such great taste eleven mo— Wait, no. You like pumpkin spice chai latte. You've got such great taste ten mo— Hang on, I just remembered Peeps. OK, for nine months a year, you've got impeccable taste, Todd. What happens to you at Christmastime? I don't understand.'

'What's that?' said Todd. 'I can't hear you over the sound of clanking chains. I think it's your business partner, Mr Marley.'

'Oh, ha-ha,' I said. 'I don't hate Christmas. I hate what you *do* to Christmas.'

'What's Bob Marley got to do with anything?' said Devin. He was a computer scientist and a testament to the problem of over-specialization in the higher education system.

'*Jacob* Marley,' said his stepson, Diego. At eight years old, he was a testament to the breadth and depth of the CUSD elementary education system. 'You know, from the Muppet movie.'

'My heart is going to break,' said Della, the third corner of this tight little triangle: Diego's mum, Devin's wife, my friend. 'My husband knows nothing and my son knows only TV.'

'MEET A MUPPETS!' shouted Hiro. I kept forgetting that the three Ds weren't actually a tight triangle anymore, not since the birth of baby Chihiro two Thanksgivings ago turned them into a sturdy square. 'LIGHT A LIGHT!' she bellowed.

'Kid's got some set a pipes on her,' said Noleen, as she always did when Hiro sang. Noleen hated kids and noise. Except for Diego, Hiro and *their* noise. As owner of the Last Ditch Motel, where we all live, she can't ban children. Most of her business is young families on road trips who can't afford anywhere nicer. She does her best, though, by having no crayons, no colour-in-able placemats at the continental breakfast station in reception, no child-friendly DVDs in the DVD library behind the desk and no cots with high sides.

'MUPPET SOW TONIGHT!' Hiro yelled. Crows in the tomato fields south of town rose and flapped away.

'She sure does,' said Kathi, Noleen's wife, co-owner of the Last Ditch and manager of the attached Skweeky-Kleen Laundromat. She was watching Hiro closely. The baby has a tendency to spit when she sings and Kathi has a bit of a germ problem (in the same way that the *Titanic* had a bit of an ice problem).

'PUT A MAKE-UP!' Hiro shrieked, after an unnecessary key change.

'No, Mami!' said Della. 'No hay segundos versos.'

'Aw, hon,' said Devin. He's a native Californian and a bit of a stoner besides, so predisposed to be a pushover to his kids. Della, in contrast, runs a tight ship. She threw her husband a look that got an 'OK' out of him and Hiro went back to smashing Lego bricks together and growling in her secret language.

'Sounds like you're coming round to the idea,' Todd said to me. 'Did you forget which side you were on?'

I opened my mouth to argue, then realized he was right. When I had agreed to go home for Christmas to let Taylor, my fiancé, meet my parents, Keith and Judith Campbell, it had felt a good long way off and quite likely to be derailed by ticket prices, COVID spikes, transport strikes, Taylor's job, my parents deciding to go on a cruise or any number of other factors. Now, here I was with less than a fortnight to go before the leaving date, staring down the barrel of it actually happening.

My last hope had been Taylor himself. He's heard enough about my mum to be wary, for a start. Also, he's Jewish so he doesn't care about Christmas, and he's Californian so he's a wimp about bad weather. Plus he's an ornithologist who hates the prospect of missing crucial migrations when he's away from the wetlands for more than a day or two. And then something else happened that made me sure he wouldn't want to witness me and my parents' tearful reunion after three and a half years. Only, because of the precise nature of the thing that happened, I pretty much had to give him final say. I hate that.

'It's Taylor's shout,' I reminded Todd. 'He hadn't decided this morning when he went to work. He said he'd tell me tonight.'

'And here he comes!' said Noleen, as we all felt the boat tip with the first foot on the bottom step near the bank. 'Place your bets, ladies and gentlemen.'

'Tenner says he wants to go,' said Todd.

'What's a tenner?' said Diego.

'Ten pounds,' I said. 'Pretty much the same as ten dollars.'

'Another good reason to go now,' Todd said. 'Fantastic exchange rate.'

'Yay,' I said. 'My country's economy tanked! Party!'

'Twenty bucks says he wants to stay home,' said Noleen. 'That's how it took me.'

'I'll split Noleen's twenty,' said Kathi, who's not much of a gambler and never disagrees with her wife.

'Does ten dollars really weigh ten pounds in Scotland?' said Diego. 'Do you use carts? Do rich people need big muscles?'

'He's a creative thinker,' Devin said to Della, who had her head in her hands.

'He should know more stuff about more things,' said Della, who had seen a documentary about Taiwanese cram schools and Googled to see if there were any in Sacramento.

'That's not Taylor,' I said. Living on a houseboat, as I do, you get to know the tread of all your friends. I would recognize Taylor's foot on the bottom step even if everyone already on board was dancing a Charleston. I could even tell the difference between him coming home from the bird reserve and from his other job at the phone shop, where he was now, making the money ornithology didn't.

The living-room door opened to reveal Roger, Todd's husband, dragging himself home from a shift as a doctor in the paediatric HDU, still in his scrubs, grey with exhaustion and wearing the expression that told us all it had been a 'bad day'. He never says any more than 'good day' or 'bad day', but it's not a tough code to crack. He kicked off his Crocs and dropped into the last remaining empty chair, stretching out a hand for the margarita Noleen was already pouring.

'I need a break,' he said, and drank the whole cocktail down in one slug. He picked Hiro up by the straps of her tiny dungarees and cuddled her. Diego immediately scrambled up on to Roger's other knee and planted a kiss on his cheek. I caught my lip in my teeth and shot a look at Todd, whose eyes had started glistening. Thing is, Roger is a rock. Scratch that; Roger makes rocks look flimsy. He never loses his temper, even with Todd, never feels sorry for himself, never complains about anything except the Giants and never makes the rest of us – makeover queen, de-cluttering guru, spa receptionist, unemployed computer scientist, motelier or even me, a marriage and family therapist – feel like lightweights. For Roger to break down far enough to chug a margarita and say he needed a break, today must have been terrible.

'*Take* a break,' said Noleen. 'There. I fixed it for ya.'

'I'm taking a break,' said Roger. 'I'm taking two weeks of a break. And that's not all.'

'Dun-dun-duh,' said Diego, to fill the pause.

'DAN-DAN-DAHHH!' said Hiro, right into Roger's ear.

'You're taking a break too,' Roger said. 'You and Kathi. Della? How do you feel about taking a break?'

'I'm begging for shifts,' said Della. 'I can't afford a break.'

'Am I taking a break?' said Todd, whose whole life was a break really.

'Taylor definitely needs a break,' said Roger, which was so true it stopped everyone squabbling while we digested it.

'I've got every intention of taking a break, no matter what,' I said. I've tried to assimilate to an extent but I will never go along with the madness that Christmas lasts one day. It's two days at least – Christmas Day and Boxing Day – and New Year the next week means it's basically eight. It's *twelve* in the song.

'Good,' said Roger. 'I bought tickets.'

'To what?' said Todd. '*The Nutcracker*? The Rockettes? Something on ice? Tickets to what?'

'Plane tickets,' Roger said. 'To Edinburgh. Ten of them. One for each of us. So we can take a break.'

'Uhhhhhhhh, what?' said Devin. He stopped smoking when he got married, but there's a hell of a tail and he's still not all that nimble, mentally.

'I can't accept an airplane ticket, Roger,' Della said.

'Edinburgh in Scotland where Lexy came from?' said Diego. 'The place with the castles?'

'FAIRY PINSISS!' said Hiro. 'LEGO! LEGO! CAN HOLD A BACK ANY MOW!'

'Dude, you can't pay for our vacations,' said Devin.

'You can pay for mine,' Noleen said. 'You owe it to me for three years of *him*.' She pointed at Todd, who closed his eyes and nodded. He knows what he's like.

'I ain't running this place on my own while you're drinking whisky up mountains,' Kathi said.

'You've got totally the wrong impression of Scotland,' I said to them, not for the first time. 'There's a Subway in Dundee. There's a KFC. There's a McDonald's.'

'MAMA! DENGO HAMBE!'

'You're always hungry,' said Diego. 'You're a donut.'

'YOU DONUT!'

'We can't take Hiro on a plane for all those hours,' Della said. 'Even if we're in a block, three sets of three and one spare, there's still across the aisle. It's not fair to the other people.'

'We're not in three sets of three on one side of a plane,' said Roger.

'We can't fly in separate seats from the baby,' Della said.

'Someone will swap,' Noleen told her. 'Anyone in their right mind would swap.'

'We're in lie-flat pods in five rows of two,' said Roger.

'Uh, hon. How much—?' said Todd.

'How the hell did you book out first class in December?' said Noleen. 'What airline is this? Tony's Cheap Flights and Grill?'

'Dude, I can't take my kids on a sketchy air—'

'I chartered a plane,' said Roger.

'Uh, hon. How much—?'

'Uh, hon,' said Roger. 'I'm a doctor. A boss doctor. We've been renting our house out to a mindlessness influencer for four years and living in two motel rooms.'

'Mindfulness,' said Todd.

'You say potato,' said Roger.

'Everyone says potato,' said Todd.

'Stop arguing!' said Roger.

There was a long whistling silence on board the boat. Diego broke it.

'Uncle Roger shouted,' he said, just as shocked as the rest of us. Roger never shouted, not even at Todd.

'DON' SOUT,' said Hiro, which at least broke the tension.

'Plus,' Roger said, 'we went nowhere and did nothing for an entire pandemic. We have so much money it's going to trigger an audit if we don't spend some. So I spent some.'

'Roger,' I said gently. I didn't want him to shout at me too. 'That is very generous of you and I hope to God you took out insurance, because Taylor hasn't said yet whether he wants to go.'

'I have twenty-four hours to confirm,' said Roger. 'But I'll tell you now: I'm going. I need to put an ocean and a continent between me and the management of that hospital just for a week or two. So we're going to Scotland with you or without you, Lexy.'

The boat dipped. Taylor was here. We waited for him in silence. All except Hiro, obviously.

TWO

The call had come at seven o'clock on a Saturday morning. I'd have ignored it, or thrown my phone out the window, or maybe answered it all set to tell the poor schlub in the overseas call centre what time it was here and curse his descendants for a thousand years. Taylor is nicer than me. He leaned over me to scrabble it into his hand and said, 'It's kinda early, bud.'

I groaned my protest – as much as I could with Taylor lying across my chest like a walrus on a rock – and not for the first time wondered if my midget houseboat bedroom really wouldn't allow for a bed that stuck out with two proper sides instead of this nook arrangement.

'What?' said Taylor in a small voice.

I opened my eyes. 'What?'

'It's Laura.'

My mental Rolodex took a minute or two, clacking through colleagues at the phone shop, fellow ornithologists, healthcare professionals and ex-girlfriends before I retrieved the information I needed: Laura was the next-door neighbour of Taylor's mum.

'Is Amaranth OK?' I said, sitting up so sharply that he rolled off my chest and banged his phone-holding elbow against the panelling.

'We'll be there in ten,' Taylor said. And then he added, 'Tell her I'm on my way.'

'Tell her?' I said as he bounded out of bed. 'So she's not—'

'Not quite. Will you drive, Lexy?'

She looked tiny, lying there in her huge seventies bed with the padded-satin headboard. She was dead centre, banked up on a dozen pillows, her twiggy little hands folded neatly on top of the blankets. Neighbour Laura was hovering near the bedroom door, a big flat patch in the shag carpet showing where she'd paced in a circle waiting for us.

'Mom.' Taylor sat on the edge of the bed and took one of the bundles of twigs in his two hands. 'She's freezing,' he said. He placed a finger against her neck at the bend of her jaw. 'But she's got a pulse. Lexy, call nine-one-one.'

'No,' Amaranth said, making all three of us jump and making Laura say 'Shit!' so loud that it reverberated around the room, despite the fact that the shag carpet, satin-covered headboard, flounced dressing table, valances, swags, throws and ruffles ate all the sounds ever made there, like those echo-suppression chambers I saw one time on *QI*.

'Mom?' Taylor said. 'Are you OK? Why are you still in bed? Why are you so cold? You need to go the ER.'

'NO!' said Amaranth. 'Yes, I'm fine. I'm in bed to die in my own bed. I'm cold because I'm dying, here in my own bed. And I don't need to go anywhere until I go to the funeral home. OK?'

'Amaranth,' I said, sitting down on her other side and taking hold of the other bundle of twigs, 'you don't— Jesus! You're like a block of ice! You're not dying, clearly.'

'Wanna bet?' said Amaranth.

'You sound fine.'

'I *said* I was fine.'

'Uhh,' said Laura, from the doorway, 'I might just . . .'

'Yeah, you get on with your day,' said Amaranth. 'Help yourself to anything in the refrigerator. I won't need it.'

'Oh, jeez,' Laura said, and scampered down the stairs.

'Busybody,' Amaranth muttered. 'Barging in here, spoiling everything.'

'You shouldn't have left the curtains open,' I said. 'Rookie mistake.'

Taylor glared at me. This, he seemed to be indicating, was no joking matter.

'So, Mom,' he said, 'can I get you some soup? Or a heat pad? You want to sit up a bit?'

'Nope, nope, nope,' said Amaranth. 'I'm done.'

'Mother, you are not dying.'

'Like you're some kind of expert,' said Amaranth. 'How many times did *you* die? Ballpark.'

'Look, we have to call a doctor,' I said. 'If we don't and you die – don't glare at me, Taylor – we could end up in jail.'

'So call my doctor,' Amaranth said. 'We discussed this. I wrote a living will and you are good so long as you don't finish me off with a pillow.'

'Jesus, Mom!'

'Calm down. She's not dying!'

And that was how she died, arguing to the end. I did call her doctor, who confirmed that she was quite within her rights to do what she was doing, that we would not get in trouble if we just sat there while she was doing it, and that he had it all in writing just in case. He stopped by early in the afternoon and asked if she was in any pain, at which point she consented to a drip. It was mostly saline solution because her kidneys were starting to ache, but he added a bit of morphine as a kind of garnish. She got somewhat loopy after that and so I suppose it's not strictly accurate to say she argued right to the end. Her second-to-last words were a heartfelt but sense-free address to someone called 'Antonio Fargas'. Her very last words were 'Be happy' which sounds like more drug stuff, but the way she said it convinced us both that she was talking to Taylor and knew what she was saying. Then, as it grew dark outside, her breathing started to slow and falter until, with no kind of fanfare at all, suddenly she breathed out and didn't breathe in again and it was over. I was still holding one of her hands.

We sat in silence for a while, then I said, 'Who's Antonio Fargas?'

'Huggy Bear,' said Taylor.

Not a bad way to go.

And a funeral always helps, of course. It was my first Jewish send-off and I had to admit it was pretty lovely. There was no recruitment drive like you get in churches sometimes, where the minister knows he's got a captive audience who might be feeling freaked out about mortality. No, this was all Amaranth: her childhood, her career, her beautiful son, her terrible jokes, her beautiful garden, her terrible cooking, her beautiful singing, her . . . striking fashion sense. Taylor recited something in Hebrew and a cantor made everyone cry. Then we all went back to the Ditch and got hammered, except the rabbi who could drink Peter O'Toole under the table apparently.

But when the funeral was over and the paperwork was done, and the realtor was there to deal with the snotty prospective buyers marching around Amaranth's gorgeous rooms, sniffing about the amount of work 'needed', that's when it really hit, as it always does, or so every grieving client I've ever had tells me.

I could have told Taylor it was a bad time to go looking for his biological parents, which presumably is why he didn't say anything until he got the letter stating his birth father was unknown and his birth mother had listed herself as uncontactable. Even then he didn't so much share it with me as be found raging drunk on the motel forecourt howling at the moon.

'I wasn't howling at the moon. I was singing.'

'It was a full moon and the lyrics were "Aaaah-oooww",' said Noleen. 'I had to comp the night for that family of uptight assholes in room two-oh-two. Trust me, kid, if I could have said it was a cabaret, I'd be a hundred and eighty dollars richer today.'

He'd been that way for four months now – no way to tell how anything was going to take him. A sad song would make him curl his lip and roll his eyes, but then an advert for assisted living would destroy him. A kid in a really good Halloween costume made his chin wobble as he remembered Amaranth hulking him up with green body paint and papier mâché muscles, but he watched the Queen's funeral dry-eyed until the corgis, which is the least amount of crying compatible with basic humanity.

And then there was the indecisiveness. He couldn't choose a pizza topping unless you threatened him with anchovies, so trying to get him to decide between his first holiday season in Cuento without his mother or his first holiday season in Scotland with mine was a challenge. Still, he had promised to tell me tonight before all the cheap seats were sold and we ended up going via Sydney.

'Hi,' he said, opening the door. 'You know something? I can tell when you're all here by how much the boat doesn't rock from the extra weight. Never try to throw a surprise party.'

'Good day?' I said uselessly while Noleen, more effectively, passed him a drink.

'I helped people choose between functionally identical over-priced baubles to give as Christmas presents to other people who'll sulk because they got it wrong,' said Taylor. 'You?'

'I listened to them sulking,' I said. 'Say, speaking of Christmas . . .'

'Yeah, fuck it,' said Taylor. 'Let's go.'

'Dude,' said Devin, meaning *please don't say that word in front of my children*.

'At least I'll be able to swear for a week or two without getting stink-eye,' said Taylor, raising his glass to Della who was, indeed, giving him an impressively filthy look.

'Ha,' I said. 'You've never met my mother. Swearing in front of Judith Campbell? Heaven forfend. My dad used to go down the garden and swear in the shed.'

'I thought all Scottish people swore like dockers,' said Kathi. 'Is it just you? And Kevin Bridges?'

'Wait and see,' I said.

Taylor had drained his glass and now he looked at me through the bottom of it. 'What do you mean, wait and see?' he said. 'Is Kathi going to Scotland? When?'

'We're all going,' I said. 'Roger got a flight and we're all going together. My mum will probably blow a gasket that I'm finally visiting and she won't get me to herself, but you lot can rent Airbnbs that are nowhere near our house and do your own thing. You don't even need to come to Dundee. You can go wherever you like.'

'No way,' Taylor said. 'If you're all coming with, I want you right there to protect me.'

'Lexy,' said Diego, 'are there castles in Dundee?'

'Oh, honey,' I told him, 'not really. I mean, there are castles nearby, but Dundee's just kind of . . . There's a big ship, though.'

'Are there pirates on it?' he said. 'Are there dragons in the sea?' And so I stopped trying to be a tour organizer and phoned my mum.

'Well?' she said, instead of 'hello'.

'You sound hollow,' I said. 'Where are you?'

'What? I'm in your bedroom, but it's empty because we're still decorating. Don't tell me I'm wasting my time. Keith! Ke-ith? It's Lexy.'

'That's my bedroom?' I said. 'It sounds like an aircraft hangar. Did you scrape off the Anaglypta?'

'Hiya, poppet,' my dad shouted. 'Put it on speaker.'

'I'm putting you on speaker, Lexy. She wants to know if we're scraping off the Anaglypta.'

My dad gave a rich chuckle that I didn't understand. Either they were doing something heinous to my old bedroom, in Taylor's honour, or he was drunk.

'Drumroll,' I said. 'We're coming. We're coming for two weeks. Roger, when are we arriving?'

'Tuesday, December twenty,' Roger said.

'Tuesday the twentieth of December,' my mum said.

'I know,' said my dad. 'We're on speaker.'

'And,' I said, 'we're not coming alone.'

'You're pregnant,' said my mum. 'You can get married while you're here. Keith, she's pregnant!'

'She's not,' said my dad. 'I know that because we're on speaker.'

'Roger and Todd are coming,' I said, testing the water. My mum had been kind of fascinated by Todd ever since she, briefly, believed he might be the man for me. And she was genetically incapable of not loving a doctor.

'Wonderful,' she said. 'About time we met them.'

'Cool.' I took a breath. 'And Kathi and Noleen are coming.'

'They're shutting the motel?' said my mum. 'Is that wise? Hospitality is a twenty-four/seven/three-six-five business.'

That, I thought, was a weird take. I quirked a look at Noleen.

'We'll get cover, Judith,' she said. 'We'll pay a guest manager.'

'Well, you deserve it,' said my mum. 'It's hard work and you should pamper yourselves for a change.'

That was an even weirder take. And it was funny to see the look on Kathi's face at the mention of 'pampering'. She can get quite fierce on the unfairness of women being asked to feel lucky for cleaning their bodies when men get baseball.

'Keith,' my mum went on, 'the two "owners" are coming.' 'Owners' was in heavy quotes because – I think – she meant 'lesbians'.

'I know, Judith. We're on speaker.'

'OK,' I said. 'And, finally, Della and Devin and Diego and Hiro are coming,' I spoke very fast as if it would sound like fewer people that way. I think it sounded like more.

'Oh, lovely!' said my mum. 'That's lovely.' Hiro had fallen

asleep and so she didn't blast a correction to this. 'Christmas is all about the children, isn't it?' my mum went on. 'How old are they? I'll get them stockings. No! I'll get everyone stockings. This is going to be the best Christmas ever. Keith, those two whoever-they-ares are coming and bringing the children with the funny names.'

'Mum,' I said. 'You're on speaker.'

'I'll get stockings!' she shouted, so they could all hear. Hardly the point, but I was so flabbergasted by how well this was going that I said nothing.

'So we're all invited for Christmas dinner?' said Taylor.

'Oh hello, Taylor,' said my mum. 'Can you eat Christmas dinner? Is it allowed? I won't put any bacon on the turkey. Or would you prefer . . .'

'I'll give you a thousand dollars if she can finish that sentence,' I told Taylor, with my hand over the phone.

'. . . brisket?' said my mum. 'And no, everyone isn't invited for Christmas dinner, Lexy. Everyone's invited for Christmas. We've plenty room.'

'Have we?' I said. 'Have you cleared the loft? How is there room for ten people in our house?'

'As long as Doo-dah and Dilbert can share with Dido and little Dingbat.'

'Jesus Christ,' I said.

'That's the spirit, Lexy,' my dad shouted. 'Plenty room in the stables! Let me know when your plane lands and I'll meet you.'

'We'll have to hire a couple of cars, Dad,' I said. Even if somehow we could all be squashed into Keith and Judith's modest bungalow, there was no way we could fit in my dad's Skoda, Octavia though it might be.

'I'll meet you,' he said again. 'Looking forward to it. Couple of weeks! Yay!'

I hung up and stared at my phone. 'My dad just said "yay".'

'Your mum said "brisket",' Taylor reminded me. 'You owe me a thousand bucks.'

'Lexy, I'm not being funny,' said Roger. 'Do your parents ever do D-R-U-G-S? Because that was weird.'

'Drugs,' said Diego.

'You're such cynics,' Kathi said. 'I might fight her off with a dry loofah if she actually tried it, but the woman said we needed pampering. She sympathized with the plight of service-industry professionals.'

'She did, didn't she?' I said. 'Roger, I don't know what to tell you. They didn't when I lived there, but if I hear tomorrow that a new neighbour brought round some funny-tasting brownies, I wouldn't be surprised.'

'Will we have to share a bathroom?' Todd said.

'No,' I lied, because I couldn't face breaking the bad news to this many Americans all at once that they might have to share actual bathwater too, unless the immersion heater was getting an upgrade along with the bumpy wallpaper of my tender years.

THREE

Tuesday 20 December

As business class ruins coach and Egyptian cotton ruins polyester, Roger's chartered jet instantly ruined every kind of travel from first class on Emirates to hanging off a trolley in the New Orleans French Quarter. I had been hoping it would go the other way: like how artisanal sourdough is all very well but you still need white sliced for a decent toastie, or how a film that won the Palme D'Or will never outshine *Mamma Mia*. But I knew, from the minute I stepped on board and saw the sheepskin slippers waiting for me, that this was going to be caviar in place of pilchards.

'Fuck me,' said Taylor. 'The inflight movie is *Wakanda Forever*.'

'Would you care for a drink while we prepare for take-off?' said Gloria, the flight attendant who had come right into the departure lounge to fetch us. She was as tall, polished and terrifying as a supermodel. That always brings out the worst in me.

'I'd like a lavender and lime gin, please,' I said, like an arse.

'Certainly, Ms Campbell.'

'Call me Lexy,' I said.

She hesitated. She wasn't going to, but she didn't feel able to say 'no' to a customer either. She was stuck.

'Or, tell you what,' I offered. 'What's *your* second name?'

'Naify,' she said, mystified.

'So I'll call you Ms Naify,' I explained. 'Or, my preference, you call me Lexy.'

'I'll call you Leagsaidh,' Gloria said. She was definitely saying it in Gaelic and with a pretty decent accent too. 'But to return to the question of your refreshment: can I just check? Do you mean our regular gin with lavender cordial and a twist of lime? Our regular gin's botanicals are juniper and cassia bark. Or do you mean a gin with lavender and lime as part of its actual botanical infusion? I'm afraid our lavender gin has rose in it too, and our only lime gin includes cucumber. You could mix them, but that number of botanicals might lead to a confusing palate experience.'

'She'll have a glass of champagne,' said Taylor. 'And I'll have the rest of the bottle.'

Gloria walked off up the aisle placing each stilettoed foot in front of the other so that her hips wiggled. Todd nodded his approval.

'You look happy,' I said accusingly.

He was instantly suspicious. 'I appreciate beauty,' he said. 'That is a beautiful woman.'

Who could open champagne bottles silently and pour it without a hint of froth, I noted two minutes later.

'Cheers, Gloria,' I said.

'Slàinte mhar, Leagsaidh,' she replied. Amazing.

I slept like the dead, on my mattress-toppered seat, under a goose-down duvet after a supper of lobster ravioli and jackfruit roulade, and, since Hiro had conked out on take-off too, I only woke when we started to come down. I opened my eyes and looked across the aisle to where Roger was still spark out. He'd been that way all night, like he'd been shot with an elephant tranquilizer. It was a pure waste of the catering. Beyond him, Diego – who had negotiated not to sit next to either of his parents since he was eight now – snuggled under a sleeved blanket with his initial on the front in 3D-effect Lego bricks. He was purple with exhaustion around the eyes and orange with cheese powder around the mouth, having reacted to finding every episode of *Paw Patrol* ever made right there on his private telly by announcing his attention to stay awake until he'd watched the lot.

'We're falling,' he said in a Zombie voice.

'We're *landing*,' I told him, and screwed round to look out the window.

Home. There it was in all its fluorescent-green glory, like the home-made surround for a toy railway. Minuscule fields, tiny snaky roads, splats of loch, smudges of forest. I held my bottom lip in my teeth to stop it wobbling as I saw the bridges over the Forth, the pink shale bings and the blue-grey roof slates. It wasn't even raining. I caught sight of Edinburgh Castle, squat on its rock, its windows blazing with reflected sunshine, and the bare hump of Arthur's Seat rising up out of the city like a . . . well, a boil.

'Is that really a volcano?' Taylor said, pressing his face beside mine.

'Blerch, your breath! You finished that champagne, didn't you?' I said.

'Oh, I'm steaming,' he assured me. 'I'm bladdered.'

'You're going to get yourself beaten up if you keep using Scottish slang,' I said. 'No one will believe you're not taking the piss. Yes, it's a volcano but it's extinct. For God's sake, get Gloria to give you a Tic-Tac.'

'Mint, orange or cinnamon?' Gloria said, instantly there. She looked as fresh and dewy this morning as she had last night, and also somehow gave off an air of having spent the in-flight hours learning Portuguese or recording talking books for the blind.

'Mint, please,' said Taylor. Then under his breath to me, 'She's been like that all night. That's why I kept drinking. Give me United any day.'

'MY TUMMY IS BUSY,' Hiro informed us and the outer suburbs of Edinburgh we were descending over.

'We're landing, dude,' said Devin. 'Wheeeeee!'

'WHEEEEEEE!' Hiro agreed.

'Uncool,' said Diego, as he fast-forwarded through a title sequence to get another episode under his belt while he still could.

And then, with a lurch and a bump and a long, terrifying hurtle along the runway, we had arrived.

'Well, dip me in chocolate and chill me,' Todd said, as we taxied in towards our gate. He reached over the seatback to shoogle Roger awake. 'Honey, look at that.'

I peered out to see what had grabbed them but couldn't spot anything except the two planes on either side of us and our own jetway being un-concertina-ed to meet us.

Roger yawned, stretched, scratched a bit and leaned over Diego to look out of the window. He gave a long, low whistle. 'I didn't believe it,' he said. 'But it's true.'

'What?' I said, standing up and crossing the aisle to get a

clue. Their faces were pressed up against the windows, misting the glass and clearing it again as they breathed out and in.

'I *still* don't believe it,' said Todd, 'and I'm looking at it.'

'What?' I said. I checked again: two planes being unloaded, a bit of tarmac and a couple of bollards.

'You told me Scotland was mono-ethnic,' Roger said. 'But I had no idea what that meant. Lexy, am I really sitting here looking at white people moving stuff around an airport? Is this real?'

'Oh,' I said. 'That. Well, Dundee's quite a big city but, yes, you are going to be kind of prominent during your stay.'

'I'll help you,' said Todd. He was barely brown, being half-Mexican, but he feels that his beauty makes him remarkable wherever he goes.

'Aha!' I said. 'See? You should have looked at Gloria with pity, not with wonder. Caught you. See?'

'What the hell are you on about?' said Todd.

Gloria, having heard her name, approached us gamely, but even she was unable to convert my outburst into a request for service.

Roger rolled his eyes but said nothing.

It's infuriating to think we got through immigration and customs quicker because we came off a chartered jet and looked rich, but suspiciously soon we had made our goodbyes to Ms Naify and were trudging along a grubby grey corridor, strewn with abandoned luggage trolleys, towards a set of scuffed swing doors.

'It's cold,' said Della. She was wearing a long black puffy coat and a hat with a pom-pom bigger than her head.

'I told you it was going to be cold,' I said.

'But why is it cold inside?'

'What can I tell you?' I said. 'It's cold inside because we're rubbish. You're going to hate it. The food's terrible too.'

'Well, Merry Fricking Christmas, Lexy,' she said.

'MELLY FICKING KISSMISS!'

'Where is the nearest castle?' said Diego.

I didn't tell him the truth, which was 'three miles off', but at least I didn't tell him the greater truth either, which was 'not as near as the nearest Burger King'.

'This airport needs a makeover,' said Todd. 'Did that carpet start life greige or did something happen?'

'Both, probably. And the whole country needs a makeover,' I said. 'I kept trying to warn you.' I had done my best to veto all seasonal Netflix in the last two weeks, urging them to watch *Trainspotting* instead. They were defiant and determined. *The Holiday*, *Bridget Jones* and even *Outlander* had been on hard rotation. 'Cotswolds, Cotswolds, fantasy,' I told them. They watched *Local Hero* and ignored me.

When the doors at the end of the corridor opened, though, I took a break from expectation management and just for a minute or two let it wash over me. The air was chilly, suffused with the smell of greasy pastry from a nearby Greggs, and clanking like a broken bell with the downbeat and lumpen sound of Scottish people talking. There were no valley girls here, no uptalk, no squees or marvelling. Just clots of Scots saying stuff, sounding like sea lions. I swallowed hard. Marks and Spencer's doorway had stands of mince pies nice and handy for the shoplifters, and I could see *Daily Mails* and cans of Irn-Bru in the McColl's. I felt tears begin to gather even before I heard their voices.

'Lexy! Lexy! Keith, look!'

'Lexy! Lexy! Taylor, is that you?'

I stopped dead in my tracks, gave in and let the tears roll down my face. It was my mum and dad. It was Keith and Judith Campbell in the flesh, waving madly and slopping their take-out coffee, eyes shining, mouths beaming, unchanged after four years.

Except they weren't unchanged at all. My dad had shaved his hair down to a wink of silver, and my mum had dyed hers ash blonde with a lilac streak tucked behind one ear. They were both wearing jeans too, and not-quite-matching (but close enough to be wrong) padded jackets with checked linings. Plus my dad had hold of two helium balloons, a stegosaurus and a unicorn.

'BOONS!' said Hiro, making all the security staff look up and take a glance our way.

'One for you,' said my mum, 'and one for you.' She bent close to Diego and said, 'I know you're a great big boy of eight, but it'll help your baby sister feel at home if you take one too.'

Then she straightened up and threw her arms round me in a sneak attack. 'Oh, Lexy,' she said. 'Welcome home!' She let go with one arm and, gripping even tighter with the other, added, 'Taylor, come on. Group hug.'

Group hug? I glanced over to where my dad was standing up on his tiptoes to reach over Roger's shoulders.

'Group hug!' said Todd, piling on. 'You know, Keith, your daughter has spent the last three years saying all Scots are as uptight as she is. What a weirdo.'

'So, Dad, did you get the hire cars sorted?' I said, extricating myself from my mum's arms.

'Your carriages await!' said my dad. 'There's a nine-seater and my Octavia, so who wants to go where?'

'You hired us a bus?' I said. 'What if people want side trips?'

'They can take my wee run-around,' said my mum.

It was news to me that she owned such a thing. We had been a one-car family my whole life.

'Not that it matters who goes where for *this* journey,' said my dad. He seemed to be bursting with some kind of suppressed excitement. 'It's not even half an hour. Let's just all stuff in and get the luggage stored.'

'It's a good hour at least,' I said. The new bridge couldn't have made that much difference.

'Oh no it's no-ot,' said my mum, whose eyes were dancing too.

'Oh what are you ta-alking about?' I said.

My mum and dad shared a look and nodded some secret agreement.

'We're not going to Dundee!'

'We're going to a holiday cottage!'

'Only it's not a cottage!'

'We're going to . . . Mistletoe Hall!'

Nine Californians said, 'Ooo-ooo-oooh!' Well, eight of them said, 'Ooo-ooo-oooh!' and Hiro said 'OOO-*OOO*-OOOH!'.

I said, 'Where the hell's Mistletoe Hall?'

'It's in a little village in Midlothian called Yule,' my mum said. 'Yule! How perfect is that? Let's go. The baby seats are in the Octavia,' she added to Della. 'And I assume you want to come with them? And, Lexy, you come with us too. Keith, wait for us if you get there first. We'll all go in together.'

'Did you know about this?' said Taylor.

'Did I know that my mum and dad were renting the kind of holiday cottage with a Christmassy name that's still available after the start of December?' I said. 'Take a guess.'

Outside the terminal, there were more people standing smoking than I had seen since first touching down in California.

'Mama, que es ese olor?' said Diego, holding his nose with one mittened hand.

'Papi—' said Della.

'Don't worry,' I told her. 'No one speaks Spanish.'

'MAMA! WHAT THAT MELL?' said Hiro, so we bundled them away from the doorway towards where the cars were waiting.

I had to pause on the way, mind you. The Greggs grease inside had filled my heart to a point I thought was bursting, but out here was even worse: there was a damp, somehow metallic tang in the air even on a dry, crisp day like this one and it filled me with an aching memory of diesel fumes from a bus in the bike lane, the sting of grit on hands and bare knees from falling over in an asphalt playground and the solidifying slush to sludge to stop of pulling over to park in litter-filled puddles. Home.

'Get a wriggle on, Lex!' my dad shouted. I shook myself back to life and saw that everyone else and all the bags were packed into a silver people carrier and my dad's car. I hurried over and folded myself into the passenger seat of the Octavia, breathing deep to smell the Murray Mints but finding only hand sanitizer. Life had moved on here too.

My phone rang before we were out of the car park. It was Todd, demanding speakerphone. I could see him in the front seat of the minibus hugging our bumper. 'More of a road trip if we all talk all the way,' he said. 'And your dad won't let me Google the place.'

'*I* Googled it,' said Noleen. 'Website under construction.'

'Oh God,' I said.

'Mistletoe Hall,' said Diego as we swung up on to the bypass. 'It sounds like a fairytale, Lexy's Mom.'

'What do you bet that name's on a decal?' I said. 'One week only. It'll have changed to Shortbread Acres by Hogmanay.'

'HOGMANAY!' said Hiro.

'Is that a curse word?' Della asked. She was still huddled in her puffy coat waiting for the car heater to kick in.

'It *looks* like a fairytale too, poppet,' my mum said, catching Diego's eye in the rear-view mirror.

'Mu-um, don't tease him.'

'What kind of place is Yule?' I heard Roger ask in the other car.

'Oh, a lovely spot,' said my dad. 'Untouched, quaint, out of time.'

'Uh-huh, uh-huh,' Roger said. 'How about the diversity?'

My dad sucked his breath over his teeth and I was flooded with love. I hadn't realized I'd missed that sound. 'Well, son, I'd have to say that you lot are probably going to add all the diversity Yule has ever seen in its life.'

'Great,' said Roger.

'But they'll love you,' said my dad. 'It's not like over by.'

'Dad!' I said. 'Stop talking.'

'We've got Graham Norton, and Stephen Fry, and Clare Balding, and what's her name, Judith?'

'Dad!' I said. 'Please stop talking.'

'Sandi Toksvig,' said my mum.

'I meant race actually,' said Roger.

'Me too,' my mum lied. 'Sandi Toksvig is Norwegian.'

'God Almighty,' I said. 'Dad, start talking again.'

'And anyway, Keith,' said my mum, 'one of the ladies on the mobile library that stops in Yule every other week is Vietnamese.'

'Now how the hell,' I asked her, 'do you know that?'

'I'm not telling you,' she said. Which I took to mean that she had made it up on the spur of the moment.

'Why is there a skid mark on that hill?' said Todd.

I peered out of the side window. 'It's a ski-slope,' I said. 'That is Edinburgh's winter sports centre.'

'That,' said Todd, 'is a tragedy.'

'I tried to tell y—'

'OH MY GOD!' said Taylor and, even though he was in the other car, it sounded like he was screaming half an inch from my earhole. I twisted round in my seat, expecting to see the minibus slewing on a patch of ice and heading for disaster.

'Steady on,' my dad said. 'Mind I'm driving.'

'Did you see that?' said Taylor. He had wound down his window and he was hanging out of the minibus to his waist.

'Someone grab him, for God's sake!' I said. 'Mum, watch the road.'

My mum was following the drama in the rear-view mirror and had strayed out of her lane.

'That was a snow bunting!' said Taylor. 'An Arctic snow bunting! Did anyone see it? It was on that branch hanging over the big puddle. A snow bunting!'

'Aye, we've had quite a cold snap, right enough,' said my dad. 'Grand frosty days. Good walking weather.'

'A snow bunting!' said Taylor.

'Yeah,' said Roger. 'Even the birds are white.'

FOUR

My mum definitely took the tourist trail. There was no way the actual sensible route to get anywhere was on these ludicrous little roads with the switchbacks and humpy bridges.

'Isn't Midlothian lovely?' she said to Della.

'Lexy told us it was a Hollywood lie,' Della said. 'Weirdo.'

'Are we going through Penicuik?' I said. 'Are you going to show everyone the shopping centre with the rusty bus shelters outside?'

'Oh My Golden Ticket to the Chocolate Factory!' came Todd's voice from the other car. 'Did that sign say *Roslin*?'

'Roslin Chapel,' I heard my dad say. 'Roslin Glen, Roslin Castle . . . That's one day out for sure.'

'What's a glen?' said Diego.

'It's a magical forest full of elves and fairies,' said my mum.

'ELLS AND FAILIES!'

When I was a kid, shouting in the car – or the street or the house for that matter – was dealt with by a swift cold swipe at my self-esteem. No one delivered disappointed like Judith Campbell in those days. Hiro's earsplitting yell produced a different response. My mum shouted back.

'*ELVES AND FAIRIES!*'

'I like your mom, Lexy,' said Diego.

I said nothing. I thought: *That's not my mum.*

'Not far to go now,' she was saying. 'Ten minutes to Mistletoe Hall!'

The roads got even smaller once we were past Roslin. Steep hills rose on either side of us and we made our way along the bottom of a glen in deep shadow, only the highest tips of the bare trees catching a bit of sunlight. Then we started to climb again, the engine straining as it hauled five people and a bootful of luggage up a gradient unknown in Cuento.

'Here we are,' said my mum, swinging on to the end of a

street that suddenly popped up in the middle of farmland, as
Scottish villages tend to do.

'Oh!' said Della softly.

She was right. It was lovely. There was a double row of low
stone cottages, most with smoke curling out of their chimneys
and wreaths on their front doors. A pub – the Holly Inn – had
a full-on fuse-buster of Christmas lights and other crap flung
over it, plus a few smokers sitting outside on picnic benches,
huddled in bobble hats and woolly scarves, holding their vapers
awkwardly in thick gloves. They waved as we passed, and my
mum gave them a toot on her horn.

'There's a shop too,' my mum said. 'Look.' A bit further on
from the pub, there was indeed a wooden lean-to tacked to the
side of a wee stone house, its walls choked with creepers and
its windows choked with small ads, curling up from condensation. *Ivy's Everyday Stop*, the sign said. *Milk, Papers, Rolls,
Gossip*. I gave it a reluctant half-smile for honesty. 'And a village
hall,' my mum said. 'Yoga, Sunday and Wednesday.'

'Right through the holidays?' said Della.

'Well, no, probably not,' said my mum. 'Still, though.'

'It's a nice wee place,' I said. 'I'll give you that much. How
was this "Mistletoe Hall" still free to be rented?'

'Why are you saying it with air quotes, Lexy?' came my dad's
voice from the other car.

'You can't "say" air qu— Oh never mind,' I said. 'Kind of
pretentious, that's all.'

'Here we are,' said my mum, swinging off the road, through
a pair of stone gateposts. We rolled around a curve made of
monster rhododendrons and came to a halt under a misshapen
and ugly-looking tree, with pom-poms of mistletoe rattling in
the breeze. The minibus drew up alongside.

'Fu-udge me,' said Taylor. 'Wow.'

'Roger? Honey? Wake up,' Todd said. 'We're here.'

'Wow,' said Roger groggily.

'Wow,' I said, staring, because it was . . . well, it was a lot of
stone: stone steps, a stone arch, stone mullions, stone crow-step
gables, a stone turret or at least a kind of a bit that looked a
hell of a lot like – no, damn it, that was a turret. And stone
crenellations guarding a walkway on the roof.

'It's a castle,' breathed Diego.

'No, it's not,' I told him. I had recovered. 'It's fake. It's Victorian Gothic.'

'Victorian?' came Kathi's voice from the other car. 'Seriously? You're saying this place is like a hundred something years old?'

'Oh, for God's sake,' I said.

'It's a castle!' said Diego. 'He unbuckled his booster seat, opened his door and jumped out. 'A castle! A castle!'

'ME OUT NOW!' said Hiro, setting off a car alarm somewhere on the street behind us.

I stepped out and looked around, at the rhododendron leaves French-tipped in frost, at the discreet white lights decorating the potted bay cones at either side of the stone porch, and at the pale plume of woodsmoke outlined against the deep blue sky.

'You did good here, Mum,' I said. 'What's wrong with it? Are we sharing with a bagpipe academy? Rehab facility?'

'We've got the whole place,' my dad said. 'Not that there's anything wrong with bagpipes. Or people in recovery.'

He marched up the steps, leaving me gaping. Again.

'I like your dad,' Taylor said. 'Sound bloke.'

'Did he teach you the phrase "sound bloke"?' I said.

'He did. OK, Todd! Let's get these bags inside.'

'That's no way to talk about our friends,' said Todd.

Kill me now, I muttered to myself. He had learned Dad jokes in a half-hour drive. This was going to be a long fortnight.

So yes, I was sulking, it's true. My parents had been taken away and replaced by people in jeans who had good ideas and were fun for tired little children; my friends had landed in Edinburgh on one of the few days it wasn't raining and thought I was a drama queen who'd lied to them about everything; our cheesy B & B was absolutely gorgeous; I was going to have to say I'd been wrong. Stuff like that. But I swear, when I got to the top of those stone steps and entered Mistletoe Hall, a shudder of pure premonitional dread shrank my scalp, stole down my spine like a stream of ice water and made my legs tingle. Honestly.

Unfortunately, in a burst of seasonal goodwill I didn't say anything, so no one will ever believe me. They might not have noticed me anyway. There was too much ooh-ing and aah-ing

going on for a 'Brrrr' to register. There was plenty to ooh
and aah at too.

A fire was crackling in the entrance-hall fireplace, underneath a
stag's head with a tinsel cat's cradle wound around its antlers. There
was a library with a lot of green velvet and leather, a pale-blue
drawing room with plasterwork that made it look like Wedgwood,
a dining room with a table to seat roughly twenty, and a billiard
room that stank of a hundred and fifty years of cigar smoke
and brandy.

'What's that green fluffy table for, Mama?' Diego said.

'It's for bad boys, Papi,' said Della, who needed to hear about
the differences between billiards and pool sometime over the
holiday.

'Upstairs!' my mum cried. 'Everybody upstairs to see your
rooms.'

We trooped up the sweeping staircase to the first floor where
my mum and dad led us through the suite of two bedrooms and
ornate bathroom that were earmarked for the Ds. Diego boggled
hard at the pattern of flowers and leaves painted on the washbasin
and toilet bowl.

'ROSA BAÑO!' said Hiro.

'Those are peonies,' said my mum. 'I think it's a pun. You're
through here, ladies.'

Kathi and Noleen's room had windows on two sides looking
out over a bare winter garden and ploughed fields beyond. There
was a fireplace with a wigwam of logs waiting for a match, and
a pair of chaises longues drawn up close to it. Kathi poked her
head into the bathroom.

'Peanut bath, babe,' she said. 'No tap end. Judith, we are going
to be pret-ty pruny for the next two weeks.'

My mum chuckled and then crooked a finger to beckon the
remaining four onwards.

'This is for Taylor and you, Lexy,' she said, opening a door.
'Naked favouritism,' she said to Todd. 'My daughter, my choice.'

Todd narrowed his eyes and entered to see what we were
getting that he wasn't. Our room had windows on two sides too,
plus a little bulge of turret with an extra window on the curve.
There was a four-poster bed, another fireplace, a glass-fronted
bookcase and a bathroom that made me catch my breath. It might

not have been longer but it was definitely wider than my entire boat. It had a fireplace too and a rocking horse.

'And we're in the attic, are we?' said Todd sourly. 'On a foldaway?'

'Well, here's the thing,' my mum said. 'There isn't another bedroom as such.'

'Uh-huh,' said Todd.

'So we've put you and Roger over the billiard room,' my mum said. 'If you come and see.' She crossed the landing and dodged into a little side hall. Todd, arms folded, followed her. Roger brought up the rear. I scuttled after them, saying, 'You can have ours. I don't know why she would be so rude, but I don't mind.' This was a lie. I had never considered how much I wanted a rocking horse in my bathroom but, now that I'd been given one, it would be a wrench to give it up.

'Oh my gorgonzola gratin,' Todd said. His voice sounded very loud and kind of echoey.

'It's the ballroom,' my mum was saying, as I stepped inside. It was too. It had to be forty foot long and twenty foot across, with gilded mirrors from waist height to vaulted ceiling and an over-the-top gilded bed on the band dais at one end. 'There's not a great deal of hanging space,' my mum said. 'And the bathroom's only got a—'

But Todd wasn't listening. He had thrown his head back and his arms wide and was spinning like a Disney princess. 'A ballroom!' he said. 'It's perfect. Hiro! Get in here!'

'Christ,' said Roger. 'This is going straight on his wish list for our forever home, isn't it Lexy? He'll want a ballroom now, as well as a spiral staircase.'

'There *is* a spiral staircase,' said my mum, missing the point. 'In the tower just opposite. It's the quickest way to the kitchen.'

'And where's the room you've picked out for you and Dad?' I said. I was back out on the landing and, as far as I could see, Della's, the kids', Kathi's and mine took up the entire floor with Todd's ballroom tacked on. There was nowhere left for my parents.

'We're downstairs in the basement,' my mum said.

'Well, that doesn't sit right,' said Kathi, coming out of her doorway. 'You found this place and you won't let us chip in to pay for it. You should at least have one of the good bedrooms.'

'Oh, we're fine where we are,' my mum said, with a lilt in her voice that sounded halfway to a giggle. 'We're perfectly comfortable. Come and see.'

So we all tramped down the stone spiral staircase with Diego saying 'wow' and Hiro briefly speechless as she negotiated the steps. We pitched out in a flagged passageway opening on to a cavernous kitchen with a slate floor, whitewashed walls, roughly a thousand copper pans hanging on hooks and a range cooker in pillar-box red belching out waves of heat.

'Um, is this the only kitchen?' I said. 'I mean, it's quaint and everything but is there a dishwasher? Is there a coffee machine?'

'It's *not* the only kitchen,' my mum said, still with that unaccountable chuckle. 'Come and see.' She took a Yale key out of her jeans pocket and opened a door opposite. 'Look,' she said. There was a very different kind of set-up in here: a modern little galley with microwave, espresso machine, rice cooker and electric kettle.

'Nice,' I said. 'It's got parsley and basil on the windowsill just the way you like, Mum.' It had just the kind of china she liked too – plain white without so much as a gold rim.

'Go through and look at the living room,' she said.

Beyond a door at the far end lay the neatest living room I'd ever seen since the last time I was in my parents' house. The plain carpet was hoovered into stripes like a lawn, and a row of cushions stood on their points along the back of the velvet couch with all the nap brushed to face the same way.

'That's the same couch as you've got,' I said. 'No wonder you said you wanted this bit. And those lamps are pretty simil— Wait. Hang on. That's— Mum, is that Dad's snoozing chair? Did you—? This is weird. Did you bring your furniture?'

'Yes!' said my mum. 'We brought all our furniture!'

'I don't—'

'I do,' said Todd. 'Come on, Lexy.'

'Well, of course you do,' I said. 'You've brought more luggage with you than Scott took to the Antarctic. You would have brought furniture if you'd thought of it.'

'Oh come *on*, Lexy,' Taylor said. 'Engage brain. We got to come here for Christmas. We're not paying. Your mom knows the ethnicity of the local librarian. All her furniture is here. Huh? Huh?'

I frowned at him, still not getting it, hampered by having known my parents my whole life. 'I give up,' I said.

'We bought it!' my mum said. 'We own it! This is our flat and upstairs is our business! You are our first guests! You are our guinea pigs!'

'But . . . but . . .' I said. I didn't know where to start. 'How could you afford it?' I went for in the end. 'There must have been a feeding frenzy when this hit the market.'

'It was a private sale,' my mum said. 'We bought it from a dear old couple who wanted to move somewhere easier to run. They're just along the street, actually. We all saved a fortune by keeping the estate agents out of it.'

'Even so,' I said.

'And we sold our old house,' said my dad.

I felt a bit of a pang then. Not that I was overly sentimental about the house where I was born and where I grew up, but I'd have liked to say goodbye.

'Yeah but . . .' I said. Because a neat bungalow in a nice-ish bit of Dundee didn't translate to a pile of Victorian stone in a posh bit of the Borders. Or even Midlothian.

'And Granny's house,' my dad said.

'Yeah but . . .' I said again. Because my gran's semi in a not-even-that-nice bit of Dundee wouldn't have bought the gateposts of this place.

'We invested wisely,' my dad said.

'Now Keith, don't fib,' said my mum. 'We invested *luckily*. When Granny's estate was all settled, we wanted a quick return. But what do we know about the stock market?'

'Nothing,' my dad said.

'No one does,' said Noleen. 'It's a bigger racket than Vegas and anyone who says different is lying to ya.'

'Exactly,' said my mum. 'So I thought I would just pick a name the way I pick a horse for the Derby. We wanted a quick return to make some money to buy a small hotel somewhere, so we invested in . . . Zoom!'

'Zoom?' I said. 'You put the whole of the proceeds of Granny's house into Zoom shares? When was this?'

'Autumn 2019,' said my mum.

'Can I ask one question?' said Noleen. 'When is the Derby and can I come with you?'

'Not till June,' said my dad. 'But could I interest you in a game of bridge tonight? If you're a gambling woman?'

'Call it poker,' said Noleen, 'and you are *on*.'

'For now,' my mum said, 'why don't you all get settled and I'll bang the gong at noon. Soup and sandwiches in the dining room. Is there anything anyone doesn't eat?'

Was there anything seven Californian adults and two picky little children didn't eat? She would be lucky to have got the full list in time for a late supper. I left them to it and wandered back out into the stone passageway to go exploring. As well as the fake kitchen and the owners' flat, there was a wine cellar down here, a laundry, a box room full of garden furniture, a dank storage room currently housing netted Christmas trees in buckets and a long corridor that turned two corners and then ended abruptly at a bare brick wall.

FIVE

'For the rest of the day,' my mum said, as she cleared plates, 'I think you should all take it easy and recover from the gruelling trip.'

'How about recovering from the gruelling lunch?' Taylor muttered under his breath. He had never experienced Scotch broth before. It was a lot of mutton fat and barley for a Californian. It didn't help that Diego had called it 'crotch broth' – an innocent mistake but one that got such a big laugh he said it ten more times, until even I had to put my spoon down.

'And what the hell was in the sandwich?' said Todd, when my parents had both left the dining room, each with a laden tray.

'Cheese and pickle,' I said. I held up a hand as he tried to interrupt. 'Not pickles as you know them, before you start arguing with me. Pickles as I know them. And cheese as I know it too. With actual flavour. Welcome to the land where Cheddar was invented and still means something.'

'Lexy,' Della said, once she had finished swishing her mouth out with water, 'would your mother be offended if I offered to help in the kitchen? Before the next meal?'

'No clue,' I said. 'I don't know who my mother is anymore.'

'But tomorrow,' my mum said, coming back with her empty tray to load up again, 'we're going to decorate the house for . . . the holidays.'

'You can say "Christmas", Judith,' Taylor told her. 'If you're putting up a tree covered in ornaments, I'd probably work it out anyway.'

'I wasn't sure,' my mum said. Then she clapped her hands together and bounced up and down on the balls of her feet. Who *was* this woman?

'We've worked so hard to get the renovations done and, all the time the place was full of plumbers and electricians and joiners, I just kept doing my yoga breathing and looking forward to the day when the paint was dry and the wood was sealed and we could decorate for' – she flicked another look at Taylor – 'the birth of our Lord.' Which was a bit much, actually.

'No plasterers then?' I said, to change the subject.

My parents both frowned at me.

'With the brickies and chippies and sparks? Hey, why do you suppose plumbers don't have a nickname?'

The frowns deepened.

'What are you wittering on about?' said Todd. 'You always say we don't understand because we're foreign, but your mom and pop don't have a clue either.'

'I found that weird bit of wall,' I said. 'Why'd you leave that?'

'Oh, I know what you mean!' said my mum. 'It was behind a false door. We took that off when we couldn't unlock it and then lost heart. There would have been so much dust and we'd painted down there by then. Like I said, we were desperate to get ready for *this*! We've got five trees!'

'I saw them,' I said.

'Five!' said my mum. 'One for the curve of the stairs, one for the drawing room, one for the dining room, one in the library and one in the children's bedroom.'

Nothing for me, then, I found myself thinking. Even though there was plenty room in that turrety bit.

'And a Nativity on the lawn,' my dad added. He glanced at Taylor. 'Since you've given us the go-ahead.'

'And speaking of the lawn,' my mother said, 'here's something you're all going to love.' She beamed around at us. Noleen, who took predictions that she was going to love something as halfway between a challenge and an insult, scowled back. 'You'll have noticed the name of the wee shop? Ivy's? And the Holly Inn? And of course you'll have seen the mistletoe when we arrived? Well tomorrow is the day of sharing.' Except she called it The Day of Sharing.

'I mean, it really is fine,' Taylor said, 'but if you're going to hold a service and pray and stuff, I might go to the pub.' He had been watching a lot of *EastEnders* in preparation for this trip and he had just about got 'go to the pub' and 'put the kettle on' off to a T.

'Not like that,' said my mum. 'It's not religious at all.'

'Pagan, I'd have thought,' said my dad. He had loaded up the last of the dishes and now he was rubbing the tabletop with a duster soaked in orange oil. He kept bending down with his head on one side to admire the sheen.

'It's mulled wine and mince pies at the pub, sherry and short-bread at the wee shop,' my mum said. 'Everyone goes round collecting greenery for their houses. They came and helped themselves here, last year when it was empty, but this year we can get right into the swing of it again.'

'I say "pagan" because holly berries are supposed to be drops of blood and mistletoe berries are drops of—'

'Keith!'

'And ivy represents—'

'KEITH!'

'But, like your mum says, that's tomorrow. *We're* doing hot chestnuts and wassail. Starts at ten.'

They left then with Della and the children in tow, because Diego wanted to choose a Christmas tree and Hiro wanted to go back to the basement, where the combination of acoustics and lung power had just given her the thrill of her short life.

The Californians managed to wait until they were long gone before losing it.

'Drops of what?' said Roger when he had stopped laughing.

'Semen,' I told him, starting him off again.

'Ewwwwww,' said Kathi.

'But why are drops of blood such a big deal?' said Todd.

'Menstrual blood.'

'Ewwwwwww,' said Todd, right in Kathi's face.

'What about the ivy?' said Noleen.

'The ivy represents *twining*. You know, close communion.'

'Ewwwwwwww,' said Devin. 'It was my turn, right?'

'Jesus Christ,' Taylor said. 'And all this sherry and mulled wine starts right after breakfast? So it's basically an orgy is what it is.'

'What's wassail?' said Kathi.

'Yeah, booze,' I told her. 'For fertility. And now you know how I felt surrounded by peppermint walking sticks for no reason.'

'Candy canes are not sex toys though,' said Devin. 'They're Js for Jesus.'

'I think that might be reverse engineering,' said Roger.

'And can we get kosher wassail?' said Taylor. 'Seriously, Lexy, is there any way you can convince them to calm down?'

'I sure didn't have "Taylor's the exotic one" on my bingo card,' said Noleen.

'I think it's more like "Taylor is taking on Lexy and we mustn't scare him off",' I told her. 'For God's sake, let's go to the pub for real, eh?'

We lost Devin, who rightly assumed that ditching the kids was a no-no, and we almost lost Roger, who bargained hard for a nap but lost, making six of us to wander down the one and only street of Yule in the sinking light and plummeting temperature of a Scottish December afternoon, to check out the Holly Inn.

What a blast of instant nostalgia! I had never been here before, but the smell of real beer, microwaved curry and an old Hoover bag – the smell of every Scottish pub since they banned smoking – was enough to bring fresh tears to my eyes.

'That was quick!' said a woman behind the bar. 'You're the Mistletoe lot, right? You must be straight off the plane.' I beamed at her but managed not to hug her. She was a barmaid – possibly landlady, given her age – in the grand tradition: her skirt was too tight, her boobs were too hiked and her tan was too deep. Her heels were too high too, so she had developed the musculature of a world-champion in some athletic discipline with a lot of heavy props and grunting. Her bum, I noticed when she turned away to lower the volume on the radio, was a shelf.

'And which one of youse is Lexy?' she said, turning back.

Noleen and Kathi both gave her a hard look, but she wasn't being funny. They would see soon enough that short hair, practical clothes and not a scrap of make-up didn't say anything about your sexuality in my homeland.

'I'm Lexy,' I said. 'Nothing you've heard about me is true.'

'Did you marry a dentist that never stopped shagging his ex-wife?' She gave a smoky laugh and told me my first drink was free, in sisterhood.

'And which one of you is Taylor?' she said next.

Todd and Roger gave her a pretty hard stare too. But again, she wasn't joking. British men all wear scarves like that.

'I'm Taylor,' Taylor said. 'This is Todd and this is Roger.'

'My God, Lexy, their teeth,' said the barmaid. 'I thought it was just on the telly. How do you dare to smile?'

'Masks were no hardship,' I said.

'And you couldn't even stick with the shagmaster until he'd sorted yours out, eh?'

I held out one hand to show her off, turned to my friends and said, 'Ladies and gentlemen, proof at last. I am not rude. I am dead normal.'

'Cheeky cow,' said the barmaid. 'I'm Beth Mullen. I'll break your fingers if you call me Elizabeth. What'll it be?'

The rest of the day was hazy. I had lost a lot of drinking form during my years in the wellness capital of the world, and it didn't take many pints of half-forgotten ales, added to the jet lag, to put me in a pleasant fug. By the time we wended our way back up the street to Mistletoe Hall, with the lights twinkling inside the cottages and the frost twinkling outside them, I felt a wide and gentle love for everyone that you might as well call goodwill to all men.

'That pub was filthy,' Kathi said. 'How often do the health inspectors come round in this neck of the woods?'

'It was fine,' Noleen said.

'I went to the bathroom and my feet stuck to the floor.'

'Aw, sticky pub floors,' I said. 'It's so nice to be home.'

'They had bar soap,' said Kathi.

'What?' I said. I had decided to climb up and down the front doorsteps of all the cottages as I passed instead of walking on the pavement and it was taking all my concentration.

'What's wrong with branded soap to promote your business, hon?' said Noleen. 'We could do that too.'

'Not bar soap. *Bar* soap. A bar of soap. That you have to touch after someone else touched it before you. That can't be legal. And a terrycloth towel.'

'Disposable bog roll, though,' I said. 'All mod cons there.'

'Ewwwww,' said Kathi.

Beside me, at the inner edge of the pavement, a clipped hedge snorted, making me jump half out my skin and skid on the icy pavement as I recovered my footing.

'Did someone say "Ewwwww"?' came a plummy voice from the other side of the bushes. 'This must be the Americans!'

Just in front of us, a head appeared as someone leaned over a garden gate. It was an elderly woman with snow-white hair, soft pink cheeks and dancing blue eyes, like someone from a fairytale.

'Oh, they're lovely, Crispin!' she said. 'They're just beautiful! Come and see.'

She was joined at the gate by the owner of the posh voice: an old man with hair brushed straight back in stripes like Prince Philip's, dressed in a shirt and tie and waistcoat and jumper and jacket and raincoat and still pretty svelte. He must have been as thin as a rake underneath it all.

'Welcome to Yule!' he said. 'One of you must be Judith and Keith's girl.'

I put my hand up.

'We're Crispin and Wilma Garmont,' said the woman. She was nothing like as posh as her husband. She reminded me of my granny.

'AKA the cheeky bastards who offloaded our crumbling pile to your poor parents,' Crispin said. 'They've been working like black slaves ever since they got the keys. Can we still say "black slaves"?' he added, addressing Roger.

'No,' Roger said. 'Thanks for asking.'

'And don't say "bastards" either,' Wilma told him. 'Half of this lot are probably Evangelicals. We love a docu-soap, don't we?' She nudged her husband. 'Evangelicals are our favourite. That and polygamists. Or are they the same thing? But yes, Mistletoe was my husband's family home for donkey's yonks.'

'It's lovely,' I said.

'Pfft,' said Wilma. 'This place' – she waved her hand at the cottage she was standing in front of – 'has got underfloor heating, a walk-in shower and an automatic garage door. We can spend all our time out in the garden instead of Polyfilla-ing walls and lagging pipes.'

'Kind of cold for gardening tonight, isn't it?' Noleen said.

'Oh, we're not gardening tonight,' said Crispin. 'We're lurking. Our daughter's coming for Christmas, and we want to jump out and surprise her.'

'Your daughter?' I said. '*She* doesn't mind you selling up the family home?'

'Camilla? Oh, bugger it! We're not supposed to call her that anymore. *Miley*. Miley was petrified we'd still be there when bits started dropping off and she'd have to choose between handling the sale herself and moving in to help us not fall over the banisters when we got wobbly. So we went against my late mother's dying wish and hawked the joint. Miley's delighted.'

'Her flat in Edinburgh's like an operating theatre,' Wilma said. 'She gives visitors these wee slippers so they don't make footprints on her Italian tiles.'

'Sounds like a woman after my own heart,' said Kathi.

'Possibly, possibly,' Crispin said, giving her a close look. 'Are you a lesbian?'

'What am I going to do with you?' his wife said. 'You can't say that.'

'Can't say anything these days,' said Todd. 'Between the gays, the God-humpers and Greta Thunberg.'

'Oh, we love Greta!' Crispin said. 'She takes no nonsense from anyone. Splendid girl!'

'Why do you ask?' said Kathi, having finally recovered the power of speech.

'Because Miley says she's not one but perhaps you'd be willing to check?'

'You can't say that,' said Todd, just ahead of Noleen, Kathi, Wilma, Roger and me.

'Speaking of,' said Crispin, as a car swung on to the street at the far end of the village and blinded us all with its full beams. 'That might be her now!'

'We'll let you welcome her home,' I said. 'See you at the Day of Sharing tomorrow?'

'Wouldn't miss it,' Crispin said. 'Planning to sneak into the old place and see what they've done.'

I looked around with his eyes when we got back inside. Surely he'd approve. The house looked beautiful, all tucked up for the evening and with firelight dancing. My dad and Devin were playing a version of tabletop hockey with Hiro as the puck, shooting her back and forth across the polished dining-room table on her fat flannel bottom. Upstairs, my mum and Della were watching Diego finish off the decorations on his bedroom tree. The smeared glasses and crumby plates suggested that they had probably drunk as much as we had and eaten even more. I'd had a packet of every kind of crisps you couldn't get in California: roast chicken, smoky bacon, prawn cocktail, tomato sauce. Despite all the beer, my tongue was glued to the roof of my mouth from the salt.

'Hungry?' said my mum. 'There's a sausage casserole in the oven. I just need to drop in the dumplings.'

'I tried,' said Della softly.

'Did you meet Beth?' asked my mum. 'Isn't she magnificent?'

'And we ran into the Garmonts too.'

'Oh lovely! Would you believe she's a retired police sergeant?'

'Beth or Wilma?' I asked.

'Well, not Wilma. She's eighty-two. I don't think they had lady policemen when she was working age.'

'I'd believe Beth was Five-Oh,' said Todd. 'She terrifies me. Even though I can't understand what she's saying.'

'And now that there's not a single branch left that you could cram another decoration on, Diego,' my mum said, 'let's all go down and have a glass of bubbly. Toast your return.'

'Another drink?' Roger said. 'I might turn in.'

'I'm going for a lie-down too,' said Todd. 'Can you bring me some dinner on a tray? No dumplings, though.' He floated off towards the ballroom.

Somehow the rest of us got through sausage casserole, dumplings, mashed potato and a serving of refried beans (to make Della feel at home; my mum had been Googling) and made it to bedtime.

'It's been an interesting start,' Taylor said.

'Yeah well, it'll be raining tomorrow and you'll be sober. You'll be begging to go back home by teatime.'

'Home,' said Taylor in a small voice.

Shit. He had forgotten about Amaranth, what with all the distractions, and then I had gone and reminded him again. So, despite the dumplings and mash and salt and beer and the two bottles of champagne we had arsed, I distracted him some more.

* * *

We were sleeping tangled up in limbs and sheets like a married couple in a PG movie when an almighty crash woke us.

'What the—?' said Taylor.

'Jesus!' came Noleen's voice, faintly, through our wall and across their bathroom and through their bedroom wall beyond. 'Are you two not done yet? That poor rocking horse!'

'Can everyone pipe down?' came Devin's voice even more faintly, through our door and across the landing and through their door. Not that the doors were more solid than the walls; just that Devin's was nowhere near Noleen's standard of bellowing.

'Puh-lease! People!' came Todd's voice, loud and clear because he had come out on to the landing to berate us and had the whole of the cupola above him to work with.

I staggered to the door. 'It's not us!' I said. 'Why the hell would everyone think that was us?' But I did wonder how noisy we'd been earlier, celebrating thick stone walls in place of a spindly boat and a motel made of sticks and plaster.

'Lexy?' came my mum's voice up the stairs. 'Was that you?'

'It came from outside,' said Taylor, appearing fully dressed and tugging his boots on.

'A burglar?' I said.

'Keith! Did you lock the cars?'

'Keith?' shouted Taylor. 'Do you have a flashlight?'

'A flashing setting on the fairy lights?' my dad shouted up. 'Wouldn't a steady beam be more—?'

'Torch, Dad,' I shouted down.

'Look,' Della said, opening her bedroom door, 'I'm not telling anyone what to do. I'm just wondering if you really want to wake Hiro.'

On tiptoe, Taylor and I headed downstairs, Todd swished back into his ballroom, kicking his dressing gown into a fan train behind him, and Noleen shut her door shut with a Hiro-non-compliant bang that she got away with, luckily for her. Roger, of course, had slept through the whole exchange as only a doctor trained in ten-minute on-call catnaps could.

Downstairs on the basement level, my dad was struggling to pack his pyjama trousers into wellies, while my mum looked on, hugging her elbows. She wasn't wearing a shawl but 'waiting at the pithead' was very much the vibe.

'Dad, don't go out there,' I said. 'I'll go. Give us those pluchs and look for a torch, eh?'

'Do you have a baseball bat, Keith?' said Taylor. 'Or a . . . like a cricket bat, I suppose it would be?'

'I haven't even got a curling brush,' my dad said. 'But they'll have run off, won't they? After making that much noise?'

'It was probably a fox in the bins,' I said, trying to convince myself.

'Too loud,' Taylor said. 'Do you get bears here?'

'How about a frying pan?' said my mum. 'A nice hefty Le Creuset frying pan?'

'Let's just go and see what's what,' I suggested. 'Where's the nearest door to the outside?'

We dragged it open, ignoring the creak of the hinge and the way it scraped against the stone flags. I also ignored the fact that there was no outside light, no streetlamp glow and no evidence of another human habitation as far as the eye could see: just the high wall of a wee courtyard jutting out on one side of us and, on the other, dark humps and shadows filling the garden, then dark fields and even darker trees stretching into the distance. I shivered and told myself there was a whole street of cottages on the far side of the house and not to be a ninny.

Taylor switched the torch on and played it around the scene, making ghosts and devils jump around in the spaces between tree trunks and bare shrubs. 'Hold it steady and move it slowly,' I said.

'There's nothing out of place,' said Taylor.

'Nothing that we can see from the doorway,' I pointed out. 'Come on.' I crept beyond the jut of the wall into the middle of the grass, waiting for Taylor's bobbling torch beam to follow. He had stopped and was bent double, torch trained straight down, concentrating hard on a patch of frosty grass.

'What is it?' I called over.

'Owl,' Taylor said.

'What? Where? I can't see anything.'

'There's a print of a pair of owl's feet,' he said.

I walked over and bent down beside him. 'Yeah?'

'Serrated toes, backward facing, clear scratches from its talons. It must have sat here for . . . Well, how long did it sit here?' He lifted one of his feet and then the other, shining the torch on his footprints as if he was dancing. 'My body temperature, compared with the temp of an owl on a cold night like this, conserving heat . . . I'd say it sat here for . . . too long.' He straightened and shone the light into my eyes. 'What kinds of owls do you get here at this time of year?'

'Or,' I said, 'just a thought – we could find out what that big noise was.'

We went clockwise round the house. My choice. I knew it was only bad luck to go anti-clockwise round a church and Mistletoe Hall *wasn't* a church, but I was experiencing another bout of that same unaccountable dread I had felt on our arrival and I saw no harm in stacking the odds in my favour.

There was nothing to see as we rounded the billiard room/ballroom extension and nothing to see at the front; just the minibus and the two cars lined up on the gravel, ice starting to form on their windscreens despite the overhanging scratchy trees. There was nothing to see on the far side either; just a broad lawn twinkling in the torchlight as the crystals formed on each blade of grass. Round again, there was a terrace I reckoned was outside the drawing-room windows, stone steps leading down to more lawn and more skeletal trees in the distance.

'Maybe it was someone pranging their car out on the road,' I said.

'You should get back inside before you freeze,' Taylor said, rounding the last corner. We were almost back where we had started.

'You're going to stake out that owl, aren't you?'

He didn't answer and I hurried after him. I banged into him, actually, because he was standing just where the last turn of the house and the jut of the drying-yard wall made a dark little neuk under yet another of those witchy trees with the thorns and the tangled branches. This one was different though: a great big lump of it had broken off and crashed into the side of the house, half flattening a sawhorse and leaving thick white scratches down the stonework as if a giant cat had attacked.

'Mystery solved,' I said. 'Good. We can clear it up in the morning.'

Taylor, though, was wading into the mess, cracking twigs

underfoot and snagging his jacket – my dad's jacket, actually – on thorns.

'When do Scottish owls mate?' he said. 'Not December, is it?'

'How the hell would I know?'

'Because this must be what spooked that bird bad enough to make it sit on the grass and melt the frost. There could be a nest of eggs here, Lexy. An injured mate.'

'There's a knackered mate,' I said. 'A hungover mate. A mate getting frostbite.'

He wasn't listening.

'Shouldn't you do this in daylight?' I said. 'In case you step on an egg?'

'That's weird,' Taylor said. He was in the branches up to his chest now, with the torchlight trained away from me. 'Oh, I see. It's gone through the tornado door.'

'The what?' I said. 'We don't get tornadoes. What are you talking about?'

'Well, what would you call that?' said Taylor, shining the light on something I couldn't see.

'Describe it,' I said. 'These are new pyjamas and I can't remember the last time I had a tetanus jab.'

'Double doors in the ground, tilted up a little?'

'For God's sake, it's a coal chute,' I said. 'Right. A branch fell off, stoved in the coal chute and scared an owl. Can we go to bed?'

'It's not a coal chute,' Taylor said. 'There are stairs. I'm going dow-waaa-ohhhh-awww-ouch.' He disappeared, taking the light with him.

SIX

'Are you OK?' I waited. 'Taylor? Are you OK?' I looked up at the windows, trying to work out whose room was above this bit of the garden. Unfortunately, I calculated that it was one side of mine and my bathroom, then the spiral staircase and the little passageway to Todd and Roger's ballroom. No point shouting for help then.

My silky pyjamas were not going to survive the next few minutes, but the possibility that my fiancé hadn't survived the last few was undeniable. I reminded myself there was no rabies in Britain and my mum always had a good stack of plasters in her medicine cabinet, then I plunged in. Taylor had broken most of the worst thorns and twigs off anyway and I got to the hole in the ground with only one bad scratch and a bit of hair pulled out at the roots.

The torch was shining straight up and I had to block it with both hands before I could see anything.

'Look, Lexy,' Taylor said in a tone of wonder. 'Come down the steps. I missed them but they look sturdy enough. Come down and see what I've found.'

'Can you turn the torch beam so I'm not blinded?' He did but he also took away most of the light, so it was by touch alone that I found the top rung of a ladder – 'steps' was over-generous – and started to climb down, getting splinters in the heels of my hands every time I moved them.

'What?' I said when I was back on level ground again. Taylor was sitting down, hunched over his splayed legs. 'Have you broken your wrist? An ankle?'

'Look at that,' he said, pointing at his crotch. I leaned over and picked up the torch. 'Don't shine it straight on! Let your eyes adjust and then look carefully.'

I closed my eyes thinking about buried treasure and opened them again, finding that they had indeed adjusted to the low light and I was looking at . . .

'A nest,' I said.

'An owl nest,' said Taylor. 'With an egg. Which survived the fall. Which survived *both* falls. The one from the branch breaking off and the one from me crashing down this hole like an idiot.'

'Cool,' I said. 'Well, pass it to me and we can—'

'We can't touch it!' said Taylor. 'It's a miracle I ended up so close and didn't brush against it. If we get human scent on it, the parents will abandon it.'

'And lay another one, right?' We had been together long enough for me to have picked up that much.

'Lexy, I have no idea what kind of owl made this nest and then alighted out there on the grass, but I've just Googled it and there is no – not a single – owl that should be nesting in December.'

'You did what?' I said. 'When I was up there thinking you were dead and calling to you and you weren't answering, that was because you were Googling owls?'

'I didn't have much time to study, after we decided we were definitely coming,' Taylor said. 'And I thought we were going to Dundee so I concentrated on seabirds.'

'I'm going back to bed,' I said.

'Mind how you step on those rungs,' said Taylor. 'That ladder looks pretty sketchy.'

'Do you realize that when you wanted me to come and see that thing, you called it a staircase and said it looked fine? And now it's a rickety ladder because I'm leaving?'

He said nothing.

'And anyway, duh! I'm not going back up the ladder to fight my way through that fairytale mess of whatever that tree is. I'm in the house now, genius. I'll go the other way.'

I shone the torch above his head to see what was behind him.

'Oh,' I said. 'Yeah, well, that's inconvenient. We're at the bit where it's bricked up.'

'What?'

'I saw this from the other side when I was exploring. Someone blocked off the passageway. Seemed weird, but it makes sense now. Those wooden doors up there aren't exactly secure.'

'Wouldn't a bolt be a better idea?' said Taylor. 'Or why not brick up the hole?'

'Duh,' I said again. 'Because horizontal bricks are a bit of a challenge, what with gravity and all.'

'Duh, yourself,' said Taylor. 'What about a sheet of metal? Or an iron grille? Or a—'

He was still coming up with suggestions when I was up the ladder, out the hole, through the branches and on my way back to the front door and my own lonely bed. Jilted for an out-of-season owl egg. Merry Christmas to me.

Wednesday 21 December

'Lexy.' Taylor was trying to wake me gently, speaking in a soft voice and stroking my arm with his fingertips. Unfortunately, his fingertips were colder than a curler's kneecap. I yelped and shrank away from him.

'What is it? What time is it? Get into bed, for God's sake. But don't touch me.'

'It's morning,' Taylor said. He breathed on his hands and rubbed them together. 'I need you to help me find out who to contact.'

'About what? At least get me a coffee if you're going to wake me up at the crack of . . . What time *is* it?'

'About the nest. The parents are both still around and uninjured, but they don't understand where it's gone. I've been watching them to see if they'll fly down the hatch, but we might need to chainsaw a bigger gap in the branches. And even then, they might not get it.'

'RSPB,' I said. 'Coffee?'

'Rescue . . . Scottish . . . P-something . . . Birds?'

'Royal Society for the Protection of. They'll put you on to the RSLC, who can advise.'

'Royal Society for . . .?'

'Lexy's Coffee.' I pulled the covers over my head. 'There's an office downstairs.'

By eight o'clock, I had made it as far as the fake kitchen and was beginning to cheer up, what with the sugar-free bread, Breton butter and Cooper's Oxford.

'This is marmalade?' Della said, peering suspiciously into the jar. 'Why is it black?'

'Is this sourdough?' Noleen said, nibbling a crust. 'How come you gave us such a hard ride if you get it too?'

'Why is this butter crunchy?' said Todd.

My mum came in with a strange woman in tow. She was dressed in wool but not woollen garments so much as loops of knitting. There didn't seem to be any ends anywhere or any definable armholes or leg parts. She was simply a big soft parcel, like an unthreatening Zombie.

'This is Leanne from the shop,' my mum said. 'Sit down and take your . . . coat off, Lee.'

Leanne unwound a few hanks from her upper half and sank down into a chair. 'Bad news,' she said. 'We've been robbed. So has Beth. And Judith says they've been at you too.'

'They fell out of the tree before they got in here,' I said. 'Thankfully.' It was my bedroom window that was closest, after all.

'No, they weren't housebreakers,' Leanne said. 'They were berry rustlers. They've stripped half the ivy off my shop and they've got Beth's holly bushes down to bare wood.'

'They were here for the mistletoe,' my mum said. 'That's what Leanne reckons. Only the branch broke and they legged it.'

'What a bunch of Scroogy bastards,' said Todd. 'What a Grinch move.'

'I said you would investigate, Lexy,' my mum said. 'Trinity. I told Leanne there was a licensed investigator and her two assistants right here ready to tackle the job, pero bueno.'

'Pero bueno?' said Della. 'What do you mean?'

'Why, what does "pero bueno" mean?' said my mum.

'It means "oh well",' I told her.

'Well what did *I* mean?' My mum blinked and frowned.

'Pro bono?' said Todd.

'Does that mean gratis?' said my mum.

'What does gratis mean?' said Della.

'Yes!' said Kathi, who is even less of a morning person than me. 'I and my two assistants will take the case. Are the crime scenes intact? Have you touched anything?'

'I was too upset even to look at it,' Leanne said. 'We're supposed to be having our Big Day of Berries today.'

'We can have a Monster Morning of Mistletoe instead,' said my mum. 'They had hardly started here. We've got tons left.'

'OK, hon?' Kathi said. 'Taking a job?'

'Ideal,' said Noleen. 'I'm going to organize the catering with Judith and Keith, giving them the benefit of my years in the hospitality trade.'

'And Roger's asleep,' said Todd. 'So I'm free too. Lexy?'

'I'm a twig widow,' I told them.

'So,' said Kathi, 'can we review your security footage?'

'My . . .?' said Leanne.

'Or we can get it from the pub,' said Todd.

'Beth hasn't got a camera either,' Leanne told him.

'Is that legal?' said Kathi. 'Is that OK with ATB?'

'With who?'

'Alcohol, Tobacco and Firearms,' I said. 'We don't really . . . Look, there won't be security footage unless someone in one of the cottages has set up a badger-cam, but let's see what we can do.'

It was a perfect winter's morning when Todd, Kathi and I stepped outside. The sky was pale blue with a lingering pink tinge in the east. Every leaf and blade and twig looked like they'd been dipped in egg white and caster sugar. And a robin was sitting on the boot scraper peering at us out of one apple-pip eye and then the other.

'No tyre marks,' Todd said, pointing at the ground. 'The rustlers must have parked on the street and sneaked in on foot.'

'No footprints though,' I said, pointing to where the gravel stopped and the grass began. 'Those are mine and Taylor's. Check the other side.'

But the grass on the billiards room and ballroom side of the house was also pristine, except for the tracks of my dad's wellies and my sturdy slippers.

'They must have come in over the fields,' I said.

Todd puffed his cheeks out and watched his breath cloud the cold air as he released it. 'Let's see what's up at the pub and the store.' He untied his ear flaps, shook them loose and set off down the drive. Dressed as he was – like the lead in a Hallmark movie – I hoped some villagers were out and about to appreciate him. Kathi was dressed as she always dressed for cold weather – like Frances McDormand.

'That is a tragedy,' Todd said when we got to the pub and saw the holly bushes on either side of the door, not to mention the big tree by the gate to the beer garden. They were wrecked: branches wrenched off, leaving white scars on the trunk and twisted rags of bark where smaller sprigs had been ripped away. Underfoot was what looked like half the berries the rustlers were after anyway.

'They can't have got anything worth selling,' I said. 'Vandals!'

'Before I get close enough to look for fibre evidence,' Todd said, 'run through the B-U-G-S round here at this time of year.'

I screwed up my face and thought hard. 'Nothing,' I said.

'Oh come on! Nothing?'

'Honestly. Nothing. It's too cold. Have at it and don't worry.'

Above us, a window rattled up and Beth stuck her head out, surrounded by a plume of steam, like she'd just taken the stage at a rock concert, except she had a towel wrapped round her body and another one twisted into a turban on her head. She already had the day's make-up on, and I found myself thinking it must be the good stuff not to melt in all that humidity. Todd had got to me, no denying it.

'It's you lot,' she said. 'Leanne texted to say she's got you on the case. But she's called the cops too, in case it's part of a crime wave. I could just cry.'

Kathi took a step back from her position under the window.

'We're on it,' I said.

'Well, they weren't in the pub,' Beth said. 'I can tell you that much. So it wasn't revenge for me cutting them off. Oh, I could just spit.'

Kathi backed away a bit more.

'Did Leanne tell you the mistletoe got off lightly?' I asked.

'Aye,' said Beth. 'But mistletoe . . . I mean, if you had to pick one out of three, it wouldn't be the seaweed with sperm balls, would it? I could puke.'

Kathi stepped right off the pavement into the gutter, but Beth drew her head in and slammed the window down without discharging any fluids at all.

We tramped on towards the shop. Things were even worse

here. The thieves had pulled whole sections of ivy off the walls, lifting paint and leaving bare wood. They had tugged big chunks of it up by the roots, dislodging soil and scattering the bulbs that had just been starting to sprout underground.

'Oh, the pigs!' I said. 'Those are snowdrops!'

Kathi was taking pictures and Todd was examining the ground and remaining branches – for unusual footprints and scraps of unique fabric, probably – when a police car drew up at the kerb and a stab-vested copper in short sleeves and tracky bums stepped out.

'Leanne McGrath?' he said, looking between Kathi and me.

'She's down the road at a neighbour's,' I said. 'Are you here about this?'

'Sick wee shites, eh?' the copper said. 'Nothing we can do except log it. Are youse tidying up?'

'We're investigating, Officer,' Kathi said. 'I'm a PI and these are my assistants.'

'Where did she dig you up from?' the cop said. 'That's not a Lothians accent.'

'Trinity for Trouble, Cuento, California,' said Todd, extracting a business card from a pocket and handing it over. 'We're here for the holidays, just by chance. Can I ask you a question?'

'One second,' said the cop, kicking at the loose dirt and snow-drop bulbs as he fished a notebook out of a pocket. He jotted something down then looked up again. 'It's like they didn't even bring a set of wots-its. They just pulled it up like spuds. Wee bastards.'

'They've trampled the holly all to hell too,' I said, 'and they haven't even gone away with proper bits of anything.'

'More like vandalism than theft,' said the cop.

'Can I ask my question now?' said Todd.

The copper inclined his head.

'Why do people do what you tell them when you don't have a gun?' Todd said.

The copper grinned, tore off a page of his notebook and handed it over.

'What does it say?' asked Kathi.

'"What authority slash no gun",' Todd said. 'Very funny. Very clever.'

'It's all Yanks ever ask,' the copper said.

'That's kind of offensive,' said Todd.

'Ocht well, you'll survive,' the cop said, and turned to leave.

'I never thought I'd be homesick for American police,' Todd said when the cop car had pulled away. 'But what a rude individual. And so puny in that ridiculous muscle shirt.'

He always hated failing to charm strangers.

'Anyway,' Kathi said. '*We* don't have to "log it and leave it".'

'Let's go over the fields to the back of my mum's garden and see if we can pick up a trace,' I suggested.

We tramped to the end of the village and kept on along the road until we found a field gate. My heart soared as I untied the orange binder twine and hefted the thing ajar on its rudimentary hinges. It had been four years since I'd tussled with the binder twine on a rusty gate and sploshed into a field through a puddle. Even better – this puddle was frozen. It creaked and clouded under our boots but stayed solid enough to walk on. Beyond it, the row of furrows swept up and over the horizon, neat as jumbo corduroy, dark as chocolate cake on their southern faces and still dusted with last night's frost in the shade.

'Is this OK?' Kathi said. 'Won't we get . . . Well, not shot because no guns but . . . chased with hounds?'

'Farmers have got guns,' I assured her.

She stopped walking.

'Oh, come on, Kathi!' said Todd. 'You've sat through the "freedom to roam" boasts just as often as I have. We can skip through these fields wearing nothing but bells and handkerchiefs and all that'll happen is we'll end up in next year's John Lewis Christmas ad.'

It was a resourceful, informed and semi-coherent take-down. I very kindly didn't tell him that Morris Men were an English thing.

'Here's the backyard wall,' Kathi said, grabbing the copestones in her mittens and toeing herself up to look over the top. 'That's definitely the turret, right?' She let go and jumped down. 'I don't see anywhere to park a vehicle, and I don't see any signs of anyone walking this way. This is weird.'

Todd put his nose up in the air and sniffed. 'Wine's a-mulling,' he said. 'Can we clamber over? Or do we need to keep stumbling through this frozen field until we find another gate? I have to say "freedom to roam" would be more of a prize in like Italy or Mustique.'

'Let's carry on and double-check the other end of the village,' I said. And thank God I did. When we were almost there, at the second-to-last garden before the field joined the edge of the road again, we found what I took at first to be fly-tipping, a big pile of black binbags up against a sagging woven fence. We were past it before my brain kicked into gear. In fact, Kathi beat me.

'Hang on,' she said, wheeling round. 'Those garbage sacks look suspiciously new. And kinda spiky.'

'Oh my God!' said Todd. 'Did we solve the case? Yeah, you're right. These sacks are brand-new.' He picked one up. 'And not heavy.'

'Open it,' I said.

Kathi laughed as if I was joking. 'Right,' she said. 'I'm going to open a garbage sack.'

'Todd?'

'I know what you said but B-U-G-S overwinter somewhere, Lexy. That twisted asshole on that lame gardening show never shuts up telling people to leave piles of logs and crap all over the place to attract the little buggers.'

'That twisted asshole Monty Don?' I said. 'That lame show *Gardener's World*? Todd, you can't say that. You practically just shot Paddington and made him into a rug.'

'I am not wrong,' said Todd. '*You* open the sack, Lexy.'

As if it's only germaphobia and parasitosis that makes clawing open binbags unappealing.

SEVEN

held my breath and poked a finger into the nearest taut section of black plastic. 'Holly!' I said. 'Ouch! Fuck!'

I got zero sympathy.

'We did it!' said Kathi. 'We cracked a case in under an hour. A personal best.'

'Yeah, but did we even negotiate a fee yet?' said Todd. 'Did anyone mention money? I thought we had time for that later.'

'Oops,' I said. 'A personal worst!'

'Enh, season of goodwill,' said Kathi. 'Grab a couple each and let's go tell the wine-mullers the good news.'

'And hope someone knows enough about gardening to fix that pruning-from-hell that's left the bushes so deformed,' I pointed out. 'And how to replant budding snowdrop bulbs.'

'Debbie Downer!' said Todd. We managed to get all the knotted bag handles securely gripped in our gloves and mittens and set off straggling back along the edge of the field.

'Anyway,' Todd went on, 'you said it yourself. That tired-ass gardening show is sacred in this sad sack of a country. Everyone in Yule probably knows how to fix the damage. It'll be the biggest excitement they've ever had since . . .'

'Since they found out their mobile librarian is Vietnamese,' said Kathi. 'And that was information worth including in the welcome pack for your mom.'

'Poor Roger,' Todd said. 'We definitely need to go to the city once while we're here.'

'Welcome pack!' I said. 'Right. Like that happened. And, Todd, if you want to take Roger to experience a rainbow of nations, Edinburgh's not really a good plan.'

'My nightmare of a Whiiiiite Christ-MAS,' sang Todd.

It was kind of lovely to see that cold weather, jet lag and prickly binbags that were lacerating us through our trousers didn't dent the warmth of our incessant bickering. Trinity was firing on all three of its grumpy cylinders and I found myself grinning as we lobbed the bags over a gate on to the verge and clambered after them.

There was just one moment when I found myself looking back to where they'd been dumped and wondering what was bothering me. 'Guys,' I said. 'Why wouldn't the thieves have taken the stuff with them? Once they'd got it all in bags and everything?'

'Duh,' said Todd. 'Because they blew it with the mistletoe and needed to get away quick.'

'But they're not heavy, are they? It's not like they would have slowed them down much.'

'Duh again,' said Kathi. 'They made a noise when the tree branch broke. So they split. And they dumped the haul in case someone stopped them and asked to search the car.'

'Yeah, that's not really . . . That's not . . . Something's bothering me.'

'Could it be that your boyfriend is probably going to spend the holidays crouched in a basement mooning over an egg?' said Todd. 'Cos that would bother me.'

But when we got back to Mistletoe Hall there was an SSPCA van in the drive and cones set up at both sides of the house to stop anyone walking round and disturbing the evicted family. In other words, it looked as if the owl element of the night's adventures was going to resolve as quickly as the berry bit. So what was wrong with me?

Nothing a good glug of mulled wine with a wassail chaser couldn't cure, I reckoned, although I'd start out with some hot chocolate to put a lining on my stomach. The Day of Sharing was ramping up in the front garden, trestle tables laden with food and booze, patio heaters melting the frost, and surely the entire population of Yule in attendance. It went into hyper-drive when we revealed that we had found the holly and ivy. My mum and Leanne set about the sprigs with secateurs and yards of wire-edged ribbon, managing to make semi-decent swags and posies, eked out with a few fake berries on sticks and one or two scraps of wool from where Leanne had got her wrappings snagged on jaggy bits. My dad appeared wearing a jumper that lit up and a Santa hat that played tunes. I raised my mug of hot chocolate and took a deep draught, not minding in the least when I discovered it was half rum.

'Where's Taylor?' I said to Noleen, who had unbent enough to be wearing a Rudolph brooch that shat chocolate buttons when you pressed his red nose.

'Where do you think?' Noleen said. 'On egg duty with his new pals. I thought I'd seen the maximum number of pockets on a single garment, Lexy. But those guys are humiliating him. They're wiping the floor. One of them has pockets in his hat.'

'You seem . . . happy,' I said. It was a serious allegation to level at her, even though I was a close friend. I waited for the scowl to develop and the swearing to begin.

'I like it here,' Noleen said. 'It's cold. It's a good place for a menopausal woman. And I walked up the street and bought a newspaper for your pop.'

'Wowsers,' I said. 'So what?'

'So the kid behind the counter in Ivy's didn't look up from his phone the whole time he served me. And that gal from the pub was pretty surly last night too. I thought you were kidding.'

'Ahh,' I said. 'No, I wasn't kidding.'

'I see why all the ass-licking bugged you so much now,' Noleen said. 'Man, I could be so happy running a motel in a country where you don't have to smile at anyone and you can swear if you feel like it.'

'I dunno,' I said. 'It might get you down in the end.'

'No way!' said Noleen. 'I ran into a mailman on the walk home and he looked at me like I was gum on his bus seat. So I said, "What's your problem, pal?" and he said, "Piss off." Plus did you meet the cop Leanne called?'

'Yeah,' I said. 'What about him?'

'Ruder than the wine waiters at The French Laundry,' Noleen said. 'And they have been at number one on my hit parade of shitty service for the last ten years.'

That had never seemed all that likely to me. It was probably more that Noleen kicked off about the price of the Chardonnay or asked for ice in her port. But I had never had enough money to check it out for myself, so who can say?

'And,' she said, sidling up close to me, 'I don't want to jinx it. I'm kinda scared to say it. But . . . doesn't Kathi seem . . . What I mean is, how does Kathi seem to you?'

'Now that you mention it,' I said, 'she hasn't been as off her rocker as she usually gets on trips.' I had put it down to the private jet at first, noting that Kathi had barely Cloroxed anything when we boarded. But then I hadn't heard her cleaning her bathroom last night after we all went to bed, and she had put her elbows on the kitchen table this morning without paper napkins under them.

'She asked me to open the binbags we thought had berries in,' I said. 'But she carried two of them round to the street. And she hasn't been to wash her hands yet. She's still standing talking to Roger.'

'Wasn't she wearing gloves?' said Noleen.

'Yeah, but mittens, not latex, and she's still wearing them.'

As we watched, Kathi laughed at something Roger was saying, then she raised a hand and used the back of her woolly glove to wipe her nose.

'Oh my gorgeous galoshes!' said Todd, suddenly right beside us. 'Did you guys see that?'

Noleen swallowed hard and said in a cracked voice, 'Kathi just touched her face.'

And that wasn't all. There were upwards of ten children milling around the front garden now. They had marvelled at my dad's jumper, stocked up on marshmallows and Smarties, and were now gravitating to Roger as all children always do. I used to think it was his LOL Surprise scrubs, but even this morning one by one they came up and started swinging on his arms, or trying to climb his legs, demanding attention and piggybacks.

'Kathi is being swarmed by alien kids in the middle of flu season and she is not backing away,' Noleen said.

'Jesus!' said Todd, pointing.

Since Roger only had two hands and two legs, one of the late arrivals had put his sticky little paw into Kathi's and was beaming up at her through a goatee of chocolate and snot. She fished a handiwipe out of her anorak pocket and wiped his face clean. We all waited with held breath to see if she would put the wipe back in her pocket again. Noleen was holding on to my arm as if she felt faint.

'OK, OK,' she said, when Kathi dropped the wipe on the ground and used her keyring sanitizer spray to disinfect her glove. 'But still, though?'

'That was a Christmas miracle,' Todd said.

She even submitted to being the tail of the conga line, with Roger at the head, heading over to the Nativity on the grass for an impromptu singsong.

'Lexy,' my mum said, rushing over. 'Are you busy?'

'I'm reeling from an astonishing incident,' I said, 'but otherwise no. What is it?'

'Can you bring another platter of mince pies up? They're in the big oven in the fake kitchen. There should be oven gloves over the rail. This is going well, don't you think?'

'It's free food and booze, Mum,' I said. 'It wasn't a long shot.' But I headed inside anyway. Halfway up the steps, I stopped and turned back to look at her. She had just said 'fake kitchen'. I had called it that yesterday, but my mum had never accepted what I called any room in her house before.

'Not the living room, Lexy, please: lounge or sitting room. Not the kludgy, please, Lexy: the cloakroom or the downstairs. No, that does *not* sound like "genitals". And don't say "genitals". Say "front" or . . . Say "front". Yes, all right, I *was* going to tell you to say "downstairs". And don't say "back bit". It's a dining nook. What? *Back bit*? Don't be so disgusting!'

'I'm going to the fake kitchen, Mum!' I called back to her, checking.

'Good!' she said, confused by the announcement, I think. 'Are you drunk?'

'A wee bit!'

'Well, don't drop my good platter!' And she turned away.

Compared with how warm they'd got the garden with the patio heaters and the chestnut brazier, it was remarkably cold in the basement of the house. I lifted the mince pies out of the oven and left it open to warm my legs while I transferred them to a turkey platter – or most of them anyway; I sampled two – and then I reloaded the oven with a fresh batch. As I made my careful way back to the bottom of the stairs, though, suddenly Taylor popped into my head. If it was chilly in the fake kitchen with an oven on full blast, he had to be frozen to the marrow sitting there on the stone floor under an open hatch, watching an egg. Even if he and his pocket friends had all huddled up together, it was kind of a sad way to spend the first day of the holidays.

I backtracked and headed to the other side of the bricked-up wall.

'Taylor?' I shouted. 'Do you want a hot drink and a pie?'

He didn't answer me.

'Taylor?' I shouted a bit louder. But still there was no reply. 'Taylor!' I bellowed as loud as I could. He would probably give me a hard time later but it wasn't as if he was babysitting the actual owls, and eggs can't hear. I was seventy-five per cent sure that was true.

I put my ear to the bricks, almost letting the pies slide off the platter.

'Lexy?' His voice was thin and tiny. He sounded like the baby bird he was hoping his precious egg would turn into.

'Speak up!' I yelled. 'Do. You. Want. Some. Grub?'

'Where are you?' came Taylor's voice back again, faint and reedy as if he was miles away. How many layers of brick had the crazy person used to stop up this passageway? It was more than the one I had assumed, that was for sure.

'I'll. Come. Round,' I screamed at him, then hotfooted it for the stairs again before the pies got cold.

'Rescue pack for Taylor and the birdy boys,' I said, when my dad caught me packing thermos cups of wassail and bowls of chestnuts into a box. 'I'm not taking the good stuff everyone's going for, so don't scowl at me.'

'That's a four-hundred-year-old recipe!' he said.

'The cooked beer with orange peel or the furry mush?' I said. 'Seriously, even the guys stuck in a cold hole with an egg might not thank you for it.'

'I've missed you, Lexy,' he said. 'Your mum's gone all nice and it's unnerving. It's good to have *you* home, for old time's sake.'

As compliments go, I thought, and slipped round the side of the house, ignoring the cones. Funny, but when I got to the fallen branch and the crashed-open hatch, it didn't seem to me that it was anywhere near the bricked-up passageway on the inside of the basement. 'Hoi!' I shouted from the top of the ladder. 'Sustenance. Sort of. I couldn't make out what you said so I just brought it anyway.'

A man in his fifties with, as Noleen had noticed, a prodigious selection of pockets about him – more zips than a punk band – came halfway up the ladder and let me lower the box down. 'Are the parents still around?' I said, showing an interest.

'Asleep for the day,' the man said. 'We're hoping to have the branch up the hatch and lashed back to the tree just about where it came off before they take flight tonight. 'We're waiting for a chainsaw.'

'Bloody hell, Taylor,' I said. 'If you're going to fire up a chainsaw down there, you could have answered me in a louder voice.'

'What the hell are those?' Taylor said.

'Chest-*nuts*,' I sang to him. 'Roasted on a you-know-wha-aaat.'

'I was shouting as loud as my voice would go,' Taylor said. 'Why were you whispering?'

'Do you want some hot chocolate and mince pies for pudding?' I said. I hate bickering in public, no matter what anyone says.

'I could eat a mince pie,' said the third man, peering at me through bottle-bottom glasses.

'And mulled wine? Or hot chocolate with rum?' I said.

'Why, what's this?' said Zippy, sniffing his thermos cup.

'Cider,' I said. 'Sort of.' And I hoofed it before they could argue.

Back in the fake kitchen, leaning against the oven door for warmth while the mince pies got the last of their heat-through, I gazed at the hanging row of copper pans, at the stone pigs full of wooden spoons and iron ladles, at the dresser shelves stocked with willow pattern and toby jugs. Everything was so solid back in those days. Maybe, if the brick wall had been put across the corridor in Victorian times, three thicknesses of brick really was the norm. But that didn't explain why the trip to the wall on the inside and the trip to the wall on the outside didn't seem to match up. My eyes fell on a wooden mallet stuck in the stone pig beside the spoons. I plucked it out and felt the heft of it in my hand. Then I trotted along the corridors to the blockage and banged those bricks like they were a dinner gong. Afterwards, I held my breath and listened. There was a faint rumble and chirp of talk, but if I hadn't had an ear out for it, I would never have noticed.

I pulled my phone out and hit the compass app Taylor had downloaded after he recovered from the news that I didn't have a compass app. East-north-east. I stuck the mallet through my belt loop and held the phone out flat in front of me while I made my way to the stairs, the side door, the grass, the drying yard and the top of the ladders. I crouched down and held my phone out, pointing it at the brick wall behind the three guys in the mess of branches. It should have said west-south-west. I took a deep breath and looked down. Almost due south.

'What are you doing?' said Taylor.

'Why have you got a meat tenderizer through your belt loop?' said Speccy, like he didn't have seventeen gadgets Velcro-ed to him.

'Your pies are nearly ready,' I said. 'What did you say about chocolate or mulled wine?'

'I could murder a cup of tea,' said Taylor. I gave him half a smile for advanced Britishness.

'Ooh, yeah, coo and two,' said Zippy.

'Splash of milk in mine,' said Speccy.

'Coming up,' I told them; then, on wobbly legs, I made my way round to the party, pausing to view the scene before I told my parents they had bought and we were all living in a house with a secret chamber in the basement, bricked up from both sides.

EIGHT

Except I didn't. My mum was busy hosting a party with all her new neighbours. And I couldn't catch my dad's eye, since he was running about with bags of chestnuts and stoups of wassail, determined not to admit he had picked both duds in the catering stakes. Kathi would react to the idea of however many years' worth of dust and crud being sealed up beneath her feet the same way she reacted anytime anyone mentioned a crawlspace in California, or showed one in a comedy, or she randomly remembered them. Which is 'not well'. Noleen would react to Kathi reacting not well . . . also not well. Todd would react to the similar – in fact, overlapping – news of subterranean cobwebs in a way that made Kathi look like a yogi. Roger would react to Todd's reaction like an exhausted doctor who had chartered a plane to get a rest and was now looking at that rest dissolving into a drama of telenovela intensity. Diego was eight and Hiro was two and Della was the mum of an eight-year-old and a two-year-old who had both been eating chocolate Santas since breakfast-time.

Which left Devin. My choice was vindicated when I sidled up to him, put my mouth close to his ear and said, 'I've just found a secret room in the basement. Sealed like a mummy's tomb.' And he turned to me and said, 'For reals? Cool. Is there a sledgehammer anywhere?'

No one even noticed us leaving. We got a sledgehammer *and* a pickaxe from my dad's tool store, where they sat neatly pegged inside outlines of themselves like I knew they would because all his tools always had, then we sneaked downstairs and tiptoed past the fake kitchen, where Noleen was decanting more pies from the oven. 'This fricking country,' we overheard her muttering. 'Raisins! Ooh. Pastry! Yay, party time,' and kept moving.

At the brick wall, Devin spat on his hands, raised the hammer and swung it like a skinny Thor tribute artist.

'Wait!' I said. 'Pictures.'

'Oh yeah,' he said. 'Or it didn't happen.' He put the hammer down, shed his coat and jumper, rolled his shirt sleeves, then picked it up again, adopting a wide stance and straining to make his pecs and biceps stand out. He looked like Shaggy from Scooby-Doo.

'I meant before-pictures of the wall,' I said. 'To document the process.'

Devin relaxed out of his muscle pose and took a few ragged breaths to recover. 'Good call, Dude. But make it a film.'

I clicked my camera over to video and panned, slow as syrup, all around the edge of the wall where the bricks met the stone, then stepped back to get a good wide-angle shot of the whole thing.

'Eleven forty-six am, twelve twenty-one twenty-two,' Devin said.

'Quarter to twelve in the morning, twenty-first of December, twenty twenty-two,' I amended.

'The beginning,' said Devin in a movie voiceover voice. Then in his normal voice, 'Are you going to keep filming? While I smash through?'

'Go for it,' I said. 'Action!'

Devin raised the hammer, lined it up like a golf shot and took his first swing.

'Ow,' he said, staggering back. I stepped forward to get a close-up of the slight dusty patch in the middle of one of the bricks where his blow had landed.

'Maybe aim for a bit of mortar,' I said. 'With the pickaxe?'

'Do you want to try?'

So I spat on my hands, hefted the axe pointy end to the wall, lined it up like a croquet shot and gave it my all.

'Ouch!' I said, reeling away. The difference this time was that the pickaxe, unlike the sledgehammer, stayed stuck in there.

'Yay!' said Devin. 'My turn again!' He doesn't have a macho bone in his body, as far as I've ever seen. He stepped up and wiggled the point of the axe free. Then he concentrated hard, with one eye shut, and did his best to make the little hole a bit bigger. The axe bounced off the middle of a brick and clattered to the floor.

'Me again,' I said. This time I heard a grating sound when I hit the mortar and a few lumps of it fell out. The brick now looked like a loose tooth.

'Try and snag it,' I said, handing the axe over again. 'Pull it.'

Devin hung off the axe handle and grunted like the old man in the story trying to pull up the ginormous turnip, but he didn't dislodge the brick or even make it grate again. 'Bang it hard,' he said, as he handed over to me again. 'See if you can knock it straight through.'

I squared up the sledgehammer, did a practice shot and walloped the brick smack in the middle. It disappeared, leaving a black hole like a letterbox. We both heard it hit the floor on the far side.

'Teamwork!' I said. 'You howk out a few more, till we can scramble through. 'It should be easier now.'

'Are you kidding?' Devin said. 'You're going to delay gratification on this? Not me.'

He plucked his phone out of his back pocket, turned on the torch app and crouched until he was peering through the hole in the wall. Then he froze. He even stopped breathing. He'd been panting from the exertion of wielding a medium-sized hand tool three times, but now he was silent.

'Dev?' I said. 'What can you see? Have you been turned to stone by an ancient curse?'

He didn't answer.

'Devin?'

Slowly, in a series of jerks, he stood up straight again. 'Take a look and tell me that's an old decoration left over from Halloween.'

'Oh, ha-ha,' I said. 'Come on. Let's burst through. If we do the other one too, we can surprise Taylor.'

'Just look, Lexy,' Devin said. 'Look through that hole and tell me what you see.'

It took a minute to get the torch beam organized, but soon enough I was peering along a cone of light, through motes of brick dust and waving veils of cobwebs, trying to see what Devin was reacting to.

'Down a bit,' he said.

I angled the light too far at first and saw nothing but the ragged edge of the hole we had made. Then I over-corrected and sent it wanging all the way up to the crumbling plaster of the ceiling. But this time, on the way past, it had picked out something that wasn't plaster, brick or stone. I steadied my hand and took another look.

'Oh my fucking God,' I said. 'That's not a leftover Halloween anything. That's a skeleton.'

'Yup,' said Devin. There was a scraping sound from beside me that I didn't understand until I felt one of his feet bash my ankle as his legs gave way. I heard him hit the floor like a sack of spuds but I couldn't peel my eyes away from the sight beyond the hole in the wall. The skeleton was sitting on the floor, propped up against a couch, right at the other side of the room or blocked-up bit of corridor or whatever this was. But the skeleton was sitting propped up, is the point. Its spine had remained intact like a grisly Jenga, held in place God knows how. I'd never seen a real skeleton before, rather than the things that hung on hooks in anatomy labs, and I might even have believed it was normal for it to stay joined together, except for the fact that the arm bones had collapsed in two piles at its sides, like a pair of dirty grey campfires, little kindling bones underneath and big straight bones crisscrossed on top. That and the fact that the skull had rolled off. At least, I really hoped it had rolled off. I really hoped it hadn't been chopped off when it was still a head and started turning into a skull right where it was now, on the floor between the outstretched legs, grinning at me.

I clicked the light off and sank down beside Devin, briefly putting my head in between my knees, until the memory of that other skull, truly between those other knees, made my stomach threaten to let go. I sat up again.

'Mhhhurrghmm,' said Devin.

'Couldn't put it better myself,' I said. 'Come on. Wake up. We need the police.'

'We need an archaeologist is what we need,' Devin said.

I was sure he was wrong, but I didn't know why. Sheer nosiness won out over feeling sick, and I stood up again and put my eye back to the hole.

'Definitely the cops. It's got some kind of jewellery on. 'I think there's a bit of its shoes left too. Soles, maybe?'

'What kind of jewellery?' said Devin.

'A chain. Like a necklace, I think, only it's not round its neck anymore. And I think there's rings in the pile of hand bones on its left side too. Loads of rings.'

'It's a woman?' said Devin.

'I think so. Its hair looks quite long.'

'But doesn't your hair keep growing?' said Devin.

'Not in a bob,' I told him.

'Right, right,' Devin said. 'Right. Well, you've got the phone, Lexy. Nine-nine-nine, isn't it?'

'No need,' I said. 'That gobby constable's up there in the garden drinking on duty. At least he was ten minutes ago.'

Actually, he was drinking coffee and letting the kids try his hat on. In other words, he was doing some pretty decent community policing. And if many more people turned up and they all drank as much as the early arrivals had, he'd be needed for crowd control.

I made my way towards him, wondering if the hat-trying-on kids were old enough to spell and, if they were, how I was going to tell him what was up without freaking them out. I needn't have worried. He glanced up, saw my face, took his hat back and came to meet me.

'What is it?' he said.

It was the end of a peaceful Christmas, for a start. It was also a death knell to my parents' new business, it was notoriety for Yule, which didn't deserve it, and it was bad news for whoever might still be waiting for that woman to come home.

'What is it?' he said again. 'The vandals? The berry thing? What's wrong?'

I told him. Then I showed him. Then I left him to decide what to do next and went round to break the news to Taylor that he was going to have to get that branch up out of the hole and lashed back to the tree pretty pronto because no one was going to care about his owl egg for much longer today.

'Oh!' I said. 'You've done it.'

'We netted it,' said Speccy. 'We got it back up and re-secured, and not a single human hand touched a single twig of the nest. Not once.'

'High five!' said Taylor, which was out of character for him, but he was performing his exoticness for his new pals. They gave him the most awkward-looking high fives in the history of bromance, Zippy missing his hand altogether and delivering a karate-chop to Taylor's shoulder instead.

'So as long as it's a nice quiet day,' Taylor said, 'we don't see any reason to worry about the parents rejecting the egg, do we, *lads*?' It was the bromance tradition's most awkward-sounding 'lads' ever. And he followed it up with some laughably unslick boyfriend moves too. 'Say, Lex,' he began, slinging an arm around my shoulder and punching me gently in the cheek with his free hand. 'I'm not a key member of a tinsel team or anything today, am I?'

'What is it and where is it?' I said. 'I'm right, right? One of you two has had an alert in a WhatsApp group about some bird that's a week early or a mile too far south or something.'

Speccy and Zippy shook their heads and frowned at me. 'There's nothing going on anywhere that's bigger than this unseasonal nesting behaviour,' Speccy said. 'We just wondered if Taylor wanted to come back to the centre with us.'

'Don't you want to stay and watch the owls?' I said.

'We're going to pick up a—' said Zippy.

'We won't see a feather till sundown now,' said Taylor, cutting him off, 'and the quieter the better, even then.'

I did wonder what he didn't want me to hear, but not as much as I wanted him to go, so all I said was, 'Have at it. Go for it. Make a day of it.'

'If there were more women like you, I'd still be married,' Speccy said.

I gave him a sickly grin. When Taylor found out I'd got rid of him so he wouldn't have to witness the monumental influx of police I had just unleashed, he might turn me over to Speccy for first refusal. And I wouldn't have a leg to stand on, except to say again that it was an egg. And they could lay another one. He had said himself that this one was too early.

I waved him off from the gate, watching the birdmobile draw into the side to let two police cars and an anonymous-looking van pass by. Anyone else would have wondered what was going on and done a U-turn, but Taylor and his new friends, as I had known they would, pulled out again and carried on their single-minded way.

I waved the two cop cars on to the drive and went to break the news to my mother.

Thankfully, the Day of Sharing was beginning to wind down on account of the aching cold, plus the fact that all the decent sprigs had been shared and the drink was running out, so it wasn't too hard to convince everyone to head to the pub for soup and a seasonal quiz. Also, and even luckier, the idea got around that the police back-up was to do with nailing the berry rustlers. The villagers and visitors trudged away, greatly cheered by the level of police attention their little upset had garnered. I overheard one of them saying, 'Say what you like about her sacking all those high heid yins. If it's meant this many bobbies on the beat, I'm all for it.'

'Who did what to who now?' said Noleen, waving them off with me.

'Nicola Sturgeon,' I said. 'Amalgamated the forces and fired the . . . commissioners, basically.'

'Risky move, defunding the police in a country with this many drunks,' Noleen said.

I thought about explaining, then decided to direct my energies elsewhere – namely to my mother, who had just been told why four coppers and a SOCO in a white jumpsuit were on her doorstep and was looking as if she might hit someone. I hurried over so she could hit me and not go to jail for assaulting an officer.

'A skeleton?' she said when we were all gathered in the library. She had wanted to go to her flat in the basement, but the cops had vetoed that on account of proximity.

'Esqueleto, Mama?' said Diego, with his eyes like soup plates.

'No, Papi,' Della said. 'Skeleton means something else in Scottish – *isn't that right, Lexy?*'

'Yes,' I said. 'Skeleton, in Scottish, means . . . racoon.'

Diego squinched his eyes up and looked hard at me. 'That's a lot of cops for a racoon,' he said. I nodded, glad that this was his problem with my cover story, not the fact that there weren't any racoons in Scotland.

'They're hard to catch,' Kathi said. 'And no one wants the

little critter to get injured. So there's a team of cops all working together. Pretty cool, huh?'

Diego unsquinched his eyes and gave her an uncertain smile.

'Diego,' my dad said. 'Have you ever had a packet of Monster Munch?' Della started to object but my dad ploughed on. 'Ever tried a Tunnock's Teacake? How about a Lion Bar? Leanne sells all of that and more along at Ivy's One Stop.'

Knowingly or unknowingly, he had just uttered some of Diego's favourite words: monster, tea, cake and lion. He turned his eyes beseechingly to Della who threw up her hands.

'Put his hat and mittens on,' she said.

Once they were gone, we could talk freely.

'Didn't you ever go down that hatch and wonder why the passageway was bricked up?' I said.

'I'm too old to run up and down ladders breaking my legs,' my mum said. 'We got all excited when we took the fake door off and found a brick wall. Then we thought we saw the other side of the wall from the garden. It didn't look very interesting, and we had a lot on getting the place ready, so we just sort of shelved it.'

'But didn't you have a survey done?' I said.

'Roof, pipes, damp, wiring,' my mum said. 'We weren't asking anyone for a mortgage, so there was no need to nitpick.'

'Unless "nitpick" means something different over here, where "skeleton" means "racoon",' Todd said, 'I don't agree. A secret room with a corpse inside is no nit.'

My mum was obviously trying to think up a smart-alec reply to this. The rest of us, though, were poleaxed. I stared at Roger who stared back, with his mouth open. Noleen and Kathi both stared at Todd, tears in their eyes. Della and Devin stared at each other. Hiro broke the silence. 'NIT!' she said. 'NIT!'

'Honey,' Roger said. 'I've never heard you use that expression before. Are you OK?'

'Ignore them, Todd,' my mum said. 'It doesn't matter what you say these days, someone will say you can't. It's my house and it's my country, and it's all right by me.'

'That's not what's going on here, Mum,' I said. 'And also, that's not how it works either. Todd?'

He was blinking really fast and had a hand pressed to his chest.

'I didn't even notice,' he said. 'It's such a useful expression. I just said it. I think it's because I was talking to your dad, Lexy.'

'What is everyone on about?' my mum said. 'Can we get back to the corpse, please?'

'This is more important,' I said. 'That corpse has been dead for years. What did he say, Todd?'

'We were moving tables for the orgy,' Todd said. 'And I asked him if he would check underneath, you know. Before I touched them. And he told me there are no Black Widows in this country. And no Brown Recluses either.'

'What's a Brown Recluse?' said my mum.

'Then I said the trestle tables seemed very solid for how long they'd been in the shed, and he was puzzled and so was I, but eventually we straightened it out, and turns out there are no termites either. And there are no stink bugs. And no pantry moths.'

'Eww, what's a pantry moth?' said my mum.

'Don't say "Eww",' I told her.

'And no ants—'

'There *are* ants,' I said.

'No ants that come into your kitchen and eat everything every summer.'

'Well, no,' I admitted. 'Did he mention midges?'

'He did,' said Todd. 'He told me about midges. They come out in the evening, in the shade, near trees and water, and they bite you and you itch.'

'Ri-ight,' I said, sharing a glance with Roger. 'So . . .?'

'But,' said Todd, holding up one finger, 'there's a crucial difference. Everyone believes in them.'

'Of course everyone believes in them,' I said. 'They're real.'

'They're so small you can't see them, Keith told me, but no one tells you they're imaginary.'

'Well, no,' I said, 'because they're not.'

'Exactly,' said Todd. 'You know what? I think I could be happy here.'

'There are wasps, bees, flies, butterflies, ordinary spiders, earwigs, slaters, beetles, daddy long legs, ladybirds, aphids . . . Help me out, Mum.'

'Maggots,' my mum said. 'Worms. Blowflies. Seriously, can we get back to talking about what's happening?'

'And you're naming them all,' said Todd. 'And yet . . . look.' He held his hand out palm down and let us all feast our eyes on how steady it was.

'What am I missing?' my mum said.

'It's a Christmas miracle,' said Todd.

'Lexy,' Devin piped up, 'is a slater a kind of insect?'

I nodded.

'So that thing you say: better than a slater up your nose?'

I nodded again.

'I get that now. I thought you meant a roof dude. I mean, that's still probably true, but it always seemed kind of random.'

'There. Is. A. Corpse. In. The. House.' I had no idea where my mum learned to slow-clap, but her timing was impeccable. In more ways than one. The last smack of her palms was still ringing in the glass shade of the antique light fitment above our heads when a soft knock came at the half-open door and a pair of police sidled in.

'Quick word, Mrs Campbell?' said the senior-looking one: a man in his fifties in the kind of suit I didn't think you could buy anymore and a tie that looked like he took it off over his head every night. His shoes had actual duct tape on them. He looked around for somewhere to sit, but the library was the smallest, cosiest room in Mistletoe Hall and there were eight of us in there already. Instead, he walked over to the fireplace and took up a position with his back to the woodstove. I hoped his trousers were cleaner than they looked or I'd be able to smell them in a minute or two.

The other one, a woman in her thirties – slim as a blade and dressed in that stretchy formal wear that makes you look like you're in a ballet about an office – perched her tiny bottom on the arm of Noleen's armchair with a nod that was not quite apologetic and certainly not in any way a request for permission. Noleen glared at the Lycra-encased buttock six inches from her nose and rolled her eyes at Kathi, who smirked back.

'So,' said Lieutenant Columbo, nodding at his sidekick to take notes, 'I believe you bought the house only a few months ago?'

'Yes, that's right,' said my mum. 'How long does it take for a corpse to turn into a skeleton?'

'You and your husband? Where is he?'

'Gone along to the wee shop to get sweeties,' said my mum. 'So probably we'd never even heard of Yule when that poor woman sealed herself up in a basement to die.'

'What poor woman is this?' said Columbo.

'Lexy said it was a woman,' my mum said. 'Is it not then?'

'I'm Lexy,' I said. 'That's my mum. I saw the skeleton through the wee hole where we knocked the brick in. Hair in a bob, a necklace and rings, right?'

'Who's we?' Columbo asked.

I nodded at Devin who stared back with his eyes so wide I could see the whites all round.

'Sir?' said Columbo.

Devin was shivering like a whippet.

'Devin Muelenbelt,' I said. 'American citizen, here for Christmas. Freaked out by this unexpected law-enforcement encounter, I think. But as innocent as the baby. That's his baby.'

'No need to be alarmed, Mr Muelenbelt,' the younger police said. 'You're in Scotland now. No strong-arm tactics here. And what about the rest of youse? Who's all been down there for a keek.'

'Everyone else was helping out with the . . . party,' I said.

'Everyone being . . .?' said Columbo.

'Doctor Roger Kroger,' I said. 'Here for Christmas. His husband, Doctor Todd Kroger, ditto. Mrs Noleen Muntz, sitting there in the shadow of your DC's arse, and her wife, Mrs Kathi Muntz. Devin's wife, Della, there. We all live together in California and we're here to spend the holidays with my parents.'

'You all live together, eh?' said Columbo. 'It's still 1968 in San Francisco, is it?'

'I'm a sergeant,' said Yoga Clothes.

'We're neighbours,' I said. 'We live together as neighbours. Plus there's my fiancé, Taylor Aaronovitch, but he's away on a jaunt today.'

'Taylor Aaronovitch,' said Columbo. 'He's no fae Bathgate, then?'

I couldn't help a quick snort at that.

Columbo rewarded me. 'It's not a woman, we don't think,' he said. 'It's not a bob, for one thing. It's a short back and sides. A fade, you'd call it these days.'

'You wouldn't, boss,' said the sergeant, rolling her eyes.

'I try,' said Columbo. 'And I fail.'

'What about the jewellery?' I asked him.

'Necklace was a good guess, but actually it's a watch chain. That got us a wee bit excited, but there's no engraving on the fob. And it wasn't rings you saw; it was coins.'

'Coins?' said Todd, perking up.

'Loose change,' said Columbo. 'Probably in the pockets before the pockets rotted away. So, what with the hair and the watch chain, we feel safe to say it's a man. The doc'll confirm when she's had a good squint at the bones, though.'

'But you can get a date from the coins, right, Officer?' Todd said.

'Inspector,' said Columbo. 'Quick thinking, Doctor Kroger. The newest one was from 1959.'

'Shit,' said my mum. I had never heard her say that word in my life. She talked about 'dirt' and 'balderdash' where other people would say 'dogshit' and 'bullshit'.

'What's up, Mum?'

'Oh, just I was hoping it was a lot older than that,' she said. 'And, when this one said "watch chain", it sounded Victorian or something. But 1959? That's living memory. That could still hurt somebody.'

I went over and perched on the arm of the couch beside her to squeeze her shoulder.

'So,' said Columbo, 'we need to start working back. You bought the house from . . .?'

'Crispin and Wilma Garmont,' said my mum. 'They live just along the road, and you won't have to keep working back any further than that because Crispin is eighty if he's a day and he was born here. He was born in the room that's your bathroom now, Lexy. That's his rocking horse.'

'Well, we'd best get ourselves along there,' Columbo said. 'You're free to use the rooms downstairs, Mrs Campbell. Just stay on this side of the tape. If you hear any noise, it'll be us but we'll come and go through the trap door, now we've opened it all up. Keep the disturbance to a minimum.'

'That's awful kind of you, Inspector,' my mum said. 'I've got a houseful, and what with Christmas . . .'

The coppers started gathering themselves to leave, but the sergeant hesitated on the threshold. 'You didn't wonder what was bricked up down there?' she said. 'I think I would have probably wanted to see. It's strange you never . . .'

'I didn't know the two sides didn't match up,' said my mum. 'I thought it was one wall. And we'd get round to it. If I'd known it was a chamber, of course I'd have wanted to see what was inside it. It's like . . . putting a warm tea cosy on your head.'

The sergeant frowned.

'Or like touching a hot plate when a waiter tells you not to,' my mum tried next.

Another frown.

'Popping bubble wrap?' My mum was starting to sound frantic.

'It doesn't work once it's popped,' was the only reply. 'The air is what makes it function as a cushion.'

'Don't go anywhere and don't call the papers,' said Columbo as the door closed on them.

'Do they have the right to ask that?' said Noleen. 'I know there's no bill of rights in this little monarchy you got going over here, but they can't tell us not to speak to anyone. Can they?'

'I don't *want* to speak to anyone,' my mum said. 'I don't want anyone to know about it. And I certainly don't want to gossip about it. Poor Crispin! Poor Wilma! This is even worse for them than it is for me.'

'What is?' came a voice from the door. Wilma Garmont was standing there with her husband right behind her looking over her shoulder. 'Judith, why are there policemen still crawling all over the place? It was only a bit of greenery.'

Everyone looked at everyone else. No one spoke for a while. Then I noticed that Todd and Kathi were both staring at me.

'Wilma,' I said as gently as I could. 'Crispin. You'd better sit down.'

NINE

So annoying. Scrap that. Absolutely infuriating. Todd is one of the most boundary-free people I have ever met in my entire life, like the love child of Miss Marple and Louis Theroux. Kathi's scalpel is more specific: she won't ask about marital status, favourite podcasts or family history, but she'll ask if you washed your hands, wormed your cat or sat next to someone who sneezed on the bus. However, if, in the course of our investigations, anyone needs to step up and say something unwelcome or potentially devastating, they always pull the 'You're a therapist, Lexy' card and leave the dirty work to muggins.

'The thing is,' I said, 'we found a body. In the basement.'

I've done courses on breaking bad news, or at least I read an online checklist one time, and I've learned to drip it bit by bit to allow for easy digestion. Serve it all up in a oney and the mark might faint, throw up or hit you.

'Did someone collapse?' said Wilma. 'Are you sure they're dead? And not just drunk? That wassail was vicious, Kei— Oh! Where's Keith? There's such a crowd I didn't miss him.' She gasped and covered her mouth with both hands. 'It's *not* Keith, is it?'

'It's not Keith,' said my mum. 'He's taken the wee boy to the shop for treats. No, not Keith. Not him. No.'

Then, as if she'd been trained by Todd and Kathi, she turned her gaze on me like the beam of a lighthouse.

'It's—' I said, which was a bit bald. I backed up. 'The thing is, this person – they think it's a man – has been dead for a long time.'

Wilma blinked at me and then turned to Crispin in search of enlightenment.

Crispin patted her arm and stepped in like a good husband. 'And then someone dug him up and dumped him downstairs?' he said. 'Why would anyone do anything so outlandish?'

They wouldn't, I thought. What a strange conclusion to jump to.

'No, he's been down there since he died,' I said. 'I saw him. He was sitting propped up as if he died peacefully.'

'Downstairs?' said Crispin. 'I don't understand. Why did no one find him?'

'Well, this is exactly what the police want to know,' I said. 'They're on their way to your house right now to ask you. You must have just missed them.'

'We caught sight of their taillights whisking off as we turned in,' said Crispin. 'I don't miss many things about this old pile but I did always like the carriage sweep.'

'Even though it meant I never learned to reverse,' said Wilma.

'The thing is,' I said, yet again. I knew I was irritating my mum, who still reckoned she had a say in my grammar and diction as I headed for forty. 'There was a door downstairs that didn't open.'

'Yes, there's always been a false door down there,' Crispin said. 'Like those false windows in Georgian houses from when there was a tax on sunshine.'

'Well, not exactly like that,' I said. 'You know the . . . coalhole, or storm shelter, or whatever. The doors like that?' I mimed opening them up like the flaps of a box.

'The what?' said Crispin.

'I remember,' Wilma said. 'It used to be a back way to the drying yard. Not exactly handy, trying to lug a basket of soaking wet sheets up a stair that was more like a ladder. But it's long gone. It's blocked off, isn't it? Overgrown anyway.'

'Right, right,' I said. 'Blocked off.' I wanted to know how Crispin's wife remembered something about his childhood home that he'd forgotten. 'But the thing is, there were *two* walls. There was the brick wall blocking off the inconvenient hatch to the drying yard. And then behind the fake door there was another brick wall. Only they weren't the same wall.'

'Not the same wall?' said Wilma.

'There was a space in between them,' I said. 'With a skeleton.'

'From 1959,' said Todd. That was the truly enraging bit. After he and Kathi left the tough bit to me, he always swooped in and grabbed the glory.

Wilma made a strange little sound that reminded me of nothing so much as a kitten stuck in a cupboard. 'The skeleton of a man from 1959?' she said.

'The police think so,' I said. 'Or no earlier than then, anyway. He had coins.'

'But, a man?' said Wilma. 'Definitely a man?'

'They think so,' I said. 'Because of the watch chain.'

'Oh,' she said, sounding as if the kitten had given up on the hope that anyone would come and free it. 'Oh.' I thought she put her head back to rest on the chair. That's what it looked like until she started to slide. Before she had quite finished slithering all the way to the carpet, however, I realized that in fact she had fainted.

It only lasted a minute. Both doctors leapt into action. Todd flipped her into recovery position and Roger had two fingers on her pulse and an eye on his phone quicker than anyone ever opened a stopwatch in the history of apps. Plus, like I said, she came round quick.

'Billy,' she said.

'Oh my darling,' said Crispin. 'I think so. It seems so. Oh my love.'

It would have taken more guts than I possessed to ask the obvious question. Thankfully, Noleen was there.

'Who's Billy?' she said.

'Would you like a small brandy, Wilma?' said my mum.

'I would like a large brandy, Judith,' said Wilma, sitting up. 'And then another one.'

My mum footered around for a good five minutes, slinging extra logs into the burner, selecting the softest cushions to put behind Wilma's head and lumbar region, lifting her feet on to the ottoman, polishing a pair of crystal balloons to fill with brandy for her and Crispin. When I was just about to scream with frustration, finally she handed over the drinks and settled down with one caring hand on Wilma's ankle.

'Tell us everything,' she said. 'Get it off your chest. You'll feel the better for it.'

'Billy was the gardener here when I was a little boy,' said Crispin, steaming in as if Todd had trained him. 'He lived in the lodge.'

'What lodge?' said my mum. 'I didn't know there was a lodge.'
I stared at her. Did she think maybe she'd overlooked it the way
she'd overlooked the bricked-up passageway? Did she seriously
think, if they hacked back a few brambles, they might find a
rentable cottage to add to their business?

'It got carved off and sold,' Crispin said. 'But when I was a
youngster, just after the war, the gardener lived there. And the
housekeeper too.'

He stalled and took a glug of brandy.

'Go on,' said Wilma. 'Tell them.'

'Then one day the gardener disappeared,' Crispin said. 'Gone.
On Tuesday he was brushing rose petals off the lawn. On
Wednesday the petals lay where they'd fallen. He was never
heard from again.'

'Open-and-shut case, it looks like,' said Kathi. She was such
a dedicated PI these days that she sounded mournful about this
boring conclusion.

'His wife, the housekeeper – no more than a girl really – was
as mystified as the rest of us,' Crispin said. 'Poor little thing.
She was hounded by the police, but she didn't know anything.
He had been a quiet, steady, faithful husband as far as ever she
knew, and then one day – pouf!'

'As far as ever she knew?' I said.

'As far as ever she knew,' said Crispin. 'So she waited, working
twice as hard as she had before, trying to keep up with the garden
as well as the house, terrified that my parents would sack her
and employ some other couple to keep the place ticking over.
My parents weren't . . . kind people.'

'She didn't do it all on her own,' said Wilma softly. 'Did she?'

'I pitched in,' Crispin said. 'I helped with the digging and the
firewood. I carried coal and pushed the lawnmower. Those heavy
old lawnmowers, can you remember?'

'And then you started pruning, and planting, and clipping,'
Wilma said.

'By 1965, I was entering veg in the Roslin show,' Crispin said.

'And bringing home rosettes,' said Wilma. 'To go with the
prizes for flowers and baking.'

'They'd be "the housekeeper's", would they?' I said. 'Flowers
and baking.'

'They would,' said Crispin, beaming. 'They would. Slowly but surely, you see, we fell in love, hiding it from my parents, of course. But determined to be together.'

'Brave stuff for those days,' said my mum. 'What happened?'

'After seven years,' Crispin said, 'the poor young wife managed to extricate herself from the marriage. And then, no matter what my parents made of it, we married.'

'You did?' said Della. I gave her a hard look but I didn't think she was kidding. She just doesn't have a suspicious nature and she hadn't twigged.

'We did,' said Wilma. Della gasped. Todd just about managed not to groan.

'And lived happily ever after,' said Wilma. 'We moved in here and lived here for decades. We brought up our daughter here. It was a happy family home.'

'A damn sight happier than in *my* childhood,' said Crispin.

'Even when we knew it was time to leave, we didn't want to go too far,' said Wilma. 'I just—' She had been dry-eyed so far, but now she plucked a tissue out from her sleeve and dabbed her cheeks. 'I haven't thought about Billy for . . . oh, many, many years. And now we find out that all the time we were falling in love, meeting on the porch of the lodge, holding hands in the dark, plotting and planning, going up to Edinburgh to speak to lawyers, all the time we waited, and then all the years afterwards, when we were so happy here, the three of us, our little band . . . you're saying Billy was down there, bricked up in the basement?'

'I'm so sorry,' Crispin said.

'What for?' said Noleen like clockwork. I wouldn't have dared but I wondered too. Was he confessing?

'For my family,' said Crispin. 'My parents. Well, my father, I suppose. Probably. I'm sorry my father put you through such hell, my darling.'

'Hang on,' said Todd. 'I mean, yes, OK, it was their house and it's hard to see how anyone else could build brick walls and hang false doors. But maybe he killed himself, or maybe it was an accident. Maybe they were trying to spare Wilma from a scandal.'

Crispin snorted. 'If only you had ever met them, you'd know

how ludicrous a notion that is,' he said. 'My parents hated Wilma. And they loathed Billy. They killed him, I assure you.'

'Why, though?' Kathi said. 'Why did they hate you both? And why didn't they just can you both? Why would they kill one and keep employing the other?'

While Kathi was speaking, Wilma flattened herself back against the cushions behind her, as if the words were blasting her in the face.

I stepped in. 'Kathi is a licensed PI, back in California,' I said. 'Trinity Investigations. She's being business-like, not unkind.'

'Trinity Investigations – in fact, the whole of Trinity – can probably help you right now,' Todd said, sweeping in again. 'Lexy is a counsellor and she can offer all kinds of support and a safe space to let you express your feelings about this traumatic discovery. I myself am a life coach. I can suggest areas of self-care you won't even have dreamed of yet.'

'That sounds marvellous,' said Wilma. 'What does it mean?'

Crispin didn't even manage that much. He was baffled by everything Todd had just said, clearly. He turned back to Kathi like a drunk to a lamp post. 'They didn't always,' he told her.

Kathi blinked and frowned. I had to scroll back a bit too, to catch what he was on about.

'Your parents didn't always hate Wilma and Billy?' Roger said, using his big brain.

'Absolutely not,' Crispin said. 'We bowled along quite the thing at first. Of course, my pa grumbled a bit about the changes, post-war. He'd been brought up on maids in black frocks with white pinnies on top. Changing for dinner and all that. He didn't much take to the fifties. But having a housekeeper and gardener installed in the lodge soothed him. It was a bit of the old days, you know?'

'Until,' Wilma said.

'Quite, quite. Until,' Crispin said. 'Do you know, old thing, as well as the shock of it and the dread of what's coming, I feel a modicum of relief. Don't you? Boot dropped and all that.'

'I know what you mean,' said Wilma. 'But I wouldn't call it a relief exactly.'

'*Until?*' said Noleen.

'It's the old story,' said Crispin. '*Cherchez la femme.*' He spoke with a flourish, but his words were met with blank looks all round. 'My sister Verity,' he explained. 'My sister Verity got herself into a spot of bother, let's say.'

'What kind of bother?' said Kathi.

'Pregnant,' Wilma said. 'Sorry, darling.'

'The parents hit the roof,' said Crispin. 'It just wasn't done. Not then, not here, not people like us. The night she told them, while he was shouting at her, I genuinely thought my father was going to have a stroke. His face was purple. Verity was crying her eyes out. My mother was as drunk as a lord. I couldn't make any headway with any of them. Couldn't get my father to calm down before he blew a gasket, couldn't get my mother to have a cup of coffee, couldn't get Verity to stop crying and tell us who the devil had taken advantage of her. So I went to the lodge to ask Wilma if poor V could come and stay the night on the zed bed in her box room.'

'I remember it like yesterday,' Wilma said. 'Your face, as white as a sheet, on the doorstep. The way you stammered to tell us.'

'And then the most surprising thing,' Crispin said. 'Billy took off across the garden as if the hounds of hell were behind him and marched straight in through the front door.'

'It didn't surprise *me*,' Wilma said. 'He had always been very fond of Verity. We both were.'

'And that was the last anyone saw of him,' Crispin said. 'Wilma and I watched him trot up the front steps and disappear into the vestibule. Then I came over a bit wobbly, didn't I darling?'

'You were so white and strained-looking,' Wilma said. 'If you'd been a stranger off the road, I would have asked you in and given you a cup of sweet tea, never mind a boy I'd known for years – ironed your shirts and everything.'

'After a bit, I crept back over,' Crispin said. 'V and my mother were nowhere to be seen, but my pa was in here, in this very room, nursing a whisky and staring into the fire. "She's going to go away and have it where no one knows her and no one knows us", he told me. "Stupid girl!"'

'What a sweetheart,' I said.

'They were different times,' said Crispin. 'I was simply grateful that Billy – as I thought – had managed to calm the old boy down. I wanted to thank him. I asked my pa where he was.'

'I remember you telling me the next day when I was so worried,' Wilma said. 'I remember what you said.'

'I asked Pa where Billy was and he said, "Gone".'

I think all of us had been waiting for a big twist of some kind. Each of us breathed out and deflated a bit.

'Of course, I took it to mean "Gone home to Wilma",' Crispin said.

'Only he never turned up,' Wilma chipped in. 'I went to bed and waited. Then I fell asleep. And when I woke up the next morning, his side of the bed hadn't been disturbed. So, eventually, I went over to the house to ask. After that, "Gone" meant something quite different. He was *gone*.'

'That's when we realized he was the father of Verity's baby,' said Crispin. 'Nothing else made sense, you see?'

'I was so ashamed,' Wilma said. 'First he seduced a young girl he'd known since she was a child, then he ran off and left her to face it all alone. The second always seemed more of a sin to me. I was so very ashamed of him. And now we find out . . .'

'. . . he didn't run away at all,' Crispin said. 'He didn't leave Verity to the brutal mercies of my pa. He . . . Well, he . . .'

'We don't know anything for sure yet,' I said. 'But the police surgeon might be able to tell something from the skeleton.'

'Oh!' said Wilma. 'I hope it was quick! Oh poor Billy.'

'Wilma,' Della piped up suddenly. 'You are a good woman. If my husband knocked up his boss's daughter, I'd still be angry, still hoping it was slow and painful, fifty years later.'

'Sixty!' said Crispin, weirdly emphatic, as if he wanted to push the ugly fact as far into the past as it would go.

Wilma seemed to be done with her reminiscing now. She heaved a massive breath, swung her feet back down and gave her husband – her second husband, her husband of so many years that surely he felt like her only husband – a brave smile. Then she turned to my mum.

'Judith, we are so very sorry.'

'It's not your fault,' my mum said.

'Do you know,' said Crispin, 'my mother tried to make sure we never had to face this. She practically made us swear we'd stay in this house for the rest of our lives.'

'Then Miley would have been stuck with the discovery!' said

Wilma. 'That's a wicked way to pay back an innocent child for being born to your precious son and a lowly housekeeper.'

'Yikes,' said my mum. 'Yes, that is pretty cold. Sorry, Crispin. I know she was your family.'

'Do not apologize to me, dear lady,' Crispin said. 'After all this!'

'We'd better go and put the police out of their misery,' Wilma said. 'They must be scratching at the door. If they've not actually started a missing-person search for us.' She turned to Della. 'When you get old, young people can be really patronizing. Thank you, pet, for speaking to me woman to woman. You've no idea how much it means.'

Crispin got himself to his feet with a bit of creaking and groaning. 'Cold weather is the devil to my knees,' he said.

'Before you go,' Kathi said, 'can I ask just one question? Crispin, you were living in the house then? That night? How did your parents explain bricking up a part of the basement? Did that never strike you as strange?'

'Oh, it struck me as very strange,' Crispin said. 'It struck me as ludicrous. But, you see, my father let it be known that that was how Billy had got into the house when it was ostensibly all locked up at night – through those trap doors, you know – and then my mother let it be known that that was where he and Verity had . . . met. In the little room that ended up being blocked off. So, in one sense, it was strange. And, in another sense, it was perfectly understandable. If you'd ever met an old sod like my father, head of the household and all that.'

'Can *I* ask a question?' Todd said. 'What happened to your sister and the baby?'

'I can tell you what was supposed to happen,' Crispin said. 'I remember my mother's voice, icy with disdain. "As soon as she shows her face, she is going to be packed off somewhere discreet. When the wretched thing is adopted, she can come home again".'

'Wretched *thing*?' said Della.

'What did she mean, "shows her face"?' I asked. 'Did she hole up in her room?'

'She took off completely,' said Crispin. 'My mother assumed she'd gone to a friend's house and would soon come crawling back.'

'*Did* she?' Todd said.

'She did not,' said Crispin, sounding oddly cheerful.

'She never turned up?' I said. 'That's unnerving. You don't think your father was angry enough to—'

'Oh!' said Wilma in a louder and brighter voice. 'No, no, no. We didn't mean to imply that at all. She never came back *here* to be shunted off to some dreadful mother-and-baby home. She took off to the Caribbean! Heaven knows where she got the money from. But she went to live in Paradise! Had the baby – a little boy! – and lived there her whole life. Died happy with pink sand between her toes and the sound of the ocean in her ears. So there. You see. You never can tell.'

'And the baby?' I said, not sure what you never could tell but willing to go along with the general sentiment. 'Did you ever have contact with him?'

'Coming for Christmas!' Wilma cried out, clapping her hands. 'Nelson. Miley didn't come last night after all, because she's meeting him at the airport and driving him down. We're having a proper family Christmas at last.'

'Family,' said Kathi, 'because Nelson is . . . your . . .?'

'I know! I'm the same!' Wilma said. 'I always think he's some kind of relation too. The son of my husband. He should be something to me.'

'He's our nephew, Wilma,' said Crispin. 'My sister's boy.'

'And we're going to have to be very gentle with him when we reveal what happened to his dad,' Wilma said. 'Let's hope the police are done and dusted by the time they arrive.'

'With that in mind,' Crispin said, smacking his hands together, 'the sooner we begin, eh?' He hauled his wife to her feet, gave her a quick hug and toddled off, with her hand tucked into his arm.

We watched them leave and then stayed sitting in a silent circle, letting the tale bed in. At least, that's what I was doing. Todd, it transpired, was in a very different frame of mind.

'Something doesn't add up about all of that,' he said.

'No shit,' said Noleen. 'They lived in a house with a rotting corpse in the basement and no one noticed?'

'Not that,' said Todd. 'Well, not just that.'

'Stone house,' I said. Stone floors. Stone flags. Bricks. You couldn't live in an American house while a human being decomposed downstairs, but I don't think there's a problem with it happening here.'

'Just one more way we suck, huh?' Roger said. 'What's bugging you, honey?'

'Hard to say,' said Todd, opening his mouth wide and using his fingers to play a little tune on his cheek. He'd stopped that, while we were all not touching our faces, and I hadn't missed it. 'I'm going to go for a walk and think back over everything we just heard,' he said. 'Dictate it into my phone. Because my Spidey sense is definitely tingling.'

Spidey sense. Todd Kroger had just said 'Spidey sense'. We were off the map and the satnav wasn't working.

TEN

I t was a glorious day to go for a tramp in the woods. If you were sick to the gills of California sunshine, that is. At the edge of the trees on the far side of the ploughed field, a raw cold was beginning to seep up from the frozen ground, penetrating our thick soles and double socks. The light was sinking too, the sun disappearing over the hill and taking the last whisper of warmth with it. The frost, briefly thawed enough to drip off twig ends, was reforming by the minute. I entertained myself by walking in the lee of a stone wall, one foot squelching where the sun had sogged the grass and one foot creaking where the shade had kept it crisp. I blew rings of steam with my breath and sniffed the heady perfume of rotting bracken, wet sheep and coal smoke. Home.

'They don't show this on BritBox,' Kathi said. 'What *is* that smell?'

'Sixty years ago,' Todd said, 'a guy completely disappears and no one looks for him? *That* stinks for a start.'

'Different times,' I said. 'No cards. No phones. No socials. And let's face it: he had a good reason to run. He'd been caught seducing his boss's daughter, cheating on his wife. He'd lost his job and none of them would have wanted him visiting the baby.'

'The baby that was supposed to be shunted off to an adoption service,' Kathi said.

'I wonder how these "Edinburgh lawyers" managed to get Crispin and Wilma married,' Todd said. He quirked a look at me. I shrugged. 'In those "different times", I mean. Could you declare people dead over here back then?' I shrugged. 'And I know he said she was a girl, but she was the housekeeper. She must have been older than him. Why couldn't his parents stop it if they wanted to?' I shrugged. It was beginning to feel like a workout. 'Does she *look* a lot older than him?' I shrugged but I backed up this one with some moaning.

'Come on! That's your area, Todd. I don't know how old people are, because I don't care. How old would *you* say?'

'I can't age people who've lived in biting winds with no facials their whole lives,' Todd said. 'Everyone over twelve looks eighty. Lord, this weather.' He pulled his scarf up until only his eyes were exposed and then pulled a pair of ski sunglasses down over them too.

'Can you still see where you're going?' I asked. 'Because, believe me, you don't want to trip over a tree root and break your ankle. NHS casualty waiting room, four days before Christmas?'

Todd took my arm, reminding me of Wilma leaning on Crispin. Kathi latched on to the other one with a death grip. 'I saw a documentary one time,' she said. '*Twenty-Four Hours in A and E*. It looked like something from Dickens.'

Joined together like that, when one stopped, all stopped. And, once we had walked on in silence for a minute or two, except for Todd muttering about the temperature, Kathi stopped dead, bringing the two of us to a ragged halt with her.

'Look!' she hissed. 'Shush and look over there. Stand still. He hasn't seen us.'

'What are you even pointing at?' said Todd. 'Oh yeah!'

Back across the field, beside the garden walls, someone was moving, slightly hunched over as if making sure he couldn't be seen from the upstairs windows of the cottages beyond, but every so often doing a short meerkat-periscope move to check where he'd got to. A slight, dark figure, hard to see clearly in the deep shadow, he crept along. Then, as we watched, he found what he had been looking for and bent right over, studying the ground.

'Fan out,' Todd said. 'Flank me. We'll kettle him.'

'Pincer,' I said. 'Not kettle.' Todd glared at me. 'Sorry. OK.'

Todd made straight for the target, while Kathi and I tacked out wide on either side, stumbling over the frozen ridges and splashing through the slushy furrows in between. I was sure that, any minute, the bent-over guy was going to hear us coming and either turn or flee, but we got right up to him, close enough to see the earbuds, close enough to hear the tsk-tsk of the rap he was listening to, and still he remained engrossed in whatever he'd found, there in the icy mud by the garden wall.

Todd leaned over and tapped him smartly on one shoulder.

'Waarrghhh!' He leapt a clear foot in the air and twisted like a salmon as he came down, ending up facing us with both hands up to ward off blows. It was the copper from this morning, in mufti.

'Consternoon, Aftable,' I said. 'That's an old joke,' I told Kathi and Todd. 'A traditional way to greet a police that stops you for a breathalyser, but it fits here too.'

'Jesus Christ!' he said. He was bent over again, but only to get a hold of his breath now. When he'd heaved in and out a couple of times, he straightened up, his face pale blue from the adrenaline rush leaving him.

'Have a sweetie,' I said. I had found a packet of Polos in the pocket of my borrowed coat. 'You need the sugar. What are you doing?'

'I'm cracking the case. That lot's sidelined me because I'm uniform and they're CID. Pillocks. So I thought I'd take a shortcut over the allotments and beat them home.'

Kathi was frowning. 'He means an end run,' I said. 'Wow, look at that! I'm translating into Sports! Are you getting anywhere with it?'

'Oh yes,' he said. 'I certainly am. I don't think it was any accident that that skeleton was found today.'

'Oh?' I said, my mind immediately on my parents and the fact that they owned the house it was found in.

'Care to elaborate?' said Todd.

'Care to meet me in the pub and buy me a drink?' said the copper.

'I'm too cold and jet-lagged to go all the way to the pub right now,' Kathi said. 'My wife makes a mean margarita, though. And it's warm and cosy in the kitchen at Mistletoe Hall.'

'Suits me,' the copper said. 'I've never had a margarita.'

Todd and Kathi boggled a bit at that. It was like he'd said he'd never had an apple.

'They've never had a black pudding,' I told him to even things back up again.

'Is that the same as treacle tart?' said Todd. 'Because, for your information, I had one once in an Irish pub in New York.'

'Yeah, exactly the same thing,' I said. 'Sorry for doubting you.'

*   *   *

The fake kitchen at Mistletoe Hall was every bit as welcoming as Kathi expected. There was another of my mum's gargantuan stews bubbling on the range and the reflections from the overhead light bouncing off all the copper pans made it look as if the place was hung around with fairy lights, like the rest of the house now that Della and my mum had been busy and every room was slowly disappearing under tinsel.

'Spill,' I said. 'What's your name, by the way?'

'Larg,' said the copper.

'Larg?' I echoed. 'Not Largs? One Larg?'

'What are Largs?' said Kathi, which was a good question.

'What the hell kind of name is Larg or Largs?' I said.

'My mum hates kids,' Larg said. 'Apparently. Right. OK. First of all, you're in trouble, all of you.'

'Did you miss out the word "not" from that sentence?' said Kathi.

'No, you're in deep trouble,' Larg said. 'You decided there had been a berry heist. And once you found the berries there wasn't any reason to keep investigating, right?'

'Uh, yeah,' I said, 'but you're the police. We might have said that – we did say that – but you bought it. You're in trouble, pal, not us.'

'Anyway,' Larg said, 'you're idiots. No way that's what happened.'

'If only Noleen was here,' Kathi said. 'She'd find this refreshing. How are we idiots, Larg? Is that like a Viking name?'

'So many reasons,' Larg said. 'First of all, if someone's rustling berries to sell at a dodgy Christmas market, they don't make such a mess of the product while they're lifting it.'

'We actually said that too,' Todd put in.

'Also, thieves tend to take the stuff away with them when they've got a hold of it.'

'But they panicked when they broke the branch off the tree and made all that noise,' I said.

'Panicked, right,' said Larg. 'Panicked so much that they scarpered, leaving the haul behind?'

'Ye— Well, nearly,' I said.

'Not even close to nearly,' said Larg. 'Your version has them taking binbags away from the back garden here, going round the end of the last house to a gate, and backtracking halfway up a field to dump them there. Also, panicked people leave footprints. Which I was just looking for and didn't find.'

'Right,' I said, but it was starting to bother me.

'It would have been quicker just to leave.'

'Huh,' I said. 'You might be right.'

'So why *didn't* they take the sacks of swag?' said Larg. No one spoke. 'Or try this one,' he continued. 'Why did they climb that tree above the trap door?'

'Duh, for mistletoe,' Kathi said.

'Duh, yourself,' said Larg. 'You're saying they ignore the trees in the front garden, hidden from the street and far from the house, including all the stuff reachable from ground level. And instead they choose the tallest tree, nearest the house – in fact right outside a window.'

'They didn't come for the berries!' I said.

'They didn't come for the berries,' said Larg in a sarcastic echo. 'They came to bring a branch down on a trap door, to make the new owners of the house look into what was *beyond* that trap door. They snatched a load of ivy and holly too, to put us off the scent, then stashed it. Because they didn't want it and they didn't want to be caught with it.'

'That doesn't make any sense,' I said.

'It fooled you,' he said. 'And it fooled the CID. It didn't fool me, though.'

'It's a little elaborate,' Todd said. 'As a way to get the secret chamber opened.'

'Oh?' said Larg. 'What would you have done?' He paused, but Todd said nothing. 'To make an owner start knocking lumps out of their house. Hmm?' Still nothing. 'How would you make me start prising up the floorboards of my flat, for instance?'

'An anonymous tip-off!' said Todd. 'I'd have sent an anonymous email, obviously.'

'You wouldn't,' Larg said. 'Not about a skeletonized corpse that had been mouldering underground for fifty years.'

Sixty! I heard an echo of Crispin's energetic correction but managed not to say it out loud.

'Oh?' said Todd, waspish as ever when someone corrected him. Like most incredibly bossy people, he didn't care for anything approaching criticism.

'Well, it's like this,' Larg said. 'Some people believe you shouldn't write your passwords down in a wee book you keep beside your laptop. They say that's dangerous. They're wrong. Some of them even say you should have the same password for everything as long as you don't save it anywhere. They're extra-wrong.'

'What's this got to do with Billy . . . What's his other name?' I said.

'I'll tell you,' said Larg. 'But not right now. See, the kind of people who break into your house and steal stuff to sell down the pub are not the kind of people who would know what to do with your passwords. The kind of people who would know what to do with your passwords will find your one and only oh-so-safe password online, on the flakiest site you ever bought something off, and clean out your bank account before breakfast. The only thing that would foil them would be if you wrote your passwords down in a wee book you kept beside your laptop.'

'Yeah, but what *does* this have to do with Billy . . . And is his name a clue?' said Kathi.

'A really ignorant boomer would send an "anonymous" email—' said Larg.

'Hey!' Todd put in.

'And make such a hash of it we'd find them without trying. A tech-head would send a good anonymous email and get away with it. The person who used the "bring a tree down" method of resurrection, therefore, is someone who understands enough about the tech to know their limits and really doesn't want to be fingered.'

'Doesn't want to be . . .?' said Kathi.

'Accused,' I said. 'Why would they be so worried about bringing a crime to light?'

'You tell me,' said Larg.

'Because they're involved?' said Todd.

'Possibly,' said Larg. 'But then why not let sleeping skeletons lie?'

'Because . . .' Todd said. 'They stand to gain something from it waking up?'

'Bingo,' said Larg. 'See? We know quite a lot about this person already, don't we?'

I didn't want to admit it, because he had worked all that out after a few minutes with the physical evidence *we'd* had since the early morning – bags of swag and lack of footprints – and he was making us look bad.

'What's Billy's other name?' I said, as a distraction.

'Promise you won't laugh,' said Larg.

'I'm jet-lagged, I'm freezing cold and we're talking about a murder,' said Kathi. 'I won't laugh. Don't know about these two.'

'There's nothing funny about any of this,' said Todd.

'I agree,' I said. 'What's his name?'

'The skeleton's name,' said Larg, 'is Mr Bone.'

Eventually, we really did go to the pub. I went because it's coded in my DNA. Todd and Kathi came with me because the other options were trying to wake Roger or listening to more of Noleen's child-like wonder at how rude everyone was – she had met an Amazon delivery woman and a florist now and enjoyed a fine sparring session with both of them.

Kathi snorted as we walked down the street. 'Mr Bone.'

'It's not funny,' said Todd. Then he said, 'Billy Bone the butler,' and cackled like a castanet.

'Handyman,' I said. 'So who would want him found? Cui bono?'

'Bono!' said Kathi. 'Sorry.' She held the pub door open for me, with her head hanging.

Once we were sitting in one of the two booths on the short wall furthest from the door – the cosiest spot in the whole pub this early in the evening before other people's breath and sweat took the chill out of the air – Todd said, 'Should we be talking about this here?' He did a big stagey look over one shoulder and then the other.

'It's either here or back at the house or out on the tundra,' said Kathi. 'I vote for here.'

'OK,' said Todd. 'Who *would* want that skeleton out of the closet, so to speak? Six months ago, your parents, Lexy.'

'They fit the profile of techno-twits,' I said. 'But apart from that . . . huh?'

'Because people trying to sell their house would want it to stay hidden, right?' Todd said. 'But people hoping to buy a house would want it to come to light – lower the price.'

'But now it makes no odds to the old owners,' Kathi said. 'And your mom and dad? Who the hell wants that kind of publicity in their kind of business?'

'But it must be related to the house being sold somehow, right?' I said. 'It's buried for decades, then my mum and dad rock up and suddenly someone wants it out in the open? Too much of a coincidence.'

'It's got to be something to do with the kid,' said Todd. 'Billy's kid. The son of the daughter of the house. The one who's suddenly coming back.'

'But to do with him *how*?' said Kathi. 'Love? Money?'

'Not love,' said Todd.

'Too late for hate,' said Kathi. 'Most of them are dead.'

'Must be money then,' I said. 'The Garmont fortune.'

Kathi and Todd said nothing.

'There's something . . .' I said. 'There's a ghost of half an idea knocking about the back of my head for some reason.' I was sitting opposite them, focused pretty hard on their faces while I wracked my brain, so I had a clear view of when they stopped looking me in the eye and, instead, let their gaze travel upwards and fix on something above my head. Their eyes widened as they stared.

'What is it?' I asked them.

'We should have gone for the tundra,' Kathi said. I twisted round in my seat and looked up to see a pair of faces side by side at the top of the booth divider. The woman was in her fifties, the man harder to pin an age on, since his face was partially obscured by the finest set of wild dreadlocks I had ever seen on a white guy. I groaned.

'Shit!' I said. 'Sorry.'

'No, no, not at all,' said the woman. 'If I don't hear my own family being gossiped about by complete strangers, I'm never sure if I'm actually back in Yule.' She had a posh Scottish accent and, on closer inspection, looked like a perfect mash-up of Crispin's bone structure and Wilma's colouring.

'Miley, right?' I said. I twisted round even further and managed to offer my hand. 'Lexy Campbell. My mum and dad bought your mum and dad's house.'

'So I gather,' said Miley. 'Care to go for the double?' She indicated the man beside her.

'You must be Verity's son,' I said. 'Nelson? Lexy Campbell. Please come and join us and let me make up for . . . what would you even call it?'

They disappeared from the top of the booth divider and, after some scuffling noises, appeared at our table.

'So,' said Nelson, as he squashed in beside Todd, 'give us more of your hot take on this skeleton in a closet at Mistletoe Hall.' He had a rich and totally incongruous Caribbean accent that would have got him smacked in the face for insensitivity in any big city in America.

'I'm really sorry,' I said. 'What are you drinking?'

'Not to mention the kid with the money,' said Nelson.

'Like Kathi just said – it makes no sense. I wasn't thinking straight. Jet lag, you know. Well, you do know, don't you? How was *your* flight?'

'I'm over the flight,' said Nelson. 'I came a few days early to hang with Miley in the city.'

'Oh you did?' said Todd. He waggled his eyebrows at me. We maybe didn't know why this guy would want Mr Bone dredged up, but it was interesting to hear he was on the spot to do the dredging.

'I needed to fortify myself before I faced my dear aunt and uncle,' Nelson told us. 'That and Christmas shopping.'

'And I can always take a bit more fortification before I face my dear parents,' Miley said, raising her wine glass.

'Hang on,' I said, a terrible notion beginning to take hold of me.

'Oh my God,' said Todd. 'You mean, you stopped off here for a drink *before* you went home?'

'You mean, you don't know?' said Kathi.

'Know what?' said Nelson.

'Didn't—?' I said, swinging round. But it wasn't Beth at the bar. It was some kid that didn't look old enough to be serving drinks. Definitely too young to care about village gossip.

'And hasn't your mom been phoning you?' said Todd. 'Or texting? Or something?'

'Oh, only all bloody day,' Miley said. 'I've learned to screen her when I'm headed down. Otherwise, I spend six hours in Marks and Sparks' food hall and another six in the offy. What is it you think she wanted to tell me?'

They did it again, the toerags! They did that thing where they both turned to me with their eyes wide open and their mouths sewn shut. *Over to you, Lexy.*

'Well,' I said, 'when we said a skeleton in the closet, that wasn't just an expression. And it wasn't in the closet. It was in the basement. There was a body in the basement at Mistletoe Hall, for the last sixty years, until it was found earlier today.'

When I had finished, they both sat for longer than people usually sit, stiller than people usually manage. Miley spoke first. 'Maybe that drink you mentioned?'

'I'll get it,' said Kathi, the weasel, leaping to her feet and practically sprinting across the floor to the bar. She wasn't complaining about the lack of waitress service in Scottish pubs, suddenly.

'Who was it? Do they know?' said Nelson.

'What?' I said. 'Oh, shit. You didn't hear that bit?'

'We were still outside,' Todd chipped in.

'We only started eavesdropping properly when we overheard "Garmont",' said Miley. 'Why? Who was it?'

I laid a firm hand on Todd's arm, in case he had any thoughts of going to help Kathi carry the glasses. I needed someone else to watch the reactions in case all of this was an act.

'Nelson,' I said. 'I'm really sorry to be the one to tell you this, but it was your dad.'

'My *dad*?' Nelson said. He looked at Miley, who shook her head. 'My dad hasn't been locked in a cupboard in someone's basement for sixty years,' he said. 'My dad was still kicking five years ago. What are you talking about?'

'OK,' I said. 'Not your dad. Obviously, not your *dad*. But I mean the man . . . your genetic . . . I mean your . . .'

'My biological father?' he said. 'Is that what you're telling me? How the hell did he get from Miami Beach to my grandma's house?'

'Huh?' I said. 'I thought your mum lived in Bermuda.'

'Barbuda,' said Kathi, back from the bar.

'Bahamas,' said Todd.

'Barbados!' said Nelson. 'Specifically, Miami Beach, Barbados. I don't understand.'

'Me neither,' I admitted. 'Maybe you should go along to . . .

Mince Pie Cottage or whatever it's called and speak to Crispin and Wilma.'

'I like the cut of your jib, Lexy Campbell,' said Miley, giving me an appraising look. 'Anyone who can't stomach Yule is my kind of people. Even if your parents have planted – I mean, found! – a bit of an embarrassment for my folks.'

There was so much wrong with that little speech that I was struck dumb. Kathi stepped in.

'You're wrong about Keith and Judith,' she said. 'I know better than most what it does to a hospitality business when a corpse turns up.'

'Or even four corpses,' I added, throwing Kathi under the bus with gay abandon in the pursuit of freaking out Miley and her cousin.

'It's only been three corpses,' said Kathi, which wasn't the knock-out punch she seemed to think it was.

'Only two that actually count,' Todd added. He probably thought he was helping.

We left them there working up to facing their relations and returned to ours.

'One thing,' Todd said, as we slipped and slithered along the pavement. 'Nelson the white Rasta? Don't tell Roger, OK?'

ELEVEN

Thursday 22 December

I opened my eyes the next morning to a different world. I knew it even through the closed curtains. The quality of the light was transformed and the sound of the silence had become something gentle and soothing. I had forgotten this, the instant certainty, and I felt an ache in my throat at being reminded.

'I think I need my ears syringed,' said Taylor beside me. 'Everything's muffled.'

'You don't,' I said.

'And my vision's . . . not blurred but . . .'

'But nothing,' I said. 'It's snowed in the night. That's all.'

'Snow?' he said, leaping out of bed. 'You told us a white Christmas was Hollywood bullshit.' I watched the goose pimples popping out on his naked bum as he crossed to the window and opened the curtains as slowly as an image downloading in dial-up days. When he had got a big enough gap to see through, he let out a huge sigh. 'All well,' he said. 'I was worried about pile-up but we've still got a fantastic view and it's fine. Come see this, Lexy.'

I grabbed my dressing gown from beside the bed and pulled it under the covers to warm up before I put it on. Winter living in my homeland was coming back to me. I had even remembered to put socks under my pillow last night. I rummaged for them and slipped them on my feet, managing not to lift the quilt and let any draughts in. By the time I slithered out and put my feet in my slippers, Taylor was shivering, so I generously didn't tie my belt but, instead, cuddled up behind him and put my dressing-gown flaps round him too.

'Oh,' I said. 'It's lovely!'

It really was. The garden was blanketed in a thick layer of pure white, broken only by the tracks of a fox or maybe a hare. The rhododendrons and lilacs by the wall were weighed down with scoops of snow on every leaf, and the fields beyond sparkled. The horizon was a perfect trans flag of pink and blue stripes, with just one spire of smoke in the distance from a woodcutter's cottage or a gingerbread house. Basically.

'You think?' said Taylor. 'Pretty plain, I'd say, although – sure – remarkable that it survived.'

I glanced at him and followed his gaze to the tree just outside our window, where the broken branch was held on with approximately fifty splints, clamps and BDSM-style jubilee clips all to protect the mess of twigs and fluff we were looking down into, in the middle of which sat a solitary pale-cream-coloured owl egg.

'Where are the par—?' I said. Then I stepped back sharply, taking my dressing gown with me, as one of the owls – bloody enormous this close up – came wheeling down to its nest, scraping the glass with the tips of its wings, then settling on top of the egg and crumpling its head down into its neck like an old CV2 parking.

'Wow,' Taylor said. He craned his neck round, quite owlishly as it happened, to look at me. 'Wow, right?'

'Wow,' I agreed. For one thing, it *was* quite cool that the egg had made it through the previous day and the parents hadn't abandoned it in all the upset. But also, when talking to Taylor, life's too short to question how amazing birds are.

'We got sidetracked yesterday, but Kev and Trev said they might have time to come back this afternoon to set up a camera. Definitely by tomorrow.'

'Cool,' I said. So Speccy and Zippy were going to be hanging out in my bedroom, were they? This, after Taylor had spent the whole previous day God-knows-where and come back frozen, starving and caked in mud. Was this maybe the time to put my foot down?

Then I looked at him, standing there bollock-naked and grinning like an idiot. 'Get back into bed before you catch pneumonia, you wazzock,' I said. 'I'll go and get some coffee for you.'

'This is the best vacation I've ever been on,' he said, burrowing back into the bedclothes. 'I definitely want to get married here, Lexy. Did you know your dad was studying to become a celebrant?'

'Dad?' I said, down in the real kitchen, where the easier-to-work coffeemaker lived. 'Is that true, what Taylor's just said, that you're branching out into weddings?'

'I am, my child,' he said in a sonorous voice. Then in his normal voice, he went on, 'That doesn't work though. Because you are my child.'

'No denying it,' I said, thinking of Nelson the night before. 'Not with your nose on my face like it is.'

'Weddings, funerals and naming ceremonies,' he said. 'Of course, only the weddings are a real moneymaker, but it seemed a bit rude not to cover the lot.'

'I love you,' I said, screwing the lids on to our two cups of coffee.

'I know, I know,' he said. 'I'll need to get used to all that mushy stuff when I start doing ceremonies. Can't say I'm keen, although I do like a good funeral. I wonder if Wilma will let me do Billy's.'

I didn't have an answer for that, so I left him planning the eulogy and trudged back upstairs. Taylor was at the window again, but he'd put some clothes on and wasn't shivering. I handed over his coffee cup and got back into bed, chasing wisps of warmth around the mattress with my bare feet. I had missed feeling cosy, in California. When it's never cold, you never appreciate being nice and warm.

'I didn't get a chance to tell you yesterday,' Taylor said, 'but I had *thee* best time at the bird reserve. It's a hell of a set-up.'

I managed not to splutter. He had talked my ear off about acreage, vehicles, hospital accommodation, feeding regimes, release protocols and even the computer network after he got home. What more could there possibly be to say?

'Their funding structure is so secure.'

Ah, right. He hadn't gone into detail about the financial arrangements.

'Is it?' I said. 'That's a surprise. Isn't it a charity?'

'Dollops of direct grants and decades of fundraising activities.'

'Cool,' I said.

'And the birds! I've never lived anywhere except California, Lex. I saw birds yesterday I've only seen on YouTube.'

'I remember the feeling,' I said. 'Like me and blue jays.'

'Kev has an *Alcedo atthis* in rehab right now that took a smelt off his fingertip.'

'Ouch,' I said.

'A smelt is a little fish.'

'What's an Attila axis?'

'Common kingfisher,' said Taylor. 'See?'

I considered it and had to go with, 'Not really.'

'A *common* kingfisher. Real basic little bird. Like these owls out here. These are not long-eareds. These are not *Bubo bubo*, Lexy. These are *Strix aluco* and I can't take my eyes off of them.'

'I'm happy for you,' I said. I hoped it sounded sincere. The truth was I remembered when I was *Strix aluco* and he couldn't keep his eyes, or hands, off me.

'And then on the way home, we stopped at a place that sells . . . I don't even know how to describe what it was. It was in tempura.'

'Batter?' I said. 'That doesn't narrow it down as much as you'd think.'

'Inside a dinky little mini-mall.'

'Probably Southern Scotland's flagship retail experience,' I said. 'Where exactly?'

Taylor shrugged. 'No clue. Off some tiny road on to an even tinier road in the dark. But that's not the point. The point is there was a phone store in there. At least, what passes for a phone store. More like a phone *truck*. Like a little hotdog stand but for phones? And it's what? Three days before Christmas? And the kid working there was doing her nails, Lexy. She had no customers. You see?'

I tried to see. He was talking about one of those market-stall things parked in the concourse of a shopping centre, selling phone accessories or hair crap. But did I see what exactly he was getting at? Again, I had to go with, 'Not really.'

'No one in this entire country gives a single flying fuck about their cellphone,' Taylor said. 'I love it here.'

'Um,' I began, then I thought back over the last couple of days. My mum and dad shared a phone. But then they were old. Zippy and Speccy each had a Samsung in a cammo case, but then they were . . . I didn't finish that thought because so was

Taylor, and I was going to marry him. I tried to think what Leanne or Beth's phone looked like and realized that neither of them had put it on the kitchen table or the bar.

'You might be right,' I said. 'Comparatively speaking.'

'I am right,' said Taylor. 'I'm telling you, I love it here. I kind of hate you for making out it was so grim and lame and all that.'

'You've been here for not quite forty-eight hours,' I said. 'Drinking and finding owls, with fairy lights everywhere. That would be fun in North Korea.'

'We've decided what to do,' Todd announced when I got to the fake kitchen, washed and dressed, an hour later.

'Snowball fight?' I said.

'Della and Devin *have* taken the kids out for a snowball fight,' said Kathi. 'In fact . . .' She put her hand to her ear as if to say 'Hark'. I harked and could just make out Hiro's voice in the distance bellowing, 'DINGO BELL, DINGO BELL!'

'Wow,' I said. 'And what have you decided for the rest of us? Taylor's pretty taken up with watching an egg. I hope you're not relying on him.'

'Hard core only, baby,' said Todd. 'Trinity business.'

'Noleen's elected to stick around here anyway,' Kathi said. 'To help your mom with . . . I have no idea.'

'Systems,' said Noleen, coming in holding a clipboard. 'I've been in this business for fifteen years and I'm ready to pass on everything I've learned.' I had seen some of Noleen's motel systems: the paperwork that built up and up until she scooped everything on her desk into a binbag and threw it away; the stockpiling of paper goods and toiletries that meant she had to list them on her tax return as depreciable goods; and, of course, her customer service which was heavy on cursing and light on smiles.

'Roger?' I asked.

'Sleeping,' said Todd. 'Hiro's right outside our window, which I cracked for a little fresh air, and he's sleeping through it.'

'Should a baby doctor be able to sleep through a baby making that much din?' I asked. No one answered. 'What business does Trinity have on hand anyway?'

'I thought of a way to shake loose some information,' Todd

said. 'Listen to this.' He moved aside a coffee cup and a jar of marmalade as if he was literally going to lay it out on the table. 'So your mom and dad bought the house, right? But not through a realtor estate sale agent.' He had learned that from me: how to say all the words and let someone else make the right selection, like holding out a handful of foreign coins.

'Estate agent,' I said.

'Right,' said Todd. 'It was a private sale to stamp out all sorts of duty, so your mom said.'

'To avoid stamp duty?' I said. 'Mum? Is that legal?' I knew she was lurking around somewhere in one of the larders or cloakrooms that led off this place. I would recognize the particular sound of her slippers shuffling on hard flooring anywhere.

'Oh you know, Lexy,' she said. I did. I knew she was well capable of fudging all the paperwork if she meant to stay in this house for the rest of her life, leaving it up to me to sort the mess out once I'd finished cling-filming the funeral leftovers.

'Anyway,' said Todd. 'Crispin and Wilma's lawyers, who held the deeds – all that jazz, you know? Turns out they've been the Garmont family lawyers since God was a toddler. So they represented the family when you-know-what.'

'Yeah, but the *firm* did,' Kathi said. 'No one who's there now did. They can't have. Even if some baby lawyer was interning from middle school sixty years ago, he – or she, but probably he – would be well retired now. It's not like Miss Marple, Todd. Am I right, Lexy? It's not like we're going to roll up and some secretary with a perm's going to tell us, "Oh, you want Old Mr Prendergast and he'll be sipping sherry in the garden right about now. Go ask his nurse to talk to him".'

'Well,' I said, 'the thing is, Kathi, it's different here. People tend to stay put, and there's nothing to do except gossip. So . . . you never know. It might be worth a try. Especially if Crispin and Wilma give us their blessing.'

'I don't think that's a good idea,' said Todd. 'My thought was we go in hard as representatives of your mom and dad, who've just been sold a house with a corpse in the basement, courtesy of Messrs . . .'

'Go for it, Todd,' Kathi said. 'Give it your best shot.'

'Cahoots, Concise, Calamity.'

'Mum?' I shouted.

'Colquhoun, Kilsyth, Kilquhanity,' my mum shouted back. 'They're in Queen Street. And it's not as daft as it sounds. No offence, Todd. Because it really isn't all that ideal to have human remains in a B & B, and I have to say, the receptionist was quite chatty anytime we popped in. Worth a try.'

'So,' said Todd. 'Road trip? If you drive, Lexy. Because I'd kill us all.'

'After the roads are ploughed? Like tomorrow?' said Kathi, with all the timidity of a native Californian.

'Nah,' I said. 'Wimpy Scottish snow won't give our tyres any trouble. And they'll all be blootered on Baileys in the break room by tomorrow. Let's pack up a picnic and go today.'

'Your dad's still got lots of chestnuts left,' my mum said, actually appearing for this announcement. 'He whizzed them up into a pâté last night. Will I make sandwiches?'

'Rewind,' I said. 'Forget the picnic. I've just remembered where I am. I'm going to eat five different kinds of hot meat encased in pastry before I'm home again. With a cold pork pie chaser and a can of Irn-Bru. Don't bother with dinner for me, Mum. I'll have my head down the bog, but it'll be worth it.'

'I'll take a sandwich, Judith,' said Kathi. I shouldn't have mentioned throwing up in front of her. 'Maybe not chestnut, though.'

I didn't want to lose face in front of the other two Trinitarians, and so I swung my mum's car out of the drive and on to the street without any audible praying, but the truth is I hadn't driven on even a smattering of snow for four years and I didn't care for the feeling of my wheels sliding sideways on the corners. High gear, low speed, I told myself. Todd and Kathi wouldn't know that growling sound was the engine protesting.

'It's really pretty,' Kathi said as we left the last cottage behind and started snaking along between glittering hedgerows with the fields flashing gold and blue in the sun and shadows.

'This won't last,' I said. 'Not the snow or the countryside. We'll be in the slushy suburbs in an hour.'

But there was no telling them. They said 'Wheeeee!' every time we went round a roundabout; they decided any stone building with a point on its roof was a castle; they even rubbernecked as we passed the hospital. 'No billing department,' Todd said. 'No accounts. I thought it would be a shack. That hospital could be in . . . maybe not California . . . but Oregon definitely. Pull over!' he said as a siren sounded behind us. 'It's a free ambulance. It looks just like a regular one.'

And, of course, Edinburgh didn't help. I'd planned to head in on one of the boring arterial routes. That would have cooled their ardour. But there was a traffic jam at the Commie Pool, so I swung round by the park to avoid it, thus giving them a view of a loch, a mountain and a certified royal palace, right there in the city.

'I know this place!' Kathi said craning out of the window. 'They brought the Queen here! It's just a slow walk behind a hearse up to the castle from this very spot. Isn't it, Lexy?'

I'm not a monster. I gave in and drove that way, past mediaeval townhouses and church after church after church, bumping along on the cobbles while Todd cracked crude jokes about no one needing sex toys.

'Who's that?' he shouted, pointing out of the window at a statue beside the cathedral.

'No clue,' I told him. 'Guy in a robe.'

'Well, who's that?' said Kathi, pointing out the other side.

'Not a scooby,' I said. 'Guy sitting down in a robe.'

'You are a shit docent,' said Todd, as we turned the corner off the Royal Mile to go down to the New Town. 'Whoaaaa! What's *that*?'

'It's a bank,' I said, turning again to drive round it. I had never noticed how solid it was before.

'Get out of town. That's not a bank. That's a palazzo. Is *that* a bank?'

'No, that's a bit of the university. New College, I think.' I took the chance while we were stopped behind a bus to look up at it, all spires and twiddly bits, looking like a gigantic grey wedding cake.

'*New* College?' said Kathi. 'What, did they distress it?'

'New for here,' I said. 'I'm not sure how old—'

'Holy *shit*!' said Todd as the bus moved away and stopped obscuring our view of the New Town at the bottom of the hill.

I turned and even I had to admit that, with the neoclassical art galleries as stately as ever, the Ferris wheel and ice rink in the gardens for Christmas, and the spike of the Scott monument piercing the blue sky, Edinburgh was putting on quite a show. We scooted across Princes Street and up into the heart of all the Georgian stuff.

'Who's that?' said Todd.

'Guy on a horse,' I informed him. 'And this,' I said, turning left and slowing, 'is Queen Street.'

'Wow,' said Todd. 'Is that a park? Another one? Another God-knows-how-many acres of prime real estate just sitting there growing trees?'

'It's a private garden,' I said. 'Like the end of Notting Hill.'

'You're such an asshole, Lexy,' Kathi said. 'Imagine not even knowing who those giant bronze dudes are.'

'I'm from Dundee!' I said.

'Don't get us started on Dundee,' said Todd. 'We thought we were *going* to Dundee. We *studied* for Dundee. Tell me, how many times have you been on board the *Discovery*?'

'No times,' I said.

'The actual ship from Captain Scott's Antarctic expedition, docked right there in your home town, and you can't even summon the courtesy to go look at it.'

'Sorry, Todd,' I said. 'But can we do that later, maybe? And try to get in to speak to the Garmont lawyers first?'

I had to trundle all the way along to the West End to find a parking space and then battle the parking app to pay for it, giving them plenty time to marvel at the architecture.

'It goes on forever! In all directions!' said Todd. 'Look up there, Kathi!'

'Do people live in these buildings?' Kathi said.

'Yeah, some of them. In flats upstairs above the offices.' I wafted them across the road on the green man, while they looked resolutely in the wrong direction for oncoming traffic.

'Would these apartments have ballrooms?' said Todd. And the thing is, probably some of them would.

'Ask Colquhoun, Kilsyth or Kilquhanity,' I said. 'They might have a bijou little one-bed one-bath one-ball on the books.'

The lawyers' premises, when we arrived a moment later, struck

Todd dumb as nothing except an A-list celebrity wedding spread in *People* had ever struck him dumb before. We mounted the stone steps, opened the double mahogany doors and stepped into a soaring entranceway with marble underfoot and a chandelier above.

'Fuck me, it's Downton Abbey,' Kathi said. 'Do we wait here for Mr Carson or try to find the library?'

'Reception,' I said, pointing at a discreet brass plaque on a nearby door, and headed that way.

Modern desks, computers, filing cabinets and outgrowths of cheap tinsel brought us all back down to earth a bit, inside the office. But the woman on the front desk made up for it. She was wearing an honest-to-God twinset and her glasses hung from a string of pearls round her neck.

'Can I help you?' she said in a voice like Miss Jean Brodie.

'I hope so,' I said. 'We're here to ask about Mistletoe Hall in Yule, lately owned by the Garmont family. I wonder if we could speak to someone who knows a bit about the place.' I paused. 'I'm guessing from your lack of reaction that you haven't heard.' She crooked an eyebrow. 'About the corpse,' I added. I had thought she was alone in the office but, on hearing those words, three heads popped up from behind various cubicle dividers.

'Corpse?' said a young man in a striped shirt.

'Skeleton,' I said. 'Bricked up in the basement. Wasn't mentioned on the homebuyer's report.'

'Is this a joke?' said Miss Jean Brodie.

'Not even slightly,' I said. 'The police will probably be in touch at some point, but we wanted to see if we could find anything out that might help my p— my, um, my . . .'

'Her private investigator,' Kathi said, stepping forward. 'No need to keep that quiet, Lexy. I'm not certified here in Scotland, but . . .' She magicked a card out of somewhere and handed it over.

'Yes indeed,' said Todd, getting in on the action third out of three, which was unusual for him. 'There has been a corpse bricked up in the cellar at Mistletoe Hall for the last sixty years. It was discovered yesterday. So your firm, which we believe has been involved with the property and the family's other business for sixty years and more, seemed like a good place to start asking questions. We have the family's blessing, which you can check if you care to call the owners.'

That was a nice touch. We did have a family's blessing. We did represent some owners. But Todd had put two sets of each in the air and hoped that Miss Brodie didn't notice him juggling.

'Of course, we realize sixty years is a long time ago,' I said. 'And no one who was across the Garmonts' private affairs back then is going to be around today. But still we thought it was worth popping up to ask, you know?'

'Well, that's where you're wrong,' said Stripy Shirt, coming forward. He gave Miss Jean Brodie a glance, as though asking permission. Getting it in the form of a stiff nod, he went on, 'Old Mr Kilquhanity didn't retire until he was pushing eighty. It drove his wife up the wall. She'd been looking forward to cruises. In the end, she went on her own, met a widower from Florida and never came back. After that, there was no way Mr K was going home to stare at his four walls.'

'You don't mean he's still working, do you?' said Todd.

'No, no, no,' said Stripes. 'He's over ninety now and even *he* can't pretend still to be that interested in the law. But he does toddle in every now and then – he only lives down on Heriot Row anyway – and although he's physically frail, he's as sharp as a tack. And . . .'

'And what?' said Kathi.

'And the most indiscreet solicitor in the whole of Edinburgh,' said Miss JB.

'Which is saying something,' added Stripes.

'Let me get this straight,' said Kathi. 'Old Mr . . . Kiltie Man City . . . is alive and kicking and just about to have tea in the garden of the old vicarage if we care to stroll along there?'

'Eh?' said Stripes. 'No, he's having lunch in a pub on George Street. But the bit about if you care to stroll along there, yeah. In fact, if you did care to stroll along there, you could bring him back. It's kind of slippy today and, like I said, he's ninety-three.'

'Shut,' said Todd, 'and I can't emphasize this enough, the front door.'

'Eh?' said Stripes again.

'He means get out of town,' said Kathi.

'What?' said Miss Jeannie B.

'They're American and they're jet-lagged,' I said. 'Nod, smile and ignore them.'

'Hey!' said Todd.

I ignored him. 'So . . . which pub is he at? We'll go and grill him then deliver him back to you safely.'

TWELVE

'Wow!' said Todd when we'd got to the right block of George Street and were looking across the traffic at the Dome. I had to hand it to him, and to the Dome management too, because it looked pretty spiffy with its Corinthian columns all wrapped in netted lights with enormous red bows tied on to the windowsills. I still couldn't believe a solicitor in his nineties was having lunch here, though. It was first dates and hen nights the last time I checked.

'This place!' said Kathi. 'This city! That looks like the Parthenon, only a little fancier. And it's a pub?'

'Well,' I said, 'it started life as a bank.'

'Don't keep wheeling that out to cover your ignorance,' said Todd. '"It's a bank! Guy in a robe!"'

'Are we going in?' I said. I hadn't missed the Festive Set Menu of home during the California years but, now I was within spitting distance of a pimped-out plate of turkey and a vertical pudding, my mouth was watering.

'Whoaaa!' said Todd when we got in the door, gazing at the Christmas tree that stretched up to fill the cupola above our heads.

'Oh come off it!' I said. 'It looks exactly like a Cheesecake Factory.'

'But, Lexy,' said Kathi, 'this place is real. That marble is marble. That carving is carved.'

'Table for three,' Todd said to a waiter who had shimmered up to where we stood.

'What name?' the waiter said.

'Oh we haven't booked,' said Todd. He batted his eyes at the guy and dropped his voice an octave before adding, 'Will that be a problem?'

Poor Todd. This bloke wasn't gay; he was European. At least that meant he wasn't homophobic either though, so he didn't recoil. He just smirked and said, 'We've been booked for lunch this week since August.'

'Ocht,' I said. 'That's a pity. Could we sit at the bar?'

'The bar's been booked since October.'

'Oh well,' I said. 'Actually we were here to see a Mr Kilquhanity, but we can wait outside for him.'

The waiter snapped to attention like he was a Barcalounger and someone had just kicked his foot pedal. 'Mr K?' he said. 'He's expecting you? Of course you can join him. He's all alone at a table for four. Step this way.'

He went zooming off at that unmistakable waiter's clip, very fast but very smooth. We hurried after him.

At one of the best tables – under the dome but out of the way of falling pine needles – a man I would have put at a rakish seventy-five sat back in his seat with his long legs casually crossed and one arm hooked over the back of his chair while he flirted with the waitress who was clearing his plate.

'Mr K,' said our waiter. 'Visitors for you.'

The old man turned our way with eyebrows raised, let them fall, then shook himself and gave us all a good look as a wolfish smile spread over his face, revealing strong yellow teeth. He even had a gap in between the two front ones. Not to mention a toothbrush moustache.

'Well, hello,' he said in excruciatingly posh Edinburgh-ese, getting seven syllables out of it. 'I thought for a minute there she'd changed her mind, Sandy, but this is even lovelier. Sit down, sit down. I've ordered an espresso martini crème brûlée, but I can nibble a breadstick and wait for you all to catch up. I highly recommend the ox cheek. My treat, naturally.'

'Ox cheek?' said Kathi. 'Does that mean the cheek of an ox?'

'The cheek of an ox as featured in the Nativity,' said Mr Kilquhanity.

'You are awful, Mr K,' said his waitress, with a nudge to his shoulder. 'I'll give you all a minute, eh?'

'Now then,' said Mr K when the four of us were alone, 'to what do I owe this unexpected pleasure? I was here to meet a young lady who'd swiped right on me but she had second thoughts when she saw me in all my raddled lack of glory. Rude, I thought. But there you go.'

'You're on a Tinder date?' I said.

'Marvellous invention,' said Mr K. 'What a boon! But quite a flooded market for old boys like me.'

'How old was the "young" lady?' said Todd. I'd been wondering too, but trust Todd to come right out and ask.

'Her profile said sixty, but that was definitely before tax,' said Mr K. 'Pouf! Forget her. On to pastures new. What can I do for you?'

In between ordering drinks and food, although not the ox cheek, we filled him in on what had happened at Mistletoe Hall since our arrival. He started out reacting like a pantomime audience with a buzz on, but his professionalism gradually took over and by the end he was nodding gravely.

'Well!' he said. 'I never thought I'd live to see the end of *that* little family drama, I must say. If I fall off the stage during karaoke tonight, I shall die happy. Dear, dear, dear. Billy Bone, eh?'

'So what all did you know before we filled you in on the latest?' I said. Mr K shifted forward in his seat and leaned over all ready to dish, so I'm not sure what made me add, 'If you feel you can tell us, that is. If it's not unethical.'

Todd kicked me under the table.

'Now, who's that playing footsie?' said Mr K. 'It's always been a game I enjoyed.' He reached for his wine glass, noticed it was empty and took a sip from his water glass instead. 'Unethical, unethical, let me see.' Then he clapped his hands together. 'Sod it,' he said. 'They're all dead except me. There should be some reward for making it into this much decrepitude. Let's order another bottle, shall we?'

'The first I knew of any trouble,' he went on, once *they'd* all got a fresh glass of something that looked delicious and *I'd* got another cup of coffee because I was driving, 'was Crispin's father ringing up to say that, if Verity got in touch with us, we were to promise to advance her whatever she needed from her trust and then let her parents know when she was coming in to collect it. Now, you must understand, you youngsters, that these were the days when one simply *didn't* ring up. One wrote a letter, licked a stamp and toddled along to the pillar box. If there was great urgency, one might include a stamped addressed envelope for a speedy reply, but ringing up the office? Not done. So, when Alex Garmont did it, we all knew something was up.'

'And did she?' said Kathi. 'Try to spring funds from her trust?'

'She didn't,' said Mr K. 'But shortly after that, Old Mr Garmont changed his will. It had been a very straightforward affair before. A few bequests, house and policies to the son, Crispin, jewellery to the daughter, Verity, paintings and cash and what have you split between the two. The terms of the *new* will were much more biblical. Old Testament. It was a nasty thing of the sort that wouldn't hold up these days – thank the Lord. *These* days, no lawyer would have anything to do with it. Brrrr.' He shuddered. 'And besides nasty, it was convoluted. He left everything he could to "future grandchildren, born in wedlock".'

'Nasty enough,' Todd said. 'But not that convoluted, I wouldn't say.'

Mr K closed his eyes and laughed silently. 'Let me explain,' he said. 'Alex Garmont left his wife a life interest in his entire estate, as was common. But then, after dispersing his movable assets – portable property as Dickens would have it – according to Scots Law, in effect the bairn's pairt, you know.'

'I can't speak for the rest of them,' Todd said, 'but I don't. I profoundly and completely have no idea what you're talking about.'

'I do love the law of my native land,' said Mr K. 'Let me enlighten you: despite the union of parliament in seventeen hundred and—' He broke off. 'No, that won't do. I need to start further back.'

I took pity on them. 'You can leave your house to whoever you want, but all the rest of your swag's got to be divided between your wife and kids and then a third of it's a wildcard. Is that about the size of it, Mr K?'

'Admirably succinct if a little informal,' he said. 'All debts once discharged, the portable property of a married man is divided in three, that of a widower in two. But – and this is the point – the fixed assets, the buildings, the land, are his to dispose of as he wishes.

'The trouble old Alex Garmont had was that he couldn't leave the property by name to a child who did not yet exist, and he couldn't leave it to "grandchildren" because there was a grandchild who did exist. I assume you know that?'

'Yup,' said Kathi. 'Nelson, over there in the Caribbean.'

'Indeed. The provision my father came up with seemed to answer the case perfectly if rather coldly.'

'Why didn't Alex just disinherit Verity and leave it all to Crispin?' Todd said. 'I mean, he might have had to change it again if he didn't approve of who Crispin married, but at the point when Crispin was single and Verity was pregnant . . . why not?'

'*Because* Crispin was single and Verity was pregnant!' said Mr K. 'And Crispin cared deeply for his sister. The old man wanted to make sure that neither Verity nor her child would ever get hold of his fortune. So he also kept his *son*, as well as his widow, to a life interest in Mistletoe Hall and the foreign holdings – i.e. the Barbados property where Verity lived and where I believe her son lives still.'

'Oh, she went off to a *family* place over there?' I said.

'And Crispin left her there in peace for the rest of her life and let the son stay on after her death. So, in that sense, his father was quite right. Crispin *would* have given it to his sister if he could. But he couldn't. Nor could he leave it to his nephew.'

'OK, you were right,' Todd said. 'It is convoluted.'

'Now let's take up the tale,' said Mr K. 'It was at this point, in late 1959 or early 1960, when Crispin's father laid down his moralizing stipulations in the new will, that everyone in the office from my father himself down through the typing pool to the cleaners as well, thought, "Ahhhh, Verity Garmont got herself in the pudding club and ran away. And her father wants to cut her off with a shilling".'

'It's a funny expression that,' I said.

'With a shilling?' said Mr K. 'You think it should be "without a shilling"? You are wrong, my dear. As we just noted, in re. the bairn's pairt. One *can't* cut off one's children without a shilling, under Scots Law. But Old Mr Garmont wanted to make sure his daughter paid for her sins – in his eyes – by preventing her from getting a penny piece more than the law decreed.'

'I meant "got herself", actually,' I told him. 'In re. "the pudding club".'

'A good point, well made,' said Mr K. 'I frequently fall asleep at the wheel of wokery. I speak metaphorically, of course. I haven't driven a car for ten years. It still feels lovely not having to be sober.'

I laughed and forgave him.

'But I'm glad you brought up the question of the father of Verity's baby,' he said. 'Because at this point, of course, we neither knew nor cared who it might be. We forgot all about it and got on with the swinging sixties. Not that they swung on much of a parabola in Edinburgh.' He dropped an eyelid. 'But there are frequent trains to Glasgow.'

I had thought the waitress who'd said, 'You are awful' and nudged him was simping for a tip but I could see myself saying it too by the end of lunch. He was. And adorable with it.

'Fast-forward seven years, though,' he said, 'and all became clear. Well, that is to say, at first things became even murkier before they became clear. First of all, Alex Garmont added *another* clause to *another* new will. My father – you must remember this detail – took care of it and I knew nothing.'

'More nastiness?' I said.

'Oh my dear,' said Mr K. 'It was no longer "future grandchildren born in wedlock" but "future grandchildren born in wedlock to a pure woman, neither divorced nor widowed". What do you think of that?'

'How is a widow not a pure woman?' said Kathi. 'They can get remarried in church.'

Mr K gave another one of his silent laughs, no more than his shoulders shaking. 'My Tinder experience would suggest there's nothing pure about a widow, you sweet innocent thing. I meant, what do you think of the clause in the will?'

'Blerch,' said Kathi.

'Indeed,' said Mr K. 'Revolting and, so we thought, unnecessary. Until, that is, Crispin came onstage in a speaking part.' He paused dramatically. 'And this time it wasn't a phone call. It was a visit! I was a partner by then, with a very swish private office in what was once the drawing room, and I remember it as if it were yesterday. Crispin, rather defiant, and with him a very diffident, not to say mousy, little woman introduced to me as Mrs Wilma Bone, whose husband had run off and left her years before. They had fallen in love, if you please, and wanted to take legal advice about how to winkle Mrs Bone out of her marriage.

'I told them, "Divorce, of course". Desertion was always grounds in Scotland, as well as adultery. In fact, I even wondered out loud why it was worth a trip to town actually. At this point, Crispin swallowed hard and said it wasn't that simple. He told me to ask my father about his – Crispin's – father's latest will. Which I did.'

Mr K whistled. I would have whistled too if I'd ever acquired the skill.

'That "pure woman" nonsense had hit Crispin like a gong,' he went on. 'They explained to me that they didn't – if they could possibly help it – want to be married as a bachelor and a divorcée, that they wanted Mrs Bone's husband declared dead, that it had been seven years and no one had heard hide nor hair of the scoundrel, so could they start the ball rolling to have him officially crrk?' He drew a finger across his throat.

'Oh right,' I said. 'Seven years. That's the cut-off, isn't it? But wouldn't that have made her a widow?'

'Patience,' said Mr K. 'First, the question of the seven years. The answer is: yes and no. Back then, before the 1977 Act – we could call it the Presumption of Death Act – we were still operating under the older 1891 Presumption of *Life* Act, you see. That was quite a change when it happened, I can tell you. A great deal of printers' ink and pulpit breath was expended, as you can imagine. The 1891 Act decreed that, after seven years, a missing person could be declared dead and – here's the point – was presumed to have died seven years to the day after they were last known to be alive. The 1977 Act, in contrast, decreed that the missing person, heretofore presumed dead and now to be declared so, died on the day they were last seen or heard from. Do you see? Presumption of life until seven years have passed, replaced with presumption of early death, rubber-stamped after seven years have passed.'

'What difference did it make to Crispin and Wilma?' said Kathi.

'Oh none at all,' said Mr K. 'With respect to the case of Billy Bone, it made no odds whatsoever. I only note it out of love for the law. You must indulge an old man, you young things with it all ahead of you.'

All three of us made some kind of reassuring noise, even though I am certain I wasn't the only one who wanted to scream at him to get on with it.

'No,' he went on, 'since there was no estate to speak of beyond a few personal belongings, and Billy's life had not been insured, the provisions of the 1891 Act suited Crispin and Wilma admirably. It was the future that mattered to them: the fact that they wished to marry. Against his parents' wishes, as evidenced by the new clause in the will about purity, divorce and widowhood.'

'But he married her anyway,' Kathi said. 'Awww.'

'This is kind of confusing,' said Todd.

'You are Correctly and Co of Correctington,' said Mr K. 'I said it was convoluted, didn't I? Let me explain in more detail.'

I managed not to groan, but I wished I was drinking. Then, before he could start up again, a terrible thought occurred to me.

'Hang on,' I said. 'If Crispin only got a life interest, never *mind* what happens after he dies, how did he manage to sell Mistletoe Hall to my mum and dad? Oh my God, could they lose it? How did the sale go through? I know you're the Garmont lawyers but didn't my parents have one?'

'Shush, shush, my dear,' said Mr K. 'People are starting to stare. Crispin sold the Hall with Miley's permission, since she'll inherit all his property when he dies and has no interest in such a white elephant of a place.'

'But hold on,' said Todd. 'You said the will hit Crispin like a gong. How does Miley inherit? How was Wilma a pure woman, neither divorced nor widowed?'

'That,' said Mr K with relish, 'is where I came in. And this is the crux of the matter now.' He paused, but he'd been saying every new thing was the key and the nub and the crux so often that none of us reacted this time.

'It still thrills me to remember it,' Mr K said. 'It was quite my Penge bungalow.'

'Huh?' said Kathi.

'Rumpole's finest hour,' I told her. 'Go on, Mr K. Thrill us too.'

He flashed another lupine grin. 'If Wilma had divorced Billy as soon as she realized he'd gone for good, she'd have been a divorcée. Impure, by anyone's reckoning in those days. Agreed?'

We nodded reluctantly.

'But the 1891 Presumption of Life Act, or even the 1977 Presumption of Death Act when it came along, necessarily had to allow for mistaken presumptions. For a return to life or a retreat from death. Do you see?'

'No,' I said.

'For insurance, inheritance and, indeed, succession where relevant, death by presumption is different from death by . . . Well, looking into a coffin and seeing a corpse. And, crucially in this instance, when it comes to *married* people presumed dead, the presumption had to be coupled with the application of the 1938 Dissolution of Marriage Act. Thus, I argued, Wilma was rendered *neither* a widow – widows do not need to dissolve their marriages – *nor* a divorcée – who nullify their marriages by decree.'

'But was she pure?' said Kathi.

'Ah!' said Mr K. 'Back to Penge. I further argued – successfully – that "pure woman, neither a divorcée nor a widow" did not constitute a list, three items long, of womanly attributes, but rather that the "neither/nor" served as explanations of – definitions of – purity. That they were intended to sum it up. And that they did *not* sum up Wilma Bone, who was therefore pure!'

'Bit of a risk, though, wasn't it?' Todd said. 'What if someone else had said it was a list, with a couple of examples.'

'Oh my dear boy, never,' said Mr K. 'No Scottish solicitor would ever allow such sloppiness. The freshest law graduate in the lowliest firm would know to say "for example but without prejudice to the generality". To miss out that phrase would be like . . . stirring one's tea with a comb.'

Kathi was so engrossed in what he was saying that she barely noticed this. 'Still a risk, though,' she said. 'Shouldn't they just have waited? What if the old man had changed his will again and left it all to a dog's home?'

'My dear, they couldn't wait! Because "born in wedlock" is inarguable. The day they came to my office to talk about a death declaration and a marriage dissolution, Wilma wasn't sitting there like a mouse because she's mousy. She was sitting there silent and grave because of morning sickness! Camilla – Miley, as she's known – was already on the way, and they had to get their skates on. Besides, Alex Garmont never had occasion to change his will a third time. He never found out that I was planning to argue Wilma out of that nasty clause. He died believing he had triumphed in his cruelty. My sweet old father chose not to disabuse him.'

'Blimey,' I said. 'You really did do them a solid then. Three cheers for Colquhoun, Kilsyth, Kilquhanity.'

'You are very kind,' said Mr K. 'Kindness, wit and beauty all rolled together in female form.'

'I'm engaged,' I said. 'Swipe left, you old bugger.'

His shoulders shook in another fit of silent laughter.

'Although that particular hurry would all have been moot within the year.' He paused to let us gather what remained of our fascination for old bits of Scottish Law. I had to rootle pretty hard for mine. 'As I said, all of this was beginning to shift and, after the 1968 Legitimation Law passed, Miley would have been the legitimate issue of Crispin and Wilma no matter how old she was when they walked down the aisle. They might have waited until she was big enough to be a flower girl, as I believe is the current fashion. They might even have waited until she was sixteen and could sign the register as one of their witnesses.' He stopped. 'Or perhaps not. Perhaps those dates wouldn't have . . . Because, eventually, the whole notion of illegitimacy was dropped in the bin where it belongs. The 1982 Act hacked at the rotten roots of it and now it's gone completely. We get there in the end, this little country. We do get there eventually. Do you know it wasn't until 2006, mind you, that adopted children got full rights? Two thousand and six! Dear, dear, dear.'

He was beginning to sound tired, and he looked, if not ninety, then north of eighty anyway. Gently, I suggested we might walk him home to Heriot Row, going heavy on the idea that Todd and Kathi would appreciate a close-up look at more of the architecture. I didn't fool him.

'Three birds with one stone,' he said. 'Some tourism for the visitors, spare me falling down drunk in the street, and let my erstwhile colleagues get on with their day. They're very kind but I must get under their feet.' He twisted round in his seat and mimed a signature at a passing waiter, taking no notice of us clamouring to split the bill.

'I'm not a lawyer,' said Todd as we picked our careful way down the Dome steps and along the shady side of the street where the snow on the pavement was getting a crust of ice. 'And

even if I was I'd be an American attorney not a Scottish . . . are
you really and truly called solicitors? Isn't that kind of confusing
in vice cases?'

'But?' I said.

'But,' said Todd, 'it's what you said about all those laws
changing, Mr K. Nelson . . . I have no idea what his last name
is, but he's here for Christmas with his aunt and uncle. And what
do you know, the skeleton of his father just happened to resurface
after sixty years. So here's what I'm wondering. After the when-
ever-it-was one that adiosed illegitimacy—'

'Oh my dear boy,' said Mr K. The cold air had revived him a
little and he sounded brighter again, his voice matching his
sprightly step. 'None of them were retroactive! Good Lord, if the
1968, 1982 or 2006 Family Law Acts had been retro*active*, there
wouldn't be enough solicitors in the whole of Christendom to
sort out the mess. Heavens, Mrs Fitzherbert's descendants would
be banging on the door of Buckingham Palace as we speak.'

'Who?' said Kathi.

'*His* mistress,' said Mr K, shaking his walking stick at a statue
in the middle of the mini-roundabout.

'Now pay attention to this, Lexy,' said Todd. I ignored him.

'Who is it?' said Kathi. 'All these guys in robes look the same
to us dummies,' she added as a sideswipe at me.

'George IV,' said Mr K. 'For whom this street is named and,
incidentally, the first one you lot didn't have to trouble yourselves with. He had one child in wedlock, a Princess Charlotte
– there's a square named after her at the far end – but she died
in childbirth while her father was still on the throne. So next
up was his little brother, William IV. If our 1968 Act had been
retroactive, it would have caused utter mayhem. Georgie Boy
had five other children scattered here and there by all accounts,
and little Willie managed twelve on the wrong side of the
blanket and only four with the blessing of the Church, all of
whom pegged out before him. But then, we know who that
paved the way for, don't we?'

'Imagine we don't,' said Todd.

'I'll give you a clue,' said Mr K. 'It was 1837.'

'I know you think that's a clue,' said Kathi, 'but all I know
about 1837 is it was the olden days.'

'It would be like us asking you who came after the 1837 president,' said Todd. 'Whoever *he* was.'

'Andrew Jackson,' said Mr K. 'And Martin Van Buren.' He turned to me. 'My retirement from the law coincided with the birth of *Pointless*. I'm a fiend on chemical elements too. But *you* must know, my dear. Who ascended the throne in 1837?'

'Victoria,' I supplied, to groans from Todd and Kathi.

'I was going to say that! Practically,' said Kathi. 'When I said "olden days" I nearly said "Victorian times".'

'Think how stupid you'd feel if you couldn't work out who was on the throne in Victorian times, though,' I pointed out to her, and she gives me a wink and finger pistol in acknowledgement.

'Anyway,' said Mr K. We had turned on to the side street heading down past the Queen Street gardens towards Heriot Row. 'Old Mr Garmont was dead by 1982, so his will was what you would call a done deal, since we never had to contend with this imagined chaos of retroactive application. And the 1968 Act wouldn't have made a difference to Nelson either, because the parents had to marry in the end to achieve legitimation. And even *these* days, one of the requirements of marriage is that both parties are alive.'

'These days?' said Todd, sounding a bit waspish. I thought I understood and hoped Mr K wasn't about to disappoint us all, after seeming so charming.

'When what matters is that two people care about one another and are sixteen and single. And not a parent, parson or any other po-faced misanthrope can stop them.'

'You're a remarkable gentleman,' said Todd, thoroughly mollified.

'Shame they've run out of statue spots in your city,' said Kathi.

'Ah, but there are always plaques, dear lady,' said Mr K. 'Mary Queen of Scots, Sean Connery . . . I think the Lionel Richie was a student rag, but it's still worth a look.'

So, all in all, when we left him at the door of his townhouse, next door to Robert Louis Stevenson as he was careful to let us know, each of us was a little bit in love with him and none of us, hand on heart, could have said which way we'd swipe if we'd been that widow.

THIRTEEN

'The wanderers return!' my mum said, as we fell into Mistletoe Hall through the back door after a hair-raising journey home. Everyone in Edinburgh was knocking off a day early for the Christmas holiday and most of them seemed to be headed south on the same slippy wee roads we'd been using, me gripping the wheel so tight my knuckles ached, while Todd and Kathi fanned on about how great Mr K was and how much I sucked.

'What's that?' they kept asking, anytime we drove past a building with any suggestion of carving in the stonework.

'Dunno,' I said over and over again. Except for once when I said, 'The Dick Vet,' and they didn't believe me.

So it was comforting to hear my mum's same old passive-aggressive greeting, even though, as I turned to roll my eyes and speak to her in a weary voice, she ruined it by beaming at me and offering a wedge of game pie.

'Your dad's clearing the freezer before the big shop tomorrow,' she said. 'I'm on a mission not to waste any of it.'

'How have you got a freezer full of game when you've only just moved in?' I said. 'And since when are you the huntin', shootin', fishin' type? Tell me it's not roadkill.'

'Ewwwww,' said Diego, after he'd spat his mouthful of pie out on to his plate. Della rattled off a cascade of Spanish – I only understood 'avergonzada' – and swiped up the discarded mouthful in a tissue. Hiro was too wee to understand and carried on doggedly chewing a mouthful so huge both her cheeks were bulging.

'Of course it's not,' said my mum. 'We inherited it from Crispin and Wilma. They didn't want a big chest freezer at the cottage, and it would have been silly to defrost it and bin the contents for us moving in.'

I said nothing. It was even more silly to make a connection between the skeletonized corpse in the back cellar and Ziploc bags of frozen 'game', but I couldn't help it. 'Was it labelled?' I said, at last.

'Of course it was labelled!' my mum said. She had a wedge of the pie on her cake slice now and was leaning over to chute it off on to the plate in front of me. 'I know you're guest guests, not paying guests, but we're using you as guinea pigs, Lexy: doing everything by the book. Haven't you noticed how the towels are folded? We're thinking of this as a dry run.'

'Let's talk it over tomorrow, Judith,' said Noleen. 'There's such a thing as being too scrupulous. I'll tell you how I keep my costs down *and* keep on the right side of the health inspector. What the customer doesn't know can't hurt him.'

I made a mental note never again to eat one of the Pop-Tarts from the complimentary continental breakfast station at the Last Ditch reception. I'd long been ignoring the fact that the ingredients were listed in a language I didn't recognize, but this was something else again.

'Speaking of things left behind when Crispin and Wilma moved on,' my mum said, 'how did you lot get on with the lawyers? Productive meeting?'

'Um,' said Kathi.

Todd played one of his little tunes on his cheeks.

'We heard a lot,' I said. 'But none of it exactly . . .' Because when you got right down to it, had we actually learned anything useful? It looked like Nelson had every right to hold a grudge against his dead grandfather. And I wouldn't judge him for wanting to embarrass his uncle and auntie to make up for them getting the Garmont fortune while he got zip. And he *was* in the country. But his alibi was their daughter. None of it seemed solid enough to put in a report just yet.

'Have *you* heard anything today?' Kathi said. 'What did we miss from here on the ground?'

'The crime-scene tape's down,' said my dad. 'I asked the CID if we could keep it for next Halloween but that went over like a cup of cold sick. I prefer the lad in uniform, I must say.'

'Leanne in the shop said the coppers were parked outside Crispin's cottage for *hours*,' said my mum. 'Poor things. They must have given them a right good grilling.'

'But they did it at home,' said Devin. 'They didn't take them in to the . . . Do they do that here? Interview people in window-less rooms with the furniture bolted down? You never see it on *McDonald and Dodds*.'

'The rooms might have windows,' my dad said, like that was the point, 'but, yes, that was a good sign. Open-and-shut case, I'd have thought. I mean, who else could brick up a' – he glanced at Diego – 'an item in a house, except the householders from back then? And the householders are both' – he glanced at Hiro – 'departed.'

'But no one's actually seen Crispin and Wilma today?' said Kathi. 'To gauge how they're holding up?'

'I didn't want to intrude,' said my mum. 'They've got a houseful.' That sounded like my mother of old, persuading herself to do nothing for a friend in need. 'I'll pop round in the morning,' she went on, though. 'Don't eat any more of the pie. If you're still hungry, have some toast. I'll take them a wedge, since it's their game in it anyway.' And, just like that, I was knocked off balance yet again, because that didn't sound like my mum at all.

'You're nothing like how Lexy described you,' said Noleen, the mind reader.

'Thanks a bunch,' I said. 'Way to drop me in it.'

'You're exactly how Lexy described all of you,' my dad said. 'Except Roger, because she described him awake. And Taylor because she described him around.'

'Don't worry about Roger,' Todd said. 'It takes him four days to catch up whenever he starts a vacation and this is only day three. He'll be Santa's enormous helper by Christmas Eve.'

'SANTA!' said Hiro, with a spray of pastry crumbs.

Diego bunched his hands up in front of his face and whispered, 'Santa!' too. 'He will find us, won't he Mama? You said he'll find us.'

'Of course he'll find you,' said my dad. 'All over the world, little boys and girls go to visit their grannies and grandads for Christmas. And Santa always finds them. In fact, since we're closer to the North Pole here than you would be in California, he might even be early.'

As soon as the words left his lips, we heard it. A faint jingling from outside and a rat-a-tat-tat on the front door.

'Wow!' said Diego softly. 'Santa?'

'I'll go and see,' I said.

It wasn't Santa. It was Miley Garmont in a Christmas jumper with battery-powered moving parts, hence the jingling. She was still jingling as she stood there on the step, because she was too drunk to keep still.

'Help, Maxie,' she slurred.

'Lexy.'

'Right, right. Well, can you and Katie and Ted help?'

'Kathi and Todd.'

'Right, right. Because the police have been nipping at my mum and dad all bloody day and never said word one about what they think or anything. Just fifty thousand questions then buggered off again. My mum was wondering if . . . your PR firm could do anything. Is it really called Tinnitus?'

'PI firm,' I said. 'Trinity. We'll come along first thing tomorrow.'

'Or tonight,' Miley said. 'I came to get you to come tonight. Because my mum's up to ninety and my dad's up to ninety. Wait. I said that. Well, they are. Only, can I have a quick wazz before we go? I'm busting.'

'Are you the most sober one?' I said. 'Is that why it was you that came? Because maybe tomorrow would be better, you know?'

'I was sober when I set off,' said Miley. 'But the thought of coming here, knowing what I know now. Wait! Knowing. What. I know. Now. Huh, I read it sight first time. Said it right. Anyway, I stopped at the Prick Inn for four pints of cider. That's what we called it when we were kids. Geddit? Geddit? Holly? Prick? Prick Inn.' She let out a long donkey honk and bray of drunken laughter. Then she cut it off dead. 'Man, Maxie, I'm going to pee myself if I don't go right now.'

I stepped back and let her go charging off towards the toilet at the top of the spiral stairs, ricocheting a little but not actually stumbling. When I was sure that she was OK – that is, when I could hear the four pints of cider start to hit the old-fashioned lavvy, shaped like the mouth of a trombone and with excellent acoustics – I nipped downstairs to scoop up Ted and Katie.

We were waiting in the hall, all three of us togged up in coats and hats, and me with a third of the pie under my arm, along with a bottle of sloe gin my mum had also unearthed from where the Garmonts had left it and a thick slab of the Christmas cake Della had knocked up during the day.

'Do you know, Lexy,' Miley said, as she shot the bolt back and rejoined us, 'I used to play in that place downstairs. I never even knew there was a brick wall behind the false door. I used to play at Dorothy in the tornado.'

She seemed to have peed herself sober.

'Will we go and look at it?' I said. 'There's nothing to see, but the police tape's down, if you want to.'

'I'll come back and bring Nelson,' she said. 'Lay some flowers or something. My God, it was his *dad*! His biological dad. Mum says she's got some old photos somewhere she's going to rake out, because she reckons Nelson *looks* like him.' She rubbed her hands over her face and shook herself. 'Let's go, eh?'

Her new sobriety didn't survive the hit of cold air and, by the time we were halfway up the street to the cottage, she had linked arms with Kathi for a bit of ballast and was interrogating us about life in California.

'Why aren't you all fat?' she said. 'Have you got guns? Do you go to a church with a congregation of thousands? Did you vote for that bawbag?'

'Choice, no, no, no,' said Todd. 'Do you play the bagpipes?'

'Yep,' said Miley. 'I started out on the tranter when I was twelve and I keep my hand in.'

'She's kidding,' I told them.

'I'm not. Do you all go to rodeos?'

'Absolutely,' said Todd. 'Every Sunday after mega-church.'

The front door opened as we turned in at the cottage gate. 'No way,' said Miley. 'It's forty years later and you're still the same witch you always were.' She fell into her mother's arms.

'Have you been pouring drink down her throat?' said Wilma, glaring at me over her daughter's shoulder.

'I used to crunch TicTacs all the way from the bus stop and practise saying "Night, Mum. Night Dad" without srurling,' said Miley. 'Sss-rrr-urrr-lling. But she always caught me.'

'Anyway,' I said, 'we're here now. How can we help?'

'I'm hungry,' Miley said, struggling out of the maternal embrace and heading along a passageway.

'Don't use the cooker!' Wilma shouted after her. 'You should be ashamed of yourselves,' she said to the three of us. 'Didn't you realize she had a problem? What were you *serving*?'

'So what can we do for you, Wilma?' Kathi said, wisely sweeping all of that aside.

'Come through,' Wilma said. 'Come in and sit down. How about a wee brandy? Whisky? It's late for port.'

She ushered us along the narrow passageway and into a living room that had been knocked through, I guessed – owing to the odd corners and the two fireplaces. It was also unmistakably a room that had been downsized into. Enormous ancestral oil paintings adorned the walls, and a fabulous antique carpet filled the entire floor and made the door hard to shove open. Also, Crispin and Nelson were sitting side by side on a Knole sofa, packed around with cushions. I concluded that the Garmonts had kept their poshest bits, their heirlooms and favoured treasures when they moved out of Mistletoe Hall, instead of trading it all in for comfort, so that – for instance – two people didn't have to sit hutched up on a hard couch as if they were waiting for a bus.

'How did it go with the cops?' Todd said, sinking down on to a footstool near the fireplace. I took the matching armless velvet chair to the one Wilma claimed, which left Kathi with a choice of squatting on the log box or ascending a kind of throne, inside an alcove, slightly outside the ring of firelight and camaraderie.

'Don't even consider it,' Crispin said. 'That bloody thing is knobblier than a shillelagh.' He fished a cushion out from behind his back and threw it on to the log box. Kathi's eyebrows drew down until she looked like an eagle, a Vulcan eagle. I had told her until I was sick of trying that Americans were much more courteous than Brits and that it was only the accent that made her think the guests on *Letterman* were charming. Now she was seeing for herself the astonishing off-handedness of not even just a Brit, but a posh, worried Scot with a few drinks inside him.

'How did it go with the *cops*?' Crispin echoed when Kathi had swallowed her pride and settled on to her cushion. 'Straight to business, eh? Well, I suppose that's what we look for in a Yank. And, if you charge by the hour, we shouldn't complain.'

Nelson opened his eyes very wide and pressed his lips together. *He* could hear it and see it – all the rudeness and rufflement – and was clearly finding entertainment in watching Brits and

Americans upset one another. I wondered briefly about life in Barbados – coconuts and reggae music as far as I was concerned – and, via wondering what on earth could have persuaded him to give all that up for a freezing cold Christmas with elderly relatives, I got even more sure that he was the chief suspect for wanting the skeleton found.

'The police are "satisfied",' Crispin said. 'And that's all they care about. They've obviously checked and they know my parents lived in the house from before Billy died until they died themselves. They know we did everything by the book in terms of having him declared dead, having the marriage dissolved and getting married ourselves. They know from speaking to your parents, Lexy, that the . . . was sealed when we left the house and they took over.'

'Chamber?' I said.

'Oh no, pet,' said Wilma. 'Not *chamber*. That's too much like Edgar Whatsisname. Is that who I mean?'

'They think they know the motive too,' Crispin continued, with a furtive glance at Nelson.

'Don't worry, Uncle Crispy,' he said. 'I'm fine.'

'And so, all in all,' Crispin said, flashing his nephew a grateful smile, 'they're happy to close the case. They'll never know which one of my parents actually did it. Probably my father, I should think. And they'll never know which one of my parents had the idea to hide . . . him where they hid him instead of burying him somewhere. But, again, since both of them are long gone, it hardly matters. So, as I say, case closed.'

He sat back. Fell back, really. He'd forgotten about giving Kathi the cushion.

'But it's different for us, isn't it?' said Wilma. 'We need to know what happened. We need to understand, don't we darling?'

'No. We don't,' Crispin said. 'Finally, we can forget all about it.'

'At the very least, we need to decide about a funeral,' Wilma said. 'Or some way to mark his passing. A memorial? It's up to you, of course, Nelson, but I think it would be fitting.'

Nelson gave a grave nod and took a huge glug of his drink, whatever it was. 'I suppose so,' he said. 'Not about the understanding. I don't feel the same urge. I never met my grandparents and I feel the police are right. We'll never know, so let it go. But about the funeral, sure.' He paused and blew his cheeks out. 'It's confusing. I mean I always knew I had three dads. There was my dad who died five years ago and loved me all my life; there was the guy I remember from when I was little, the one she only ever called "scumbag". And before them there was the first one, the one that made me. If I think, "What will I do with my first father's remains?" I want to take them home and scatter them in the sea by his favourite beach. But that's the guy – the imaginary guy – that my muma always *told* me was my biological father. The one who came with her to Barbados and lived there in Paradise. She really put effort into that story, by the way. She told me he was good with his hands, fixed up our house by the sweat of his brow after he knocked off from his job at night. Loved a bit of fishing. Loved swimming in the blue sea. Loved her. Loved me.'

He had been talking more and more quietly and now he wound down into total silence.

'So how come he left?' said Kathi. I winced along with the rest of them this time. There *was* a brusqueness there. 'In this story, I mean. How did she square all that with the fact that he was gone?'

'No squaring needed,' Nelson said. 'It made sense to me. Island kid. He made a baby, fixed him and his muma a comfortable home, and then he turned his face to the blue ocean and drifted away. She used to say to me, "There are seven hundred islands in our heaven here, baby, and your daddy loves them all".' He drained his glass. 'So sure,' he said. '*That* guy should be taken home and scattered on a beach. Trouble is that guy doesn't exist. The real guy – married man, seduced his boss's daughter and got himself murdered when he tried to handle it? What do we do with *his* ashes? You tell me.'

'Got "himself" murdered is a wee bit harsh, son,' said Wilma. 'And I must say, if I can forgive him for his infidelity to me then surely you can do the same.'

'And as for trying to handle it,' said Crispin, 'he was braver than me that night. I crept away from my father's wrath. He marched towards it. Of course, at the time we thought it was pure chivalry. We never dreamed it was "hands off my woman".'

'That's still a *kind* of chivalry,' Wilma said.

'And you had no idea?' I said. 'Afterwards, I mean? Not to

be indelicate or anything, but if someone goes into a house and never comes out again and immediately afterwards a bit of that house gets bricked up, didn't you even wonder?'

'I wasn't there,' Wilma said.

'What? Where were you?' said Todd.

'I was at the lodge,' said Wilma. 'Mrs Garmont told me, when I went to work the next morning – it was a Wednesday as I remember and there was a pile of ironing – she told me I wasn't needed and she would tell me if and when that changed. So I went creeping back to the lodge cottage, shaking in my boots. My husband was missing, my job was looking precarious and the family I'd worked for ever since I left school was falling apart. I stayed at home, waiting for Billy to come back or Mrs Garmont to sack me, whichever happened first.'

'I hate to think of it,' Crispin said. 'My poor little robin. My poor little wren. I'm ashamed to say that was the furthest thing from my mind.'

'Because *you* were living in a house where someone had disappeared and immediately afterwards a bit of the house got bricked up?' said Todd.

'No, because I wasn't there either,' said Crispin. 'I took off to try to find V. The next morning, when it became clear that she'd packed her belongings, not just fled into the night with a view to returning, I followed.'

'Where did you look?' I said.

'Well, not the passenger lists for ships headed to the Caribbean!' said Crispin. 'That never occurred to me. Stupid, I suppose, since we had family connections there in the dim and distant past.'

'A lot darker than "dim" and not so "distant" either,' said Nelson, sounding grim.

Crispin gave an awkward laugh. 'Yes, I'm afraid the Garmont fortune was made in sugar,' he said. 'It was sugar that built Mistletoe Hall. My father used to make a rather tasteless joke – one that my mother found most amusing too – saying that was why the house was named after a parasite.'

'Ewww,' said Todd. 'Do Keith and Judith know that?'

'Because a skeleton in the cellar is one thing,' said Kathi.

'Yeah,' I said. 'But you know what? If you're going to try to not get "sugar" on you, in this country, you're pretty constrained about where you can live. It's not as easy as not buying a house with pillars in a Southern state.'

'Really?' said Kathi.

'Oh honey,' said Nelson. 'You have no idea. How any Brit has the gall to sniff at America.'

We sat for a minute bathed in our white guilt until Nelson broke the silence. 'So where *did* you look, Uncle Crisp?'

'The thing you need to remember is that this was the old days,' Crispin said. 'First, I asked around Verity's friends – discreetly though; not saying why she might have been in touch but merely asking if she had been. When that turned up nothing, I tried all of the mother-and-baby homes. Nuns, chiefly, but it wasn't only nuns and I went round every one in Edinburgh and then Glasgow, the cities in the north of England and finally London. When all of that produced nary a whisper of Verity or anyone under a different name who looked like her, I threw in the towel and came home. Thereafter, beyond putting a small ad in the *Times* on her birthday each year, I'm afraid I gave her up as lost. It was a terrible, terrible time for all of us.'

'Not for Muma,' said Nelson. 'She was living the dream.'

'When did she get back in touch?' I said.

'She sent a letter with a picture of the baby,' said Crispin. 'Which would make it nine months more or less.'

'And in that nine months, you didn't ever wonder about the bricks?' said Todd. 'Your sister's missing after disgracing the good name of Garmont and there's a new development in the basement of the last place she was seen? Because what goes for Billy surely goes for her twice over?'

'I believed what my parents told me,' Crispin said. He turned to Nelson. 'They said they had screwed it out of Verity that she and Billy met in that little room – she creeping down the stairs and along from one end, he opening the trap doors and coming down the ladder to meet her. There was a couch. Heaven knows why.'

'Still is,' I said. 'What's left of it, anyway. Yellow with dark flocking?'

Too late, I saw Wilma's face change colour and realized I shouldn't have blurted that out.

'Oh God,' she said. 'Of course it's still there. Was he . . . Was he lying on it? I forgot, in all the upset, that you saw him, Lexy.'

'He was . . . Are you sure you want to know this?'

Wilma nodded, her eyes closed.

'He was sitting on the floor, propped against it,' I said. I missed out the bit where his head had rolled off his neck and his arm bones had settled into piles of kindling.

'That makes sense, I suppose,' Crispin said. 'Wherever in the house he was killed, it would have been easy to drag him to where they left him, but a lot harder to lift him up off the floor. Yes, I can see that. I suppose so.'

'You know, Nelson,' Wilma said, 'when I think about him spending all those years in that dark basement, the thought of his ashes scattered in a blue ocean by pink sand sounds lovely. Even if he only ever went there in your mother's dreams.'

That was the cue for another silence.

'But to return to the question, Crispin,' I said, after a while, 'your parents explained the bricks on account of trying to seal up the way Billy got in and the way Verity went to meet him?' A shadow of irritation crossed Crispin's face before he answered me, and the answer when it came was no more than a sharp nod. 'And you believed that?'

'Of course!' he barked at me. 'Why wouldn't I? It accorded with everything I knew. Verity was pregnant by the gardener, they'd run off together and my parents were angry. Actually, my parents were shattered. Nothing in their lives had prepared them for such a shock. For the shame and the grief. They were never the same ag—'

'Well, no,' I said. 'They wouldn't be. Because what shattered them was not only the fact that their daughter had done what girls have been doing since we all lived in the garden but, more to the point, the fact that one or both of them had committed a murder. If you saw shame and grief, that's what lay behind it.'

'It killed them,' Crispin said in a dry, harsh voice as if his throat had contracted. 'It killed my father. We weren't long married when he had a stroke. He wasn't even sixty. And my mother faded away once he was gone. We always thought—' He stopped and stared at Wilma. She was gazing back at him with tears in her eyes.

'I didn't,' she said.

'Oh my darling,' said Crispin. He swiped at his cheeks and

gave an enormous wet sniff. 'You are very kind but you know you did, deep down. We blamed ourselves. Falling in love and marrying against their wishes and then, of course, Baby Camilla – Miley – coming along rather early. We tried to tell ourselves that, compared to what V had done, our little romance was nothing to trouble them. Only . . . when my father died and then my mother followed him into the grave months later, it seemed as if our marriage had finished what Verity started. And although we've been very happy all these long years, that was always a cloud. Until now.'

'There was a cloud for you,' said Wilma, even more vehemently. 'I always knew there was something else going on. People don't just up and die like that.'

'But it doesn't matter now,' said Crispin. 'We are out from under the cloud at last. We have an answer.' His words were mild, but his tone was anything but.

'I need to know more,' said Wilma. Her tone saw his and upped it plenty. 'I need to know which one of them did it.'

So, all in all, this third silence was in a league of its own. Those first two silences had been its support bands.

It was still on the go when Miley reappeared, carrying a roughly hacked and even more roughly assembled sandwich with two mince pies balanced on top.

'I haven't had these wee white pickled onions for years, Mum,' she said. Then she frowned. 'Why's everybody . . . Are you having a séance?'

'Not the worst idea I've ever heard,' Todd muttered.

'So will you help us?' Wilma said. 'Fresh eyes and trained minds. Will you try to work out which one of them killed Billy? For Nelson? And for me?'

What could we say? To the accompaniment of Miley's pickled-onion burps, we made our arrangements, starting with a commitment to examine all the old photos and papers Wilma had brought to the cottage, in case they held any clues.

Kathi was keen. Todd is the nosiest person I know. I can't say the idea of rootling through moth-eaten crap to find out which of two dead racists was also a murderer struck me as particularly festive, but it was better than watching an egg or listening to Hiro, so I was in too.

FOURTEEN

'No use asking Lexy,' Todd said when we were back out on the road again. 'Her eyes were rolling around like pinballs, but what did *you* think, Kathi?'

'Hey!' I said. 'What are you even talking about?'

'See?' said Todd. 'Oblivious. Not a clue.'

'You think I don't know you're randomly attacking me over nothing?' I said. 'Yeek!' I had skidded on a patch of ice. I grabbed on to Todd's arm and steadied myself.

'Don't you dare take me down with you!' he said. 'You said it yourself and it's a whole day closer to Christmas now. The ER will be like a war zone. I can't believe Roger—' He shut his mouth so quickly his teeth snapped.

'Can't believe Roger what?' I said.

'Ask him yourself,' said Todd. '*You'll* have all the facts at your fingertips to shoot him down with.' He huffed out a huge white puff of breath into the light of the lamp post we were passing. 'Briefly though: he woke up and went out for a walk while we were in the city. Do you call it a city when it's so titchy? Anyway, he met the local doc and . . . Oh, ask him yourself, like I told you. And I'm not attacking you, randomly or otherwise. I'm talking to Kathi about the case.'

'What I thought,' said Kathi, who'd been waiting patiently, 'was Nelson's a fantastic actor or we're wrong.'

'Ab—' I said, and managed to finish it off with '-solutely,' instead of '-out what?'

'Oh puh-lease,' said Todd. 'You have no idea what we're talking about. Listen and learn. It was when Wilma started in on how she wanted answers and wasn't satisfied with "one of them did it, who cares which?" Someone digging around should have been Nelson's worst nightmare right there, if he came here to make sure the skeleton turned up. Right? If he's got something to hide. Right?'

'Unless he needed to out the skeleton to get the very same answers Wilma's after,' I said.

'Hmm,' said Todd. 'Wouldn't that have required him to know that the skeleton was his father? And why wouldn't he have just told the cops?'

'Larg said an anonymous report is hard to pull off,' Kathi said. 'But it's got to be easier than bringing a branch down right on target in pitch blackness.'

'Maybe it really was berry rustlers,' I said. 'A complete coincidence?'

'And Nelson being here when it happened is another one?' said Kathi.

'Bor-ing!' Todd said.

'OK,' I said, 'when we go back in the morning, let's turn the screw.'

'What screw?' said Todd.

'Tell Crispin and Wilma we went to speak to Mr K,' I said. 'Tell them he had lots to say, but some of it was confidential; ask for their permission to hear it. Make sure Nelson hears us asking. Watch how he reacts.'

'That is not your dumbest idea you've ever had, Lexy,' said Todd. 'It's actually pretty smart. For a change.'

'Where's this *coming* from?' I said. 'Is it to do with what I've got to ask Roger?'

'All I'm saying is your parents didn't notice that there was a part of their house missing, and you know what they say about apples and trees.'

'That is totally unfair. It was me who *did* notice there was a bit of the house missing. It was me who noticed the inside brick wall and the outside brick wall didn't match up. It was me who cracked this case wide open. Devin couldn't even aim the sledgehammer.'

'Could you just stop!' said Kathi. 'It's a beautiful night and it's Christmas, and we've got a case that might pay for the walking-around money on our free vacation. Will you quit ripping into each other and look at the stars?'

So we were all standing in a row gawping at Orion's Belt when my mum's little car came trundling up the street and stopped beside us.

'Watcha doin'?' said Taylor, hanging out of the driver's side window.

'Star-gazin',' I said in the same flirty tone.

'I know, right!' he said, getting out and standing next to me. 'I've been watching them all the way up from the reserve. Thank God these roads are quiet! I can't have been on the left more than half the time.'

'Not you too!' Todd turned away and stamped off back to Mistletoe Hall, leaving us gaping.

'So, good day at the empty bit of freezing cold wasteland, honey?' I said.

'Full of life if you know where to look,' said Taylor. 'You?'

'We've got a case,' said Kathi. 'Finding out all we can about what really happened to Billy Bone.'

'You won't need to disturb the nest again, will you?'

'Why the hell would we need to disturb the nest again?' I said. Then I followed it up with, 'Sorry. Todd was nipping at me, but that's no reason to be nipping at you.'

Taylor gave me a squeeze. 'Enh, it's not a family Christmas without a bust-up. Or so they tell me.'

Devin had definitely got the memo. He was in the library, sitting with his arms and legs crossed and his foot jiggling up and down, glaring daggers at Della in a very festive way. Roger and Noleen were playing cards with my parents, all pretending they couldn't see him.

'What's going on here?' I said.

'Nothing!' said Della. 'It's been a lovely day. *I've* had a lovely day.'

'And I've been cut to the quick,' said Devin.

'Where did you hear that?' Noleen shouted over. 'Do you even know what a quick is?'

'*What's* going on?' said Kathi, settling down by the fireside to unwind her scarf and shrug out of her jacket.

'I took Hiro and Diego to look at the little Christmas tree in the little park by the little kindergarten,' Della said. 'And we met some of the children who go there. And they had a snowball fight and made snow angels and everyone was very friendly. Look.' She opened her camera app and passed her phone over.

'Aww,' I said, scrolling through half a dozen pics of our little ones and some other little ones, all rosy-cheeked and snotty-nosed in a snowy playground.

'Their mothers were *very* friendly,' Della said. 'At first they thought I was Spanish.'

'Oh,' I said. 'Well, yeah, they would. Spain's just down the road.'

'But then I told them I'm Mexican,' Della said. 'And . . . nothing! It was like I'd told them I was from Delaware. Lexy, when you said Scotland was whitey-white-white, I always thought you meant it was racy-race-racist. But Diego spoke to them in Spanish because – well, you know, with the accent and everything, he didn't realize they were using English – and these mothers were *impressed*. They thought two languages was just wonderful.'

'Hmm,' I said. 'Try them with English and Urdu and see what happens.'

'Why did you never tell me there is no anti-Mexican feeling in Scotland?'

'Why would that ever come up?' I said.

'Why would there be anti-Mexican feeling?' said my dad. The card game was more or less abandoned. 'What did Mexico ever do?'

'Da-ad,' I said. 'What did *anyone* ever do?'

'You know,' Roger said, 'it hasn't been the nightmare I was expecting either. Once you get used to it.'

Todd, who had not said a word so far, stood up and swept out. We all heard him stamping upstairs.

'I don't get it,' I said. 'Devin, why would you be upset that Della had a nice day and the kids met some little friends?'

'Tell her,' said Devin. I had never heard his voice so flat, so stern.

'I want to stay,' Della said. 'I don't want to go back to America.'

'You—' I said. 'You just got citizenship. You really want to go through all of that again in a different country? A different bureaucracy? And pledge allegiance to the Quing?'

'How long is that poor man going to keep on being called the Quing?' said Taylor.

'And don't let this weather fool you,' I said. 'It'll melt tomorrow and be endless plotching rain till Easter, then one sunny day and then endless plotching rain that's a bit warmer till August. Then freezing cold again.'

'And no drought and no wildfires and no empty reservoirs,' said Della.

'You can't just move here though,' I said. 'Unless you're a millionaire.'

'Or a coder,' said Della. 'Like Devin.'

'Right, right, right,' I said. 'Because how could a coder ever get work in California? Where Silicon Valley is? And Google.'

'But Silicon Valley and Google don't offer six weeks of paid vacation, paid sick leave, free healthcare and a pension that kicks in automatically.'

'How did you find out all that?' I asked.

'Wait for it,' said Devin. 'You'll love this.'

'It's on the website,' said Della. 'It's right there in the job description.'

'Job?' I said.

'Told ya,' Devin said.

'There's an actual job?'

'There's an actual printed-out set of position particulars and an application form in our bedroom,' Devin said. 'And about five thousand pages of immigration stuff too.'

'And free schooling,' said Della.

'There's free schooling in California,' I said. 'CUSD is free.'

'What's cuzzed?' said my mum.

'Cuento Unified School District,' said all the Cuento-ites in a chorus.

'And free university tuition,' said Della. Which was a point, it was true. 'And while we're talking about school and university campuses . . .'

'Don't say it,' said Devin. 'Don't even.'

'What?' said my dad.

'And playgrounds, and movie theatres, and shopping malls,' said Della.

'We don't really do shopping malls,' I said. 'I mean there's sometimes a big garden centre, and there's a place in Edinburgh, if they've finished it.'

'Oh they've finished it,' said my mum. 'Except for the roads. And the trams. But the overpriced bling is all there to bankrupt yourself for.'

'Don't say what?' said my dad, completely ruining a decent diversionary tactic.

'Sports arenas, concert venues,' said Della.

'I can't believe you're going there,' said Devin.

'It's pretty low, Della,' said Noleen.

'True though,' said Kathi.

'We've got Murrayfield for the rugby and Meadowbank for athletics,' said my dad. 'And Easter Road and Tynecastle. Does the wee man like his footie?'

'And as for concerts,' said my mum, 'well, it's Edinburgh. The Festival, you know? And a fair few theatres the rest of the year round. In fact . . . it's supposed to be a surprise for Boxing Day, but since it's come up—'

'It hasn't, Judith,' Devin said. 'That's not what she's talking about.'

'What *is* she talking about?' said my mum. 'What are you talking about, Della? Schools, playgrounds, cinemas, shopping centres, sports halls and theatres? Surely you've got all those things in California too? If the wee ones are hobby-daft, like you're saying.'

'See? They don't even know what I'm referring to,' said Della. 'They're wracking their brains and they can't think what I'm saying. I want Diego and Hiro to grow up where that's true.'

No one said anything for a good while and, when Noleen broke the silence, it was to start making goodnight noises. One by one, we followed her. Because the trouble was, it *was* true. And Devin knew that, but Della making out he didn't care was beyond shabby. And, as well as the personal angle, Della had just broken the immigrant's deal in the worst possible way. In Britain, you can diss the weather and the dentistry, but you can't say David Attenborough's a prick or someone will hurt you. In America, you can take a pop at the portions and even the president, but you can't do what Della just did. Even I knew that.

FIFTEEN

Friday 23 December

Their bedroom door was still closed when I got up the next morning, and I saw from the big window halfway down the stairs that Noleen and Kathi had the kids out in the snow in their jammies and wellies playing some kind of ball game with a cricket bat. It wasn't cricket, mind you.

Roger, wonder of wonders, was up before Todd. He was sitting in a Windsor chair at the head of the table in the fake kitchen, making it look spindly.

'Your mom's fixing pancakes,' he said, nodding at where my mum was standing by the range with her back to us. Her apron strings were wrapped twice around her middle and tied with a double knot as if she could literally gird herself into knowing what American pancakes should turn out like. I looked over her shoulder.

'Crêpes?' I said.

'Unkind,' said my mum. It was a Campbell family joke. 'I'm using up what we've got. It's the big shop today, Lexy. Are you coming with me?'

Was I going to Tesco the day before Christmas Eve to buy a week's worth of feasting food for twelve people. 'I've got the case, Mum,' I said. 'We're going to be flat out to try to get Wilma and Crispin some answers so they can relax and have a nice Christmas after all the upset.'

My mum pressed a hand to her heart and nodded gravely, buying it hook, line and sinker. Roger poked his tongue in his cheek and shook his head slowly at me, buying nothing.

'Is Todd talking to you yet?' I asked him, to deflect. 'What's up with him anyway?'

'Same as Devin,' Roger said. 'Only worse, because Della knows Devin didn't fake an entire vacation with a hidden agenda.'

'I have no idea what you're talking about,' I said.

My mum turned round, splattering a bit of raw pancake batter off her ladle. 'Same here,' she said. 'But I love it. It's like watching an episode of *The West Wing*. Not a clue what's happening but everyone really means it.'

'I got into it with the local PCP yesterday,' said Roger.

'Is that drugs?' said my mum. 'I don't want to be a party-pooper but . . .'

'Primary care physician, Mum,' I said. 'He means the GP.'

'Yes!' said my mum. 'Dak, the dishy doctor! I completely forgot about him. He's Indian, Lexy. He's got eyes as brown and shiny as two plates of oxtail soup.'

'Do you know,' said Roger, 'I asked him about indemnity insurance and he didn't know what I meant. He's forty-three and he's never been sued by a patient.'

'Well, no, I should hope not,' said my mum. 'I wouldn't like to think our local doctor was incompetent enough to be sued by people.'

'And what Devin said about benefits is all true,' said Roger. 'If we lived here, I could catch a train to work, do nine hours in a ward full of kids whose parents would never sue me and come home again. Two weeks in Italy every summer. Two weeks here every Christmas. And I'd never see another GSW even if I didn't retire till I was eighty.'

'What's a GSW?' said my mum.

Roger held out a hand inviting me to feast my eyes on someone who didn't know what a GSW was. 'Global search word,' he said. 'Paperwork.' Because Roger has cover stories for all the upsetting medical terms, in case his baby patients overhear. I once heard him say a catheter was a kind of elf that lived in a fountain.

'Get that, would you?' said my mum, as the front doorbell rang upstairs.

I tramped up the spiral staircase, meeting Todd on his way down, then together we crossed the hallway to lug the enormous oak door back on its enormous iron hinges. Outside on the step stood Larg.

'Mornin' all,' he said, doing a PC Plod plié that it was impossible not to laugh at.

'Are your boxers too tight?' Todd asked him. 'I can probably fit you in for a wardrobe blitz if you commit by the end of today.' He was feeling a bit better then.

'My box—?' said Larg, and then shook his head as if to clear his ears of water. 'Right then, I'm here with an update.'

'I thought you were banned from this case,' I said, ushering him back downstairs.

'I was when it was interesting,' he said. 'But coming along after the horses with a shovel is the kind of job I was made for, so they tell me. I've come to fill your parents in.'

When he was installed at the table in the fake kitchen with the first pancake – and the second one, which didn't look all that different – he got going.

'William Bone,' he said. 'ID'd by his watch – according to his ex-wife. Cause of death, a blow to the head from our old favourite, the blunt instrument. Date of death, Tuesday August the ninth, 1959. Perpetrator, Alexander Garmont, deceased, and/ or Jemima Garmont, deceased. No other suspects. No other avenues being pursued. Thank you very much and goodnight.'

'That's a pretty shaky ID,' I said. 'Isn't it?'

'Do you have any reason to think it's someone else?' said Larg. 'Not that I'm disagreeing, but we – and when I say "we", I mean my superiors in the CID – we didn't have any luck with dental records. He had some fillings and one crown, but his wife can't remember who his dentist was and we haven't got the resources to go on a nationwide dentist hunt when there's nothing to be gained.'

'You really believe Crispin and Wilma didn't know he was in there?' said Todd.

'I know, right?' said Larg. 'But actually, I do. The brother went off on a wild goose chase to find the sister – that's true enough, because he kept records of where he searched. Names of nuns and what have you. And the wife kept away from the big house, panicking that she was going to be sacked and turned out. Then, eventually, one day, Mrs Blunt Instrument said, "Oh Wilma, how about running the Ewbank round this avvy?" and everything went back to normal. Except for a bricked-up room.' He nodded towards it as he took a slurp of tea. 'And they explained that away on account of that's where their innocent daughter was seduced and they wanted never to see the place again.'

'Then guilt about what they'd done ate away at the both of them and they died years before their time,' I finished up.

'They can't have been all bad then,' my mum put in.

'Except for trying to keep their good name beyond the grave,' said Larg. 'Crispin told the boss and the boss told me that, before the old girl croaked, she said her dying wish was that he would stop on, not sell up. Not rent it out. Not muck it up.'

'I'll bet,' I said. 'And she was right. It stayed hidden as long as they lived here. My God, it nearly stayed hidden a lot longer.'

'Until Lexy Campbell, Super Surveyor, came on the scene,' said my mum, sliding a plate of pancakes in front of me. They were proper old-fashioned Scottish pancakes, paper-thin and frilly round the edges, a world away from the fluffy wonders Todd was used to. I spread jam on one, rolled it up and ate it like a chimichanga. Todd watched, nodded and reached for the jam jar.

'And that's that, Mrs Campbell,' Larg said. 'Case closed. You can do whatever you want with your own basement and the Garmonts can decide what to do with the remains. As long as the press don't get a whiff, it should all blow over soon enough. Thank God for Christmas, eh? No one wants to be sniffing out a story when they could be drinking in front of the telly.'

'But it's OK by you if *we* do a little more digging?' Todd said. 'The family would like some answers, if we can find any.'

'The same crack team that thought we had berry rustlers?' said Larg. 'I don't see how you could do much harm. Have at it.'

'Condescending much?' said Todd as we left the kitchen. 'Now I really do want to turn up some big-ticket info just to shove it in his face.'

'So the default rudeness hasn't taken you the way it's taken Noleen?'

'Don't even,' said Todd. 'Can you believe these people?' He opened the door to the spiral staircase and ushered me through ahead of him. He had obviously got used to it in the last couple of days and no longer wanted someone behind him to break his fall if he lost his footing.

'What people?' I said. 'Roger and Della? That's just the mark of a good holiday. I always start daydreaming about how to stay forever. Don't you?'

'Yeah, on Maui. In Cabo.'

'None taken.'

'So you *don't* think they mean it?' he asked me. 'You don't think Taylor's serious? He sounded pretty serious to me.'

'Taylor?' I said it so loud it echoed, in spite of the close stone walls pressing in on us all around.

'You called?' came Taylor's voice from above us. 'I love the acoustic in here.'

'Are you coming down?' said Todd. 'Because I am not trying to pass. Go back up and let us out first.'

'I'm not coming down,' said Taylor. 'I'm sitting here like Christopher Robin waiting for Lexy. Lex? I've got something I need to discuss with you.'

'Nope,' I said, scuttling up the last few steps to the ground floor. 'No can do. Not today. Busy, busy.' I let the door bang shut behind me and strode across the hall, slowing down just a touch as I realized I didn't know where I was going.

'Not so breezy now,' said Todd behind me.

'They can't be for real,' I said. 'Della and Roger and Taylor want to stay here? Want to *live* here?'

'Perhaps the bird place is looking for a . . . oh I don't know . . . feather fluffer or something.'

'This can't happen,' I said. 'We need to . . . take them to – I don't know – a Semichem in Broxburn.'

Todd mimed puzzlement.

'Like a Dollar General in Scranton,' I said. 'Only so much worse. They need to get a night bus from Kilmarnock. They need to go to a Scottish barbecue. Or try to find a watermelon. This is insanity!'

'That's what I was trying to tell you.'

'Does Devin know weed is illegal here?' I asked.

'No,' said Todd darkly. 'But Della does.'

His voice already sounded like he was announcing the death of someone fairly important, but just at that moment he got back-up from the clanging of the front doorbell. Before we could get over there to open it, the handle turned and Miley Garmont poked her head round.

'Yoo-hoo,' she said, in a tone more suited to saying 'cat sick'. Then she caught sight of us. 'I'm not being rude. It's just I remember what it was like traipsing all the way to the front door of this place, and I wanted to spare you. Only I didn't want to go downstairs. Even though that's exactly why I've come: to bring Nelson and go downstairs.'

'So let me in,' came Nelson's voice from the doorstep. 'I'm freezing my backside off out here.'

Miley came forward, with her cousin jostling close behind. 'I am so sorry about last night. I was bladdered. If I wasn't fifty-odd with a face like a boxing glove, I'd say someone spiked me in the Prick. I only had four pints.'

'On top of Uncle Crispy's pours,' said Nelson.

'So I apologize for anything I said or did,' said Miley. 'But don't think up any punishments because how I feel this morning is payback enough.'

She did look pretty rough. I had forgotten what a hangover looked like in my California years, because no one except me drinks enough to make it worth opening a second bottle, and I'm careful never to look in the mirror till it's steamed up from my shower water.

'Do you want some coffee?' I asked her.

'She already drank the world's coffee supplies down to half a jar of instant granules,' said Nelson. 'Come on, girl! We said we wouldn't be long.' He turned back to us. 'Uncle Crispy is in the attic looking for those family papers to show you all. How can an attic in a cottage they've lived in less than a year be so full of junk that he's got to rummage? Search me. What are you supposed to do with a pile of old crap they should have thrown out before they moved? Search me harder. But whatever. Nothing about this family makes any sense anymore. Who does what they did? Who lives in a house after they did it?' He had started off sounding as laid-back as ever but ended up kind of frantic.

'We don't have to do this, Nelson,' said Miley.

'Oh I want to do it,' Nelson said. 'Let's go.'

'Would you like some flowers?' I said. My mum would kill me for tugging stems out of her Christmas arrangements but we were going to visit the place where this man's father had died, after all.

'You got any rum?'

Miley groaned softly.

'Or let's just go and stand awhile.'

So we collected Kathi and trooped down the spiral stairs, me with an ear cocked in case Taylor was still lurking. At the bottom, we skirted the door to my parents' flat and let Miley lead the way around the twists and turns of the passageway until we reached the place where the brick wall sat half demolished, jagged-edged, rising out of a pile of dust and rubble.

'And this was covered by the door?' Miley said. 'Because I don't remember bricks.'

'A false door, yes,' I said.

Todd was picking his way through the hole and into the chamber. I wished I could stop thinking 'chamber'. Miley followed and then Nelson, with a shrug, squeezed through too. Kathi waited outside.

By the light of three phones, we had a forensic view of the battered brocade couch and the dark patch on the floor in front of it.

'My blood,' said Nelson. 'My flesh and blood. This is too much.'

Miley put an arm round him but said nothing. She had gone even whiter and there was a sheen to her pasty face.

'You OK?' I said. Not laying flowers was one thing but throwing up was something else.

'Just got the willies. I remember that fabric. It must have been a suite at one time. There must have been an armchair. I remember sitting and picking the velvet bits off the arm. I remember my mum scolding me for spoiling it.'

'I used to pick labels off everything that didn't move,' I said. 'It drove my mum nuts.'

'You still do it,' said Todd. 'It drives *me* nuts. But you're a different story, Miley. If someone's got poor enough taste to have flocking around toddlers, they deserve what they get.'

Nelson hadn't been listening. 'How could a man be so unmissed?' he said. 'No father or mother to wonder where he went? His wife lets him go without question? His girlfriend never asks? And didn't he have friends? Men in the village that he went for a pint with? How can someone leave no hole when they go? What kind of man is that?'

These were good questions and I had no answers. Thankfully

Nelson supplied those himself. 'Nothing like any other man Muma ever kept company with,' he said. 'That's for sure. She liked fun. She liked a man who laughed. She liked a singsong. Even the scumbag was a good laugh. He was a perfect playmate for a little guy like me. And my real dad – my last dad, my *dad* – couldn't get locked in a toilet stall without a dozen friends getting up a search party.'

'Maybe,' I began, then I caught hold of myself. I had been going to wonder aloud whether something worse than an assignation had happened here on that threadbare couch. Whether Verity ran away from a trauma as much as from an angry father. Whether Old Mr Garmont had a deeper grievance against Billy Bone than we had thought. Whether this married gardener was different from every other boyfriend Verity had chosen because she didn't choose him.

The same thought had occurred to Todd but he flashed his eyes at Nelson and then frowned at me. He was right. The poor guy was going through plenty already today without facing that.

Miley saw the look too and, sick or not, she sprang into action to distract her cousin. 'And that?' she said, pointing to the other stretch of broken brickwork. 'That sealed it off from the Wizard of Oz end, did it? See, that's where I played, not in here.' She stepped over and slipped through the gap. 'I used to pretend there was a tornado coming and scamper down the ladder, batten those doors behind me and talk to my imaginary friends.' She gave a gruff laugh. 'It all seems so much smaller now.'

'If this place feels smaller now you're grown up, my childhood home would be like a dolls house!' Nelson said.

'So you visited your aunt and cousin in Paradise?' I said. I was inching my way towards the questions I wanted to ask. 'And, Nelson, did you come over here?'

'Not here,' Nelson said. 'We went to London on a trip but never made this far up.'

'Yeah, I went to Barbados a couple of times when I was a student,' Miley said. 'I couldn't handle the thought that my dad had a sister and I never knew her, that I had a cousin and didn't know him.'

'Oh sure,' said Nelson. 'And if we'd been in . . . Mogadishu, you'd have been just as keen, right?'

'Why the hell would you be in Mogadishu?' said Miley.

'I'm just saying, living in Barbados sure does make people stay in touch.'

'Same as California,' said Todd.

'And Yule?' I said, pressing one last time. 'I mean, what made you come over for Christmas this year suddenly?'

'Muma died,' Nelson said. I felt my pulse quicken. 'So Uncle Crispy and Auntie Wilma were all that was left from that generation.' My pulse slowed. 'But,' he went on,' that's not the whole story.' My pulse picked up again. 'I reckoned everyone deserves a break from the wife and kids sometimes.'

My pulse was beginning to bug me.

'Do you buy that?' said Miley, with a sharp look at me that made her wince and put a hand to her head.

'Well, not now we don't,' said Todd. 'What do you mean, "buy"?'

'And do you trust them?' Miley asked Nelson, with another skewering look. This one turned her pale.

'What choice have I got?' said Nelson. He took a deep breath, blew it out through pursed lips and reached for his phone. 'I've got the original but I thought it was better not to bring it. Zoom in if it's too small to read.'

Todd and I rejoined Kathi and we all huddled together over the screen. It was a photograph of a letter:

My dearest son, I have made many mistakes in my life but you are not one of them, no matter what my family might say. I have done my best to give you a good life, even though that sidetracked me from what my purpose was when I came here. I want you to carry on my mission and don't give up like I did. Grief is a terrible thing. Grief clouded my eyes for years. I was so hurt that your papa left me waiting for him, all alone and abandoned. It's only in these later years that I have come to see he would never have done that to me if he had a choice. Go back and find the truth. The world has changed. The world is listening with different ears. I trust you to make it a better place, with my love, Muma.

'What does that mean?' I said. 'What purpose? What truth? What dream?'

'Search me,' said Nelson. 'She was all about restitution and reparations when I was a kid. Dismantling – what did she call it? – the long tail of privilege that hangs from the beast of colonialism.' He grinned. 'Fun at parties, huh? But that didn't have anything to do with Scotland. With Yule. It's like she mixed two different things up together at the end. Billy disappearing without a trace and what the Garmonts did in Barbados.'

'And she never said any more than what's in this letter?' asked Todd.

'Not a word.'

'So . . . how did you know the truth was in this cellar?' said Kathi. 'That's a heck of a leap.'

The cousins looked at one another, hoping the other one understood. Or maybe Miley was hoping someone would give her a bacon sandwich and a mug of tea.

'I need to sit down,' she said, sinking on to the old couch. It released a puff of mouldy dust, and she sprang back to her feet again.

'What did you mean?' Nelson asked. 'What leap?'

'We thought you brought the tree down on the hatch to alert everyone to what was down here.'

'Seriously?'

It did sound a bit bonkers when you heard it said out loud.

'Because it wasn't a proper berry heist,' said Todd.

'A "proper berry heist"?' said Nelson.

That sounded pretty unhinged too.

'And who else would want him found?' said Kathi.

'Who else apart from someone who didn't even know he existed?' said Nelson.

Which made it sound like our theory was total garbage and we were idiots. Rather than say that, though – I thought it might undermine his faith in us as investigators – I focused on the future. 'Let's get along to the cottage. Where better to find the truth about old secrets than in boxes of old . . . What is it we're going to see exactly? And what's supposed to be hidden there?'

'Wow,' Nelson said. 'I'm glad it's not me that's paying you. OK, though, yeah. Let's go.'

SIXTEEN

'It's not the first time,' Todd said, as the three of us togged up for the walk along Yule High Street. Once Kathi had studied the letter on Nelson's phone, he and Miley had gone ahead since she urgently needed the fresh air. 'We've been employed by Person A and worked for Person B before.'

'We're not working for Person B,' I said, watching Todd tying on a scarf like he was making a pretzel the old-fashioned way. 'If that means Nelson. We're gratefully accepting his trust and hoping to find out what he might be hiding, in pursuit of fulfilling our commitment to Person A – Wilma, plus a reluctant Crispin.'

'Who, if you think about it,' said Kathi – she wound her scarf twice round her neck and tucked the ends into her body-warmer – 'told us she wanted the truth to come out.'

'Did she, though?' Todd said. He screwed his eyes up as if the sight of me throwing one end of my scarf over my shoulder to hang down my back while the other end hung down my front was causing him physical pain. 'As I recall, Wilma asked us to see if we could find out which one of the two parents killed Billy Bone. Like those were the options.'

'They probably are,' I said. 'Let's see what they've unearthed at least. It might all be moving in the same direction.'

Outside, the morning was yet another winter wonderland: it was colder than ever and the frost fractals looked more elaborate than they had yesterday. The icicles were longer too and the snow was not yet grey-yellow because this was such a quiet road. We could still see individual tyre tracks and, although a sheep had got out of a field at some point, even that looked like chocolate chips in whipped cream.

'Hell,' said Todd, looking around. 'It's so pretty. And with the agreement about the existence of midges and everything.'

'I know,' said Kathi. 'I tried to tell Noleen there are no dry-cleaners on this backwards little rock and she said, "Oh no! A gap in the market for you to fill" in this really sarcastic voice.'

'No dry-cleaners?' Todd said. 'Seriously?'

'Not *no* dry-cleaners,' I said. 'Just not like you've got.'

'But how do people get their formal shirts washed?' said Todd.

'They wash them,' I said.

'How do they get them ironed?' said Kathi.

'They iron them,' I said.

'Hmph,' said Kathi.

We were up to the shop now. Todd tapped on the window and waved in at Leanne behind the counter. 'Maybe that explains Leanne's wardrobe,' he said. 'Maybe it happened in a laundry incident.'

'So where's the nearest dry-cleaner to here?' said Kathi. I frowned, pretending to think about it. 'I'll ask your mom.'

'She won't know,' I said. 'Unless they've had to go to a funeral and my dad got coronation chicken on his suit at the purvey. Even then she'd probably just dab it with something.'

We'd got as far as the pub now and Beth, slapped up for the day, came out to empty a dust buster into the wheelie bin. She raised it in salute like a sword.

'Bloody freezing,' she said. 'I'm putting up the price of my soup at lunchtime.'

'We might be in for a hot toddy,' I said.

'Also at a premium price,' said Beth. 'You think I'm kidding?' She went inside again.

'HotToddy was my Twitter name before Roger made me change it,' Todd said. 'I've basically spent my whole life bending over backwards for that man. Probably my own fault he thinks he can railroad me with this nonsense now.'

Kathi and I said nothing. Roger lived in a motel to make Todd happy and that was just the beginning of his forbearance and sanguinity.

'I can hear you thinking,' Todd said.

'Here we are!' I opened the cottage gate and followed them up the path, wondering who would greet us: our actual client or the guy I couldn't help thinking of as our side hustle.

'Come in, come in, come in,' Wilma said, sweeping the door wide. She was wearing a scarf on her hair and a cross-over apron on top of her clothes, like someone playing a cleaner on a vintage telly programme. 'We've been right through the attic and brought down everything we can lay our hands on. Stuff we'd forgotten all about, actually.'

'Have you looked through it then?' I said.

Wilma paused. 'We've left it for you. I hope that's OK. Crispin's all for getting rid of the lot once you're finished. He's been on the phone to see about a big shredder. Did you know you can rent great big shredders?'

'It's going to be into the new year, they think,' Crispin called from the telephone table by the stairway. They had actually moved a telephone table into their new house and set up their landline there. 'How do you feel about a brazier, my dear?'

'We've put you in the dining room,' Wilma said. 'Coffee in a thermos on the sideboard. I made a tray of flapjacks. Masks, gloves, if you'd like them. It's all very dusty. It's quite handy how we've all got masks and gloves around the house these days, don't you think?' She kept on wittering and hopping about like a sparrow till Kathi stepped up in front of her.

'Ma'am,' she said, 'we seem to have everything we could ask for and more. You just go right ahead and get on with your day. We'll holler if we need you.'

'Such beautiful manners!' said Wilma. 'You sound like a sheriff in a western.'

'Th–thanks?' Kathi said to the back of Wilma's pinny as she whisked out of the room.

'Are you going to be OK?' I asked Kathi, surveying the metropolis of cardboard boxes, biscuit tins and cigar cases crowded on to a dustsheet on the dining table.

'Me? Why?' said Kathi. 'Oh, dust, you mean? Yeah, I think so. How about you, Todd?'

'What because of spiders?' said Todd. 'Uh-huh.'

It was torture to hear this with no one else around. I started to text Roger and Noleen, then realized that would only add more fuel to the 'move to Scotland' fire. I slipped my phone back into my pocket and advanced on the nearest crisp box, to see what treasure was in store.

'Ooft, diaries,' I said, flipping the cover open on the top one. 'Great! Mrs Garmont's old-lady diaries from the olden days, written in spidery old-lady writing also from the olden days.'

'Luck of the draw, Lexy,' said Todd. 'I got photographs. Yay me.'

'And this,' said Kathi, prising open an outsize biscuit tin, 'is letters. Postmarked . . . who am I, Benedict Cumberbatch? But the stamps are Bar-something.'

'Letters,' I said. 'Ha-ha.'

'Ha-ha yourself,' said Kathi. 'They're typed.' She blew a cheek raspberry and settled down to start reading.

The diaries in my box started in 1955. The early ones were embossed with the year on the cover but the later ones were simply posh notebooks that Mrs Garmont had written in every so often. 'I don't have to start at the beginning, do I?' I said.

'Um, I'd start on Tuesday August ninth, 1959, Lexy,' Todd said. 'The night Verity broke the news.'

'Oh yeah,' I said. 'Brain fart. Sorry.' I dipped my head to hide my shame. Then I lifted it again. 'But *would* Verity really have misjudged her family so badly that she chose to break the news?'

'Maybe her mom suspected and finally faced her with it,' Kathi said. 'See if you can find a hint in a diary just before that night and I'll see if Verity said anything about it in her letters.'

'And I'll waste my time with photographs,' Todd said. 'They're all of Crispin's family anyway,' he added, flipping through a leatherette album with a faded tassel. 'They'd hardly have pictures of the gardener, so I guess I can skip them. Oh!'

Kathi and I both looked up as if our chins were on strings. 'They take some shots of the servants after all?' Kathi said.

'Nah, just that couch in happier days,' Todd said, turning the album to face us and holding it wide open so its stiff binding squeaked. Held on to the rough card page was a yellowed photograph obviously taken in the drawing room at Mistletoe Hall, showing a fat baby in an explosion of lacy ruffles propped up with cushions halfway along that same brocade sofa we had all just seen in its basement grave.

'My mum and dad have done a pretty good job,' I said, because apart from the fact that it was black and white, this photograph of sofas with spindly legs, club chairs with footstools and little tables covered in magazines and silver photo frames was identical to the current look, save the telly. 'God knows where they learned stately-pile chic but they've nailed it.'

Todd clapped the album shut and laid it aside, returning to the table to look for something more useful.

'These letters are definitely from Verity,' Kathi said. 'From Barbados. Listen to this: "I am typing for practice, Mother. I am studying secretarial and business with a view to contributing to this little family after my confinement". Confinement!'

'It doesn't mean jail,' I said. 'It means childbirth. What's the date?'

'Yep, yep, that tracks,' said Kathi. 'October 1959.'

'And I don't think Old Mrs Garmont suspected anything in advance,' I said. 'Listen to this from the first of August.' I cracked the notebook open to get daylight on to the page. '"Garden all day. Delphiniums going over, but montbretia glorious, roses too. Sprayed all for greenfly. Picked last of runner beans".' I flipped forward a few pages. '"Beautiful day in the garden. Picked five pounds of apples and made jelly. Peelings to Margery's pig".' I flipped again. 'Then she went quiet. Nothing for the second half of August at all. Or September.'

But after that, and in a very different vein, she started up again. Towards the end of November, in an undated entry, Old Mrs Garmont had written: *The joy has left this house. I wonder if I will ever see my son or my daughter again. If they came back now, they could live here in comfort with us. The worst is over.*

'What do you reckon this means?' I said and read it out to the others.

'If we didn't know what we know,' said Kathi, 'I'd say that meant the head of the house has gotten over his hissy fit and it's safe for my children to come home where they belong.'

'But given what we *do* know?' I asked.

'The decomposition is past the stinky bit,' said Kathi.

I shuddered and kept reading.

'Found him,' said Todd, who was standing up at the table, leafing through some loose snaps. 'Billy and Wilma's wedding day.'

She was dressed like Grace Kelly, covered in lace from neck to wrist to ankle, and Billy was in a Fred MacMurray lounge suit. I could see a section of the famous watch chain stretched over his waistcoat. And I could just about see the seeds of eighty-year-old Wilma in the girl holding on to Fred MacMurray's arm.

Did Nelson look like him? I couldn't see it, but maybe it was more in the expression, and only Wilma, who had been married to the man who fathered the boy, would be struck by the resemblance.

'Holy crap, but it all came down to earth pretty quick,' Todd said, handing me another pair of photographs. In one, Billy Bone was posing halfway up a ladder, leaning against a gnarled tree. He was in dungarees and an open-necked shirt, heavy boots on his feet, but he was smiling down at – I assumed – his wife just as cheerfully as he'd been smiling on his wedding day. In the other photograph, Wilma was holding a wicker basket full of white washing. It looked wet and heavy, judging by the way she was straining to keep it balanced on her hip. She was wearing wellingtons and a pleated skirt with a hand-knitted jumper – a badly hand-knitted jumper – and her hair was in an overtight perm. It must have seemed like a good, no-nonsense, easily maintained choice, but when you put it together with not a scrap of make-up, it left her looking like Vivienne Westwood pushing seventy-five.

'"I will not bring the subject up again",' Kathi read out from her current letter. '"All I ask is that, if anyone" – that's underlined – "asks after me, you have my permission to give him my address and the message that I would like to be in contact". Wow. Christmas Eve, 1959.'

'That's your wow, right?' I said. 'Not Miley's.'

'That's my wow.'

'So they told her to drop the subject of where her boyfriend and the father of her baby had gone, and she told them she was open to contact if he came looking for her,' said Todd. 'Wow.'

'My God, what a letter to send to your parents on Christmas Eve,' I said. 'When you're thousands of miles from home, pregnant and all alone.'

'In Barbados,' said Todd. 'Like Nelson pointed out. Not Mogadishu.'

I calculated a fortnight for the letter to reach Yule, what with Christmas and New Year, and went rummaging for Mrs Garmont's journal from January 1960.

My heart is broken, I read in one entry – an entry that had runs in the ink as if she'd been crying as she wrote – *the return*

of my son should comfort me, but all I can think of is my daughter.
I want to buy passage on a ship and go to her, to be there when
she passes through that gateway of pain.

'Blimey,' I said out loud.

'What?' said Todd.

'Nothing, just Old Mrs G spreading it on thick.' I returned to
the diary. *But then Verity would return. And she would ask ques-*
tions and know too much of the truth to believe our slippery
answers. So we must remain here in this mausoleum, living a
hollowed-out life. I sometimes wonder if prison wouldn't be
preferrable to this. It would be prison, not the noose. They
wouldn't hang a woman for a crime of passion. Nor a man for
protecting his wife.

'Jesus fucking Christ!' I said.

'Lexy!' said Todd, half-serious. 'It's Christmas.'

'Sorry. Baby Jesus fucking Christ.'

Kathi snorted. 'What is it?'

'Brace yourselves,' I said.

'Hmph,' said Todd. 'And all I found were more photos of
Billy and Wilma – at the seaside, on Christmas morning, at a
dance . . .'

'All *I've* got is a blow-by-blow account of learning to touch-type
and take shorthand,' said Kathi. 'You don't think of secretaries in
the Caribbean, but they must have needed them, I guess.'

'I win for sure,' I said. 'Get ready for this. It was the mother
who did it. Whatever Billy got clobbered with, it was Mrs who
did the clobbering. She says she wouldn't hang if she confessed.'

'Because it's Britain,' said Todd. 'We know. You never tire of
telling us.'

'No, I'm pretty sure we were still hanging people then,' I said.
'She thought she wouldn't get hanged because she was a woman,
and her husband wouldn't get hanged because he was an accom-
plice – and I quote – "protecting his wife". Ergo, she did it. And
that's not all.'

'That's quite a lot,' said Kathi.

'She said Verity knew too much to be fobbed off with their
"slippery" answers.'

'What does that mean?' said Todd.

'OK, I'm guessing,' I said, 'but I *think* it means Verity knew damn well where she met Billy for their assignations and it wasn't that old couch in the basement, so she wouldn't buy the cover story for why it was bricked up.'

'Wow,' said Kathi.

'Told you.'

I opened up one or two more journals at random pages and read isolated words – 'grief', 'regret', 'impossible' – then set to, to try to find the last one of all. I couldn't read everything but I definitely wanted to read that.

And here it was. No more plush, moleskin journals; this one was a spiral-bound notebook from William Low. Mrs Garmont had tried to make it a bit less bargain-basement by scratching out the price tag with black ink and writing her name and the year – 1966 – on the front in her copperplate handwriting.

'God, Wullie Low's!' I said. 'I'd completely forgotten about that place.'

I flipped to the last page and read the final entry: *I have told Crispin and Wilma to be happy here. To be as happy here as we were once. To be happier here than I have been for such a long time. I begged them to live in the house, cherish it, enjoy it. I told them not to be boring and subdivide it simply because it's a big place for a modern family. I cannot say more than that without arousing suspicions, but I pray that, out of sentiment, they will chance never to find the secret of Mistletoe Hall.*

'Oh come on!' I said. 'This is pure Enid Blyton!'

'Who?' said Todd.

'Virginia Andrews.'

'Ewww,' said Kathi.

'Without the incest. Can you believe Mrs Garmont on her deathbed wrote "the secret of Mistletoe Hall"?' I read the entry out loud to them.

'If you can't get maudlin on your deathbed, when can you?' Todd said, trying to be kind, I think.

'Plus it was to a purpose,' Kathi said. 'If she made sure Crispin and Wilma never sold the house and never knocked it around, then they'd never have to deal with Billy Bone. She was trying to spare them.'

'Still weird, though,' I said.

'Weird how?' said Kathi. 'I get it.'

'Just . . . if she's ill enough to be dying, you'd think she'd be past caring. What did they say she died of? Old Mrs? Because her handwriting in her last diary is exactly the same as all the earlier years.'

'Didn't Crispin say she faded away? *He* had a heart attack and *she* faded away.'

'How old were they?'

'We can work it out roughly,' Todd said. 'If Crispin is eighty now then, in 1959 . . .'

'I'm crap at this,' I said.

'He was about twenty,' Kathi said. 'So his mom would be what? Forty-five? Fifty? Fifty-five at most. Todd, does she look old in the family snaps? Does her husband look old enough to drop dead clutching his chest?'

'Hmm?' said Todd, half listening. 'I'm finding lots of pics of Billy and Wilma in their little love nest. I think it was Wilma's camera. She's documented everything he did. Here he is digging the garden and here he is hanging wallpaper. Sorry, what did you ask?'

'How old were Mr and Mrs Garmont when they died?'

Todd abandoned the box of snaps and went back to one of the leatherette albums with the tassels. 'This is quite a late one,' he said. 'Crispin looks like a Rock-a-Billy in the Christmas family portrait anyway. How old . . .? How old . . .?' He passed the album to me.

'Bloody hell, it's the whole household,' I said. A young man with extravagant sideburns who was just about recognizable as Crispin stood on one side of a pair of armchairs. At the other side was a young woman in a twinset and tweed skirt, scowling at the camera. Enthroned between them sat their parents, the father in layers of tweed and twill and wool with a stiff-looking collar and a knotted tie, the mother in identical clothes to her daughter. It was impossible to say how old they were: between the black-and-white photograph, the poor lighting and the costumes, they looked like ghosts. What *was* interesting – and I was surprised Todd hadn't mentioned it – was that Billy and Wilma were there too, standing off to the side, dressed in their apron and dungarees. They were holding hands, but Billy's eyes were not on his wife, nor looking at the lens, but focused intently on the side of Verity Garmont's head.

I nudged Kathi and handed the album over, pointing to Billy and tracing the line of his gaze.

Kathi whistled. 'I can't blame him for being smitten, to be honest,' she said. 'I would have liked Verity too. She makes sure and says in every letter, "I am complying with your demand to stay off the forbidden topic". Rubbing her parents' nose in it, you know? I love a bit of passive aggression.'

'Shame Noleen only does aggressive aggression,' I said, making her laugh. 'And the forbidden topic is the baby born out of wedlock?'

'Definitely not,' said Kathi. 'She tells them everything about the baby. Butt and teeth and stuff.'

'Butt and teeth?'

'Teething,' said Kathi. 'You know. Potty training.'

'The frequency must drop off if you're up to teething already,' I said. We were all experts in the milestones of infancy and early childhood, because of Hiro.

'Yeah, I'm skimming,' Kathi said. 'I'm on 1965 now but she's still saying, "As per our agreement, I'm saying nothing. I'm surprised you're questioning me".'

'World-class shade,' I said. 'So the forbidden subject is Billy Bone? And her parents are covering up what they did to him by asking her if he's been in touch? Sneaky.'

'Awww,' said Todd, holding up a photograph he had unearthed from a new box. 'Nelson's first day at school. Cuter than an upside-down panda. Lexy,' he added, 'you're getting on my last nerve.'

I had been absent-mindedly peeling the blacked-out price sticker off the shiny cover of the journal in my hands. He was right, like my mum was right: it's a disgusting habit – beer labels, barcodes, Reese's Book Club screamers, loose varnish on garden furniture, shelf liners – I pick away at all of them, without knowing, just like Miley destroying flocked upholstery, except worse because she was a little girl and I should know better by now.

'Sorry,' I said, balling up the little scrap of gummy paper and stuffing it into my pocket. 'You must be nearly finished too if you're up to Nelson's school days.'

'Yep,' said Todd, 'we're done. What are we going to tell them?'

'That it was her, and he protected her. That Billy had his eye on Verity for a while. That the old girl was scheming, even as she died, to keep the secret hidden. Do you think knowing any of that will help them?'

'Definitely,' Kathi said. 'And then Crispin can fire up the furnace and get rid of it all.'

'Except the pictures,' said Todd.

'Well, except most of the pictures,' I said. 'Maybe slip that one of Billy making cow eyes in with the burn pile. It's strange that they kept that at all, if you ask me. Did no one notice, until us, just now?'

'I might take it and show it to Nelson,' Todd said. 'He's the only one who would be happy to see that his father cared for his mother, once upon a time. Even if he is holding another woman's hand. My God, what a mess. Families, huh?'

'Families,' I agreed. 'Speaking of which, I'm about to go round Tesco on the busiest day of the year with my closest relation. Do either of you two want to come and dilute her for me?'

SEVENTEEN

In the end, my mum and I took Noleen and Hiro, which had to be the worst possible combination that could be formed out of the entire household: two women who had been getting on each other's nerves in supermarkets since before barcodes; a curmudgeon who gets grumpy in Costco with the free snacks; and a foghorn-voiced baby who had never been away from her mother in a strange place before.

'Did I ever tell you about my friend Sarah in the M&S food hall on Christmas Eve,' said my mum, as we were waiting by the empty trolley thing for someone to relinquish one. We hadn't seen a single abandoned trolley en route from the far corner of the car park near the clothes donation bins which was the only bit we could find a space in. 'She lost it. She sat down on the floor near the rum butter and started to sob.'

'Not surprised,' I said. 'Don't judge her until we get round here without doing the same.'

'That's not the story,' my mum said. 'A security guard came, got her on her feet, took her through the back, gave her a cup of tea, finished her shopping for her, rang it through on her credit card and called her a taxi.'

'Service!' said Noleen. 'Was that in this country?'

'Sarah said she was going to do it every year from then on,' my mum said. 'In a different branch. Of course, it would only work if you took a list.'

I rolled my eyes and huffed out such a fierce breath that I managed to make my mum's fringe move. This was an old fight.

'There's one,' she said, leaping to intercept a trolley that a knackered-looking woman had sent towards the trolley park from eight feet away, with a heartfelt kick.

'Hey!' said a man who had been jogging across the path towards it.

My mum ignored him, steered the trolley round in a tight circle and waited for Noleen to stick Hiro's chubby little padded legs through the holes in the baby seat. Then she unfolded her printed-out shopping list and said, 'Sprouts.'

'POUTS!' said Hiro.

'Bean sprouts?' said Noleen. 'We having Chinese food? Is this for Taylor?'

And we were off.

'So, let me get this straight,' Noleen said, once we were finished in the fruit and veg bit and had washed up by the sushi bar for a breather, 'it's the biggest, fanciest meal of the year and the sides are boiled carrots, boiled Brussels sprouts and two kinds of white potatoes?'

'TATOES!'

'Yep,' I said. 'It's payback time for Thanksgiving.'

'No mac and cheese? No casseroles? No yams? No beans? How about dressing?'

'What would we dress?' my mum said. 'I used to make a prawn cocktail starter, but it spoils the main. I just do sorbet these days. What did you think all the lemons were for?'

'I was hoping gin,' said Noleen.

'DIN!'

'She doesn't mean dressing, Mum. She means stuffing.'

'Let's get the wine next,' my mum said. 'Lay it on the trolley bottom where it can't squash anything.'

She darted across the top of the aisles, with Hiro going, 'WHEEEEE!'

'What the—?' Noleen said as we swung round the gondola end. 'Have they just announced Prohibition starting tomorrow?'

'Welcome to Scotland,' I said. I could feel a lump forming in my throat as I watched the raging battle for the booze. I would have loved to claim it was balletic, a people brought together by their rich heritage of dysfunctional drinking, a collective celebration of appetite. In fact, it was more like a rugby scrum, naked ambition for the bargains winning out over any seasonal goodwill, and good use being made of the ankle-height knobbly bits on the trolley wheels.

'Get twelve bottles of Freixenet, Lex,' said my mum. 'You've got bigger hands than me.'

I turned sideways on to make myself a more effective wedge

and drove my shoulder into the crowd until I had got to the front at the sparkling section.

'Lexy!' my mum's voice came loud and clear. I thought she might be cupping her hands to make a megaphone. 'Make it twenty. I forgot about breakfast.'

'Here,' said Noleen, who was right behind me. 'Relay them to me and I'll pass them back.'

Twenty-one bottles later, because I lost count, I turned to face into the wall of bodies building up behind me.

'That won't work,' Noleen said. 'Turn around and I'll pull you. Just try to stay on your feet.'

I've never been dragged through a hedge backwards but, judging by the way Hiro burst into peals of uncontrollable giggles when she saw me, being dragged by the scruff of the neck through Tesco shoppers in the Christmas booze aisle is much the same thing.

'That was cool!' Noleen said. 'I'm sorry it's over.'

'It's not over,' said my mum. 'We need to do it again next week for Hogmanay, and right now, we're off to snag a turkey.'

'GOBBLE, GOBBLE!'

We got the turkey, sausages, bacon, puddings, cream, Quality Street and After Eights, and rounded off the trip on the snacks aisle.

'Will I go get another cart?' said Noleen. 'These dinky ones aren't made for days like this.'

But my mum was a past master at building a solid pyramid on top of an already full trolley. She stabilized it with Pringles, packed the centre with Kettle Chips and infilled the gaps with Twiglets and other sundries. At the end, she could have rolled that thing over cobbled streets with no wheelchair dips and not lost a single Marmite cashew.

'Jam,' she said, as we joined the end of a check-out queue that reached halfway up the aisle. 'Custard powder, jelly, Swiss roll. Tick, Tick, Tick, Tick.'

'TICK-TOCK! TICK-TOCK!'

'You're making a trifle?' I said. It brought back a wave of memory: me so full of Christmas pudding that I couldn't eat another bite but saying yes to a big helping of raspberry mush. The way it slipped so easily down the throat and stopped under the ribs, waiting there for the traffic ahead to ease. 'Have you got Alka Seltzer?'

'How dare you?' said my mum. 'Of course I have. And peppermint tea. Should we go back and get another pâté?'

'Another one of those great big round bowls of pâté like from a deli counter?' said Noleen. 'I think one will do.'

My mum looked at her with mystification. Noleen didn't know that, during the Christmas shop, the only answer to 'Do we need another?' is a 'yes', definite but sheepish because you hadn't picked it up already.

'Hey, look who's here,' said Noleen, nodding towards a pair trying to ram sideways through the till queues to get along the width of the shop. It was Wilma and Miley Garmont, with an empty shopping basket each.

'They're off their rockers,' my mum said. 'Everyone knows there's no free passage at this end today. You need to scoot straight up past the bakery and go along the top. And as for making the attempt without a trolley . . . Bonkers. Yoo-hoo! Wilma!'

She didn't hear, but Hiro helped.

'YOO-HOO!'

Everyone for yards around looked up and the baby got the kind of spontaneous round of applause usually reserved for barmaids dropping trays of glasses.

'You should have told us if you're only here for a few bits,' my mum said, pointing at the handbaskets. 'We could have picked them up for you.'

'Too kind,' said Wilma. 'But we need to do this ourselves. We're after Christmas decorations.'

'Bit late,' my mum said.

'I gave them to Miley when we moved. She's got acres of storage in that space-age flat of hers. And – get this – she's chucked them out. The whole lot.' She turned on her daughter. 'I thought you'd bring them down, since you were coming for Christmas.'

'I think Christmas should be elegant and understated,' Miley said. 'Some of that crap was crocheted.'

'CAP A COCHET!'

'Wow,' Miley said. 'Anyway, if you can bin them, why can't I?'

'I didn't "bin" them. I passed them down to my daughter.'

'And I passed them down to landfill.'

We shuffled forward as the customer at the head of the queue jammed the last of her load on to the conveyor belt and it shifted six inches. I noticed that the woman behind us was watching Miley like a hungry hawk. The handbaskets were empty but that didn't save anyone from being accused of pushing in. Not today.

'But you didn't have to,' Wilma said. 'We had to. Moving from the Hall to the cottage. Dad offed a lot of his books too.'

'Well, he left them behind anyway,' said my mum. 'And we're very grateful. They fill up the library just grand until we can get a chance to buy something someone might actually want to . . . Well, most of them are pretty tough going.'

Miley snorted. 'Understatement,' she said. 'They make Walter Scott's collected works look like the *Beano*.'

'I don't suppose you might have left some Christmas stuff behind too?' said my mum. 'In the attics? Is it worth us checking?'

'No, no, no,' said Wilma. 'We cleared the attics completely and went through everything. We didn't leave anything behind that we didn't mean to.'

The thought struck all of us at the same second that, in fact, they had left something fairly significant behind that they didn't mean to. Miley's face flushed, although that might have been her age or the fact that she was in Christmas Eve Eve Tesco with her coat on. Wilma's face paled, but that might have been the next step after over-heating when you fall into a faint.

Thankfully, at that point, the woman behind us could contain herself no longer.

'Are you in this queue?' she said. 'Because if you are, it starts back there.'

'Season of goodwill going great guns,' Miley said. 'No, we're not in the queue. Merry Christmas.'

'Sarky bitch,' the woman said.

'I hope your next shite's a hedgehog,' said Noleen. She had learned it from me but the trouble with swearing in a foreign language is you never really get how to pitch it at the right level and that was far too aggressive for this moment. A quick 'miserable cow' would have been satisfactory all round, but the only way we managed to smooth things over was to let the woman go in front of us and send Noleen to wait in the car. Wilma and Miley were gone the next time we looked.

'Imagine throwing out your Xmas dex,' said my mum. 'That's cold. I promise you, Lexy, I'll be hanging that Play-Doh reindeer that looks like a pig until I'm too old and frail to lift my arms.'

'I know you will, Mum,' I said. 'And yes, it *is* weird that they threw out stuff they've got to replace now, when you consider what they saved. What they took with them.' In my pocket, I was rolling the price ticket from that last journal into a ball between my finger and thumb, while my brain clacked fruitlessly over something I couldn't quite get a grip on.

Back in Yule, things had stepped up a gear. If we thought the berry swap was the pinnacle of Disneyfying a Scottish village, we were wrong. The main street was still choked with snow and, in the light of the setting sun, all the trees were twinkling with strings of bulbs. The chimneys were smoking, someone was unloading logs from a pick-up into a red wheelbarrow and there were real, live, actual bloody carol singers gathering at the cenotaph, Santa hats, lanterns and all. Someone had dressed up their dog.

'What the hell?' I said. 'Mum, there's a dog in a costume!'

'Aww,' my mum said. 'Cute.'

'But . . . but . . .' I said.

'BUTT BUTT POOPY BUTT!' Hiro had been dozing but was back in the game now.

'But it's only Americans who do that,' I said. 'I've been scoffing at them for four years.'

'It's spread,' said my mum. 'Like Black Friday sales and pumpkins.'

'Heh-heh-heh,' said Noleen. She had been in a bad mood after the hedgehog incident, but watching me face my culture being overrun with nonsense straightened her face right out again.

So I was distracted as I helped my mum hump the seven thousand bags of grub and booze in the side door and along to the owners' flat. Noleen had elected to take Hiro – and her nappy – to be dealt with or, ideally, handed back to Della.

'I'll put the nibbles in the fake kitchen,' my mum said. 'And the drinks and the cheeseboard can go there so everyone can help themselves. Chocolates. Mince pies. Shortbread. Stollen. Panettone.'

'I still don't know why you bought a Panettone. No one'll eat it.'

'I'll use it for a trifle base if it goes stale.'

'You bought Swiss rolls for the trifle base.'

'Not *the* trifle, Lexy. A trifle. In January.'

'Why, what's in January?'

'Our Burns Supper weekend special. Once you guinea pigs all go home, we've got a few weekends booked out before our soft opening at Easter. Burns Night, Valentine's Day and St Patrick's. Oof.' She hefted the four carrier bags she was carrying up on to the kitchen bunker and shook her hands where the straps had been digging in.

'So, if you're booking February,' I said, 'you don't believe everyone's guff about staying?'

'Of course not,' she said. 'Not here. They can't stay here – this is a business, Lexy. But I've been looking at short lets of flats and chalets with Della. That would buy them a few months till they've got their feet under them.'

'Mum,' I said. 'I went to Hawaii. I would have loved to stay forever, but I knew it was just a dream. This is no different.'

'Well,' she said, very long and drawn out, 'the thing is they *are* crying out for doctors, and I'm not saying I understand what Roger said about Todd's parasite – would it die in the cold weather? – but he was pretty firm. And Noleen's probably right that a good dry-cleaners could make a killing, like I just said.'

'Like you just said what?' I heard my voice getting yelpy but I couldn't do anything about it.

'Like I just said about everything from over there coming over here when you saw that dog in a jumper. Come on, Lexy, two more loads and we're done.'

'So how long have you got for a proper rest after we all bugger off again?' I said, trailing after her, back to the car.

'*You* don't have to bugger— Actually, don't use that language, please. You don't have to go. You're my daughter. We can always squeeze *you* in. But it wouldn't be practical long-term. What a nightmare of a commute.'

'Ha-ha,' I said, thinking she meant to Cuento.

'For Taylor, that is. I know you can do your thing online, from anywhere.'

'I'm back face-to-face now,' I said, reaching deep into the boot for the last of the bags.

'Hmm,' said my mum. 'Pass me the loo rolls. I'll tuck them under my arm and carry something else light on that side. Would you need to be closer into the city, then? Or would nearer Taylor's have enough of a – what do you call it? – patient pool?'

'Eh?' I said. I stood up too fast and cracked my head on the boot latch. 'Ow.'

'They do say rural communities have horrendous mental health. But also not much money. On the other hand, Taylor can't spend all *his* life commuting. Not on our roads.'

'Mum,' I said, 'what are you talking about? Commuting to where?'

'What?' she said, staring at me very hard while two pink spots grew on her cheeks. 'Is that the phone?' she said, feinting to break away.

'No, it's not the phone,' I said, putting a foot out to block her. 'What are you talking about?'

'I think that's for Taylor to tell you,' my mum said. 'Which, obviously, I thought he had.'

'Obviously he told *you* instead, so why not help me out here?'

'We need to get this shopping in before the frozen stuff starts to thaw.'

'It's bloody freezing out here, Mum. Nothing's thawing.'

'He didn't tell me anything really. He just asked me to help him print out something he called his . . .'

Now, there weren't many ways to finish this sentence. 'Print out my' only ever goes with 'boarding pass', 'speech' or – and I'd put good money on this one – 'CV'.

'Resumé?' I said, translating it for her.

She swallowed hard and looked over my shoulder. 'Look!' she said. 'Here he is!'

As I turned to see her car arriving at the gate, she made a second, successful, attempt to get past me and scuttled into the house with carrier bags banging off her legs. Unless those were loaves of bread or bags of crisps, she'd have bruises tomorrow.

I set my armload back down in the open boot and faced the approaching car, putting my hands on my hips and spreading my feet so I looked – I hoped – like Wonder Woman. The car came on, slower and slower, before rolling to a stop a foot from my toes. I stared through the windscreen. He was wearing a collar and tie and a dark jacket that was either the top half of a suit or a blazer.

Slowly, as if trying not to startle a deer, or maybe anger a bear, he opened his door and stepped out. It was a suit. He had brogues on too.

'Have you looked in the nest today?' he said. 'How's the egg?'

Granted, I was already angry, but that put the tin lid on it.

'Where did you get that clobber?' I said.

'Your dad.'

'Of course,' I said, finally recognizing my dad's funeral suit now I was looking right at it. 'Because you wouldn't have packed *interview* clothes for a holiday, would you? Because deciding to move to a different country for a job isn't the sort of thing you just decide to do on a whim one day, without – you know – talking to your fiancée about it first.'

'Le-ex,' he said.

'Don't!'

'No, I was just going to say, can we go inside because these thin-soled shoes are turning my feet into ice cubes.'

'What if I go home and leave you to live here without me?' I said, standing my ground on account of how he wouldn't be wearing my dad's thin-soled shoes if he wasn't a furtive wee get, so his cold feet were his problem. 'What if I go home and take all your stuff and drop it in the slough and write an article in the *Voyager* about that time you laughed at *The Minions* and shat yourself in a cinema seat?'

'You couldn't,' said Taylor. 'I could never do it without you.'

'OK.' That was more like it.

'Because you're the citizen,' he said. 'In fact, we need to get married before the start date, so I get fast-track residency.'

'Wow,' I said. 'We've barely started thinking about our wedding. We haven't even decided which country to do it in or whether to have a religious bit and what religion, or just a hooley. I haven't tried on a single dress, off my head on free Prosecco.

And now you suddenly need the business taken care of so you can spend the rest of your life at a different bird reserve looking at different birds? What if you go to Iceland or Antarctica? Will you woo some Tarty Skankusdottir to get a green card off *her*, once you've divorced me?'

'Lexy,' he said, and even I knew I was losing it so I was open to the idea of listening to what he said next as long as it was reasonable. Unfortunately, what he said next was 'Calm down.'

'Calm down?' I said. 'I am dealing with the fact that my parents sold my childhood home, that there was a corpse in their new basement, that there are police crawling all over my life again and that I was handed yet another murder to solve that everyone thinks is solved already – and whatever it is that's bugging me about it is so far under the surface I can't even work out where to look for it. I'm not calm because everything is unravelling, Taylor! And, if you would take your selfish head out of the cloaca of the nearest passing random Canadian goose for one minute, you might give a shit about that. There is more going on here than an owl egg in a bloody nest that frankly has had more of your support and attention than me, my family, our friends or the pressing question of a murder victim all put together!'

'Canada goose,' he said. 'Not Canadian.'

So I stamped up the steps and locked the front door, hoping that, as he went round the house to find a way in, he would slip on his stupid leather soles and break his neck.

EIGHTEEN

Saturday 24 December

There are those who would say when you're just about to
have a blow-out, you should abstain for a bit beforehand
to prepare. Others insist you need to ramp up to a feast.
When I woke up on the morning of Christmas Eve, I felt fine
for about a second and then, when I opened one eye to gauge
what sort of time it was, I remembered deciding to start ramping
up the night before. We'd opened with Snack Olympics, Devin
in particular taking to it with gusto as we pitched crisp flavour
against crisp flavour and wasabi pea against Frazzle. The salt
sent us straight to the Cava, which delivered us to the bread
basket, which softened us up for the venison casserole, washed
down by the claret, so that by the time my mum wheeled out a
baked cheesecake, all I said was did she have any jam to go on
top. I remembered having to stop swirling my brandy round in
its balloon because I couldn't focus and it was making me dizzy.
Getting to bed was a blur.

I opened my other eye and carefully swivelled my head round
to face Taylor's pillow. He wasn't there.

'Thank God for that,' I croaked.

'What?' said Taylor from the window, where he was watching
the nest.

'I had a bad dream,' I lied. 'It's nice to be awake.'

'If it was about singing all seventeen verses of "The Teacher
Whey Comfrey Sky", that wasn't a dream.'

'Oh God,' I said. 'Not "The Tewchter Whae Come Frae Skye"!
I'm sorry.' I had had a short but intense relationship with a posh
bloke when I was a student and it had left me with an unfortunate
tendency to sing rugby songs when I was legless, like a gut
parasite after a dip in the Congo.

'I forgive you,' Taylor said. 'For everything.'

'That *is* everything,' I told him. 'I didn't do anything else to

be sorry about, did I?' I waited and cast my foggy mind back
as best I could. '*Did* I?'

He was never going to answer so the knock at the door didn't
really interrupt our conversation. Todd breezed in.

'You look like you should, you total disgrace to womanhood,'
he said. 'Where did you learn those lyrics? I thought I had heard
every bawdy ballad ever written – between Fire Island, Key West
and the Castro – but kudos to you, Lexy.'

'What do you want?' I said, using the last of my energy to
flip the covers up over my face. I had been enjoying the early
mornings without Todd barging into my bedroom. I knew it
couldn't last forever but why did it have to end today?

'I brought you a bacon and egg roll and a cup of tea with milk
and sugar,' he said. 'I told Judith you usually go for coffee and
Danish, but she insisted.'

I struggled upright and looked at the cup and plate in his hand.
'I go for coffee and Danish because the tea stinks, the bacon's
worse and the rolls are bog-awful,' I said. 'Hand it over.'

'You OK then?' Taylor said, waiting until my mouth was full
of yolky roll, the weasel. 'Cool. See you later. Text me if you
need anything. Bye.'

'You didn't make up, I see,' Todd said. 'When he carried you
up here like a caveman.'

'Wh—?'

'I meant fireman,' Todd said. 'What the hell are we going to
do, Lexy?'

'Whatever it is,' came a voice from the door Taylor had left
swinging, 'can I do it too?'

Kathi looked a hell of a lot better than I felt but she was
obviously hungover, because she was wearing one of the silk
robes my mum had put on hooks on the backs of all our bedroom
doors and it takes a lot for Kathi to be seen without her jeans,
even by us.

'Can I get in?' she said, not waiting to be answered but sliding
her bare legs under the covers beside me. 'And can you hold that
toxic bun to the other side? What *is* that?'

'Brown sauce,' I said.

'Ewww, why is it so much worse that it sounds so generic?'
said Kathi. 'What are we going to do? Noleen's busy digging

herself in here, and your mom is lapping it up. Roger's in talks with that PCP from along the road and Taylor's practically ordering a muffin basket for his first day. What the hell happened?'

'Short-lived collective madness,' I said. 'It must be. It's the snow and the lights and the booze. Once the weather turns, they'll remember the swimming pool and the oranges and Target, and come to their senses.'

'I dunno about Target,' said Kathi. 'Noleen was pretty warm about Tesco.'

'In the meantime,' said Todd, 'I suggest concentrating on the case and solving the riddle. Apart from anything else, it'll be good publicity if we . . .'

'If we?' I said.

'You know, if we do . . .?'

'If we *stay*?' said Kathi. 'Is that what you mean? Are you crumbling?'

'I'm . . . It's been a long time since I heard Roger sound so happy and hopeful,' Todd said.

'Because he's on vacation!' Kathi spoke very firmly. 'We all feel happy and hopeful when we're on vacation. He's daydreaming. He'll stop.' Her firmness had turned to desperation by the end of this speech. 'What's that noise?' she went on.

'Sorry,' I said. My phone was ringing. 'Hello?' I said when I'd got a hold of it and accepted the call.

'Lexy? It's Gloria.'

'Who?'

'Gloria Naify. Your flight attendant?'

'Oh! Sorry. Right. Hi.' If one of us had left something on the plane, I thought, she had taken her sweet time letting us know.

'I didn't want to disturb you on the holiday,' she said, 'but I wanted to set your mind at rest about the return journey, next week.'

'Are you a witch?' I said. 'How the hell did you know we were worried about the return journey?' I covered the phone. 'It's Gloria from the private jet people phoning up to reassure us that we're still going home.'

'Huh?' said Todd.

'I'm not a witch,' Gloria said. 'Would you prefer Wiccan crew? I can look into it but probably not until after tomorrow. No, what

I wanted to tell you is that we've managed to source the lavender gin you requested. So please don't worry.'

'I'll try,' I said. Then I realized I was being a boot. 'Thank you, Gloria. You're amazing. I hope you've got something lovely planned for Christmas.'

'Veil,' Gloria said. 'And you?'

'Me too,' I said. 'Veil, like you said. See you soon.' I hung up. 'What's veil in a Christmas context?' I asked Todd and Kathi.

'Vail? The ski resort in Colorado?' said Todd.

'Oh hell, she's going to think I'm a total nutter now,' I said.

'Not if we stay,' said Kathi, 'and you never have to see her again.' I think she was joking, but she's very dry. Todd didn't think she was joking, clearly. He drew himself up to lay into her, but I held my flat hand out in front of his face.

'Let's not argue,' I said. 'What we need is something to focus on. Todd, thank you for suggesting that we buy all the presents at home and wrap them before we came. We are the only people in the world looking for a job to do on Christmas Eve.'

Todd gave me a long look. He couldn't work out if I was being sarcastic or sincere. Which was fair enough because I wasn't sure myself.

'So,' I said, 'everything we've seen chimes in one melodious chord. Billy Bone came into this house all fired up one night. He was never seen again. Because Mrs Garmont killed him with a blunt instrument, for knocking up her daughter. Wilma and Crispin weren't in the house for a while, during which time his corpse was bricked up in the cellar by Mr Garmont, who said he was sealing off the place the seduction happened. Verity flees to Barbados and stays there. Mr and Mrs Garmont, haunted by what they've done, peg out one after the other in the following few years. Wilma has Billy declared dead and gets her marriage dissolved. Crispin marries her, Miley comes along. Mr K sorts out the inheritance problem. The families stay in contact with letters between Barbados and Scotland, and Miley visiting occasionally, but otherwise lead separate lives.'

'Good summary,' said Kathi. '*Why* are we still saying there's a riddle to be solved?'

'I wasn't finished,' I said. 'Then Verity, at the end of her life, leaves a letter for Nelson saying she's charging him with carrying on her mission; she says the truth is in Scotland and she wants him to come over here and sniff it out. So he invites himself for Christmas. Trouble is, Crispin and Wilma have sold the house with the secret in it. But, thankfully and by complete coincidence, the skeleton comes to light after a fake berry heist and, also thankfully, Crispin and Wilma have saved all the relevant bits and bobs of diaries and photographs and letters that document that period of the family history, and they even employ a private detective to look at it all and say, "Yeah, that's what happened".'

'When you put it like that,' said Todd, 'it's as sketchy as hell.'

'Or,' said Kathi, 'Crispin and Wilma kept the stuff for the reason people usually do – nostalgia – and it's not *that* part that's sketchy at all. It's the melodramatic deathbed letter from Verity to Nelson.'

'Could be both,' I said. 'Or neither.'

'Both,' said Todd. 'The letter *and* the diaries were pure Harlequin romance, supposedly written by typical Brits, frozen, repressed and dysfunctional.'

'OK,' I said. 'Bit of editorializing but fair point.'

'Verity's letters from her early years in Barbados are pretty brisk, when you think about it,' Kathi said. 'But I don't think it's weird that deathbed notes and near-death diary entries are a little different from usual.'

'Hmm,' Todd said. 'So maybe there is no puzzle? Verity said there was a secret over here. There was. She said Billy wouldn't have abandoned her. He didn't. Mrs Garmont died feeling guilty. So she should! We're done here.'

'Except what is it that's bugging me?' I said.

'Taylor?' said Todd. 'Your mom?'

'Kathi, are you even listening?' I asked her.

'Got it!' she said, looking up suddenly, with a big grin on her face. 'Yes, I was listening. Well, no, I wasn't. I was checking something. Verity's letters home, right?'

'Right,' said Todd.

'They were typed. Because she was learning office skills to support her little family.'

'We know that,' I said.

'But she still signed them with a pen. I mean, a letter to her mother – of course she did.'

'Uh-huh,' I said, trying not to scream at her to spit it out.

'And she wrote the deathbed note to Nelson and signed that too.'

'For God's sake!' said Todd, doing my dirty work for me.

'Look.' She held out her phone, where somehow there were two images on a split screen both bearing the name 'Verity' but in totally different – wildly different – styles.

'How did you get *them*?' I said.

'Hello, my name is Kathi Muntz and I'm a practising PI,' she said. 'I took pictures of everything we looked at in the cottage the other morning. Representative sample anyway.'

'You did?' said Todd, taking her phone. 'What were *we* doing?'

'I ask myself that question a lot,' said Kathi. 'If I ever work it out, I'll let you know.'

'But how did you get the signature from the letter on Nelson's phone?' I said.

'I airdropped it to myself while I was checking it out,' said Kathi. 'It's like a magic Polaroid, Lexy. You should look it up in an encyclopedia when the reference libraries are open again after the holiday.' I loved this woman. Every time she got arsey and I remembered the shrinking little puppy she had been when I met her, my heart swelled.

'You know what this means, don't you?' said Todd.

'I do.' Kathi abandoned her sarcasm for a smug smile. 'Those two "Veritys" were not signed by the same person.'

'Let's see,' I said, snapping my fingers for the phone. 'Remember this was decades apart. Fifty going on sixty years. A young woman and an old woman.'

'Which would explain firm lines and shaky lines,' Todd said, 'but wouldn't explain that.'

He handed over the phone and I bent my head, ready to argue. The argument died inside me. One signature had a round-bottomed V, an e like a back-to-front figure three and a big looping tail on the y. The other had a sharp V like an arrowhead, an ordinary e and a y with a spiky tail jabbing straight down.

'One of these is a forgery,' I said.

'No duh,' said Kathi. 'But how do we decide which?'

'The letters can't be forgeries,' Todd said. 'The envelopes had stamps and postmarks.'

'So the *envelopes* can't be forgeries,' Kathi said. 'But the envelopes' contents might be.'

'Or the letter might be a forgery,' said Todd.

'Even less duh,' said Kathi. 'We just said that.'

'How *do* we decide which?' I said.

'And that!' said Kathi. 'We're looping. Come on, people! We've got detecting to do.'

Downstairs, the house was fizzing with that unmistakable Christmas Eve energy. Diego and Hiro were the main conductors of it, naturally, as if all the cladding had been stripped off their wires and they'd both been connected to the mains.

'SAAAAANTA CLOD A COMIN A TOWN!' Hiro informed me from the main hallway when I was halfway down the stairs. '*SAAAAAAAANTA* CLOD A COMIN A TOWN,' she added when I didn't answer her.

'Lexy!' came a whisper from beside me, making me jump in the air, never a good idea when you're on a staircase, never mind with a brutal hangover. It was Diego, hopping from foot to foot as if he needed a pee.

'You know where the bathrooms are,' I said.

He shook that nonsense off and beckoned me to bend down and put my ear close to his mouth. 'Is Santa Claus coming tonight?' he breathed.

'Yes,' I said. 'It's not a secret.'

'I was testing you,' he said. 'Jareth in my class said Santa Claus wasn't . . . coming . . . because we're eight. But Abuela Judith is making little cakes for him and Abuelo Keith said we need to let the fire go out early so he doesn't burn his bum.' At that big swear, he lost control of himself and burst into giggles. When he'd breathed his way through the attack, he carried on. 'Also, there are a lot of presents under the big tree already. But Santa is supposed to bring the presents. But Jareth said he isn't . . . coming . . . so I feel funny in my tummy.'

I felt funny in my tummy too. That 'also' had nearly killed me. Plus, I wanted five minutes alone with this Jareth kid.

'Hiro,' said Diego solemnly, 'would be upset if Santa isn't . . . coming . . . like Jareth said.'

'Hiro, eh?' I asked him, but he didn't get it, which was just as well. 'Well, she can relax. Santa *is* coming, but only for Hiro and you. The rest of the presents are what the big people give each other now that we've got jobs and money. So Santa isn't too busy and he's got enough time for children.'

'Promise?'

'I swear on my drain plug,' I said, high stakes for anyone who lives on a boat.

'That Jareth!' said Diego. 'What a mean meanie! Will Santa come to his house?'

'That's up to Santa,' I said. 'But I hope so, don't you?'

He tussled for a moment, then nodded, good soul that he was. 'Hiro! Hiro! Hiro!' he shouted, scampering down the rest of the stairs. 'Who's coming tonight?'

'SAAAAAAAAANTA CLOD!'

Thank God they took their racket into the three interconnecting rooms on the ground floor and left the spiral stairs to the basement clear for me. That voice reverberating off the stone would have finished me.

My mum had carols on the radio in the real kitchen, so I swerved. But she had the same carols on in the fake kitchen, with better acoustics too. And my dad was singing along as he clanked bottles in the wine store.

'Da-ad!' I said, sinking down on to the bottom step. 'Can you . . .?'

'Not today, Lexy,' he said. 'You can have Baileys on your cornflakes tomorrow but I'm not uncorking anything this early today.'

'Oh my God,' I said. 'I wasn't panting for a drink! I'm asking if you could not smash the bottles together so much. I've got a headache.'

Then 'Ding Dong Merrily on High' came on and I had to get out before my ears started bleeding.

In the courtyard, it was so cold the air hurt my nostrils, as if I'd lined them with toothpaste, and the bench by the kitchen door was damp too, but it was completely quiet except for the slow drip of a thawing icicle at a bend in the roan pipe. I tried to concentrate on the plink-plink-plink while my head and stomach settled again.

Which signature was the real one? Which *Verity* was the real one? The good girl who was seduced by an unscrupulous older man? The adventurer who took off to Barbados? The rabble-rouser incensed by the Garmonts' past in the Caribbean? The no-nonsense single mother who sent bald little letters back home? Or the tortured woman who left that tantalizing note to be read after her death?

'I've had an idea,' came Kathi's voice at my elbow, setting my heart hammering. 'Well, two ideas. One, come inside before you freeze to that bench and we have to prise you off with a chisel. But, as well as that, remember what Mr K was saying about the family business, trusts, and bequests and everything?'

'Yeah?'

'Well, Verity was eighteen when she left home, wasn't she? I wonder if she ever signed anything for . . . him.'

'Were you trying to remember the name of the firm?' I asked. 'Go on, give it a go. I need a laugh.'

'Racoon, Silk Ties, Inanity.'

'That is pretty close,' I said. Then I sighed. 'I wish you'd thought of this yesterday. We could have phoned them. But it's Saturday and it's Christmas Eve. There is zero chance in hell anyone'll be in the office.'

Kathi, in her disappointment, flopped down beside me on the damp bench and slumped forward with her hands hanging between her knees.

'It's not the end of the world,' I said. 'It would have been nice to tie it up in a red bow and put it under the tree tonight, but it's not like Wilma and Crispin gave us a deadline.'

'Not the point,' said Kathi. 'Unless we think of another lead to pursue, I'm going to have to spend the day in the kitchen with the women.'

'You're a woman.'

'Your mom wants me to peel chestnuts. Has this country never had a canning industry? Who peels chestnuts?'

I hadn't noticed that there was a window behind our heads. This house was enormous, and in keeping with the Scots baronial style, there were pointless little sash windows all over it, as if the builder had thrown them at the walls and stuck them down wherever they landed. So, when someone banged on the glass right by my ear, sending flakes of old paint and a chunk of dried-out putty down my neck, it shook my hangover badly enough to turn me dizzy.

'To-odd!' Kathi said. 'What the hell?'

'Sorry,' said Todd, emerging from the door. He didn't look sorry. 'I'm calibrated for triple-paned sealed units. I overdid it.'

'What is it anyway?' I asked him.

'You will have noticed that I am robed and coiffed for the day?' He was dressed, with dry hair, so technically it was true, if unremarkable. 'Well, I was thinking in the bathtub. I never realized how much more time there is to think, in a tub, compared with in a shower. Filling it, adjusting the temperature, soaking, scrubbing . . . But I had the chance to review everything we've learned and see where the possible points of entry are.'

'Cool,' I said. 'And?'

'The one thing we don't know much about,' said Todd, 'is this "mission" of Verity's that Nelson spoke of.'

'That's true,' I said. 'If it exists. If the deathbed note is genuine and what he told us about her is true. We've only got his word for it, after all.'

'What we *do* know,' Todd went on, 'is that, if it's true, it's a public thing, right? Not a personal thing.' He waited until we nodded before continuing. 'Reparations, social justice, all that. So, I wondered if there might be a fiduciary angle.' He spread his hands out waiting for praise.

'Uft,' said Kathi, which wasn't the reaction he was hoping for.

'Pretend for a minute I don't know what "fiduciary" means,' I said, which wasn't much better.

'The thing is, Todd,' Kathi said, 'it's Saturday and it's Christmas Eve so, even if Verity's mission needed that kind of help, we're sunk.'

'Huh?' said Todd.

'What *does* "fiduciary" mean?' I said. 'I only know it from *Mary Poppins*.'

'The office is closed,' said Kathi.

'So what?' said Todd. 'We know where he lives.'

'Yay!' said Kathi, leaping to her feet. 'No chestnuts for me!'

'These local expressions don't get any more normal,' said Todd. 'Road trip, Lexy?'

*   *   *

We got away, but it wasn't easy. In my opinion, Christmas Day was the time for a three-line whip on togetherness, where side trips were an insult to family and a nappy pin in the peachy backside of the Baby Jesus. If we had suggested nipping up to Edinburgh tomorrow, they would all have had a point. But Christmas Eve is a normal day if you're not Polish, and Trinity is a 24/7 business and we were working.

Nevertheless, Roger had a cob on, which took a lot of gall considering Todd had been entertaining himself for days waiting for the great nap to be over. Noleen was always in a bad mood, but it was rare for her to aim it in Kathi's direction. She managed it this morning. Taylor, of course, couldn't care less and didn't bother to hide the fact. I pretended not to care that he didn't care, and we parted with barely a grunt. It gave me a pang to hear how much more lively he sounded on the phone to Speccy or Zippy as he walked away. 'Yeah, my day freed up,' he said. 'Which hide are you headed to?'

And then there was my mum. And my dad. And their look of bewildered, crestfallen pain when I told them I was going out but would be back for dinner.

'Again?' my mum said. 'We've hardly seen you.'

'I'll come into your room with my stocking at six o'clock tomorrow morning,' I said. 'Like I always used to.'

'Big talk,' said my dad. 'I'll believe it when I see it.'

Damn. They *were* doing me a stocking then. I had meant to wrongfoot them and slip away while they were feeling guilty. 'The thing is,' I said, 'I don't want to tell you and blow it, but I'm organizing a surprise.'

'Awww,' said my mum, letting her pastry brush fall into the bowl of brandy she was painting on to a warm cake just out of the oven. The splashes sizzled as they hit the hot cooker top, filling the kitchen with booze fumes. 'I should have known, Lexy. You're such a good girl. Mummy's treasure!'

'How long have you been inhaling that?' I said. 'Dad, make sure she gets some coffee, eh?'

I took a different route up to the city to show them some more of the countryside, which was my first mistake. Passing an IKEA put a real dent in the wonder of foreign travel for both of them, and the bypass was choked solid. It got warmer and greener as we went too, the sky lowering, black clouds with purple edges rolling down on a scudding wind. When we were almost at the start of the suburbs – in fact, passing the crematorium – the rain began to hit the windscreen in big leathery splotches. By the time we'd got down to the scruffy area where the students all live, the wipers were straining to keep up and grey slush was spraying out from under the bus wheels and splatting on the side windows.

'That's another bit of the university,' I said, trying for more of the other day's New College vibe. Kathi peered out and craned up to see the top of the David Hume Tower.

'Soviet,' she said, which was fair.

Even the Mound and the galleries, the New Town, were different today: rain-sodden and sparsely peopled as some of the shops started to close their doors. The coloured lights looked smeary through the downpour and the black streets were plastered with handbills from the Christmas market, all disintegrating as people trod on them.

Heriot Row is hard to spoil with a bit of weather, though, and finding a parking space right outside Mr K's door was an added bonus.

'What if he's not in,' Kathi said.

'He's in his nineties and it's pouring with rain,' I said.

'What if he's halfway through an intimate date with the latest Tinder match?' said Todd.

'Eww,' I said. 'Let's hope he tells us to get lost and not wait in the next room so's not to waste the Viagra.' Sometimes jokes come out a lot cruder than you expect them to. To hide my regret about that one, I got out and scurried up the steps to shelter in the shallow overhang of the entranceway while I rang the bell.

It took a long time for anyone to answer, and I wished I hadn't planted the image of Mr K and a date in my own mind.

'Hello?' came a querulous voice.

'Mr Kilquhanity?' I asked.

'Who's this?'

'Lexy Campbell, from the other day? At the Dome? With Todd and Kathi? We've got some more questions for you about the Garmonts, but we didn't know your phone number.'

'And you've never heard of Twitter?' said the voice. 'I always answer my DMs.'

'Oh,' I said. 'Look, it's raining quite hard out here.'

'I'm only kidding,' he said over the buzz of the door catch releasing. 'Come up, come up, and keep me company!'

'So . . . is every one of these houses like this?' said Kathi as we tramped up the sumptuous staircase to get to Mr K's flat. The carpet was deep, the banister rail was polished mahogany and the plasterwork looked like a wedding cake. Not the new kind where they've scraped off half the icing to show the crumbs.

'Yep,' I said. 'I could draw you a floor plan of any house in a mile's radius of right here.'

'Welcome, welcome,' said Mr K, out on the landing in his slippers to greet us. 'Come away in, as they say in these parts. Have some Madeira, m'dears,' he added, shooing us through an over-furnished hallway into the original drawing room of the house, a vast space with two fireplaces – both lit – and three long windows looking out over the park.

'I never tried Madeira before,' said Todd. 'Count me in.'

'I'm driving,' I said, 'so just a small one.'

'What is it?' said Kathi.

Mr K waggled his wiry white eyebrows at her and turned to the drinks tray on a behemoth of a sideboard. 'What can I do for you today of all days?' he said.

'Oh God, I know,' I told him. 'What a cheek. You must have so much to be getting on with for tomorrow. But we've got a couple of questions that shouldn't take too long.'

'So much to be getting on with?' he said. 'It's been a lot of years since I could claim to be busy, young lady. Putting in the hours till *Countdown* is more my thing these days. No one wants to go out on a date on Christmas Eve. It's a time for family.'

'Who are you spending tomorrow with?' Todd asked him.

He passed out the glasses, set a plate of shortbread within reach of us all and settled himself down in his chair, the one with the flattened cushions and discoloured headrest, where he obviously sat every day.

'Well, spit it out,' he said. 'Question one!'

'Do you have an example of Verity Garmont's signature?' I said.

He opened his eyes very wide and pulled his chin back into his neck, causing a ruff of whiskery wrinkles to appear. 'If I'd been given thirty-three guesses, I shouldn't have come up with that,' he said. 'Why, might I ask, do you need to see the signature of a deceased woman? What will it tell you?'

'Possibly nothing,' I said. 'Possibly which of two different pieces of writing she actually wrote and which is a forgery.'

'How exciting!' said Mr K. 'I'm sorry I can't help you with it. What's the other question?'

'This one's a little more of an ethical workout,' said Kathi. 'It's about what Verity said *in* one of these pieces of writing, if she did. We wondered if she ever consulted you about it. And after you were so open about the will the other day . . .'

'Ah, but wills are public documents,' Mr K said. 'If you're asking me about a consultation, that's quite another matter.' He sniffed. 'Tell me and we shall see.'

'The thing we want to find out more about,' said Kathi, 'is the thing that made her leave a note for Nelson, on her deathbed. She told him to carry on her "mission" and hinted that the key to it all was back here in Scotland. Do you know anything about that? If the note's real, that is.'

Mr K had been blinking at us benignly as he sipped his Madeira and nibbled his shortbread finger, but now his expression hardened. 'Oh yes,' he said. 'Verity's mission. I remember that episode very well. In one respect, though, you are mistaken. It was early in her adulthood, not on her deathbed. So I should say the deathbed note is the forgery.'

'How can you be so sure?' said Todd.

Mr K gave a theatrical sigh. 'I've watched enough American drama on Netflix to know that attorney–client privilege isn't an alien concept to you,' he said.

'But?' said Kathi hopefully.

'*And*,' he said, 'I couldn't break it even after her death,' he continued. 'Or mine, for that matter.'

We all took a sip of Madeira. When a man in his nineties started talking about dying, there was nothing to say. The Queen had destroyed our ability to pretend people were endless.

'Of course,' he went on, 'I can always speak hypothetically. And it most certainly would be hypothetical, if we're considering

Verity as an old woman. Because, as I told you, wills are not executed retroactively.'

'Wills?' said Todd.

'Oops,' said Mr K, not very convincingly at all.

'So . . .' I said. 'Verity's mission had something to do with a past will? And it wasn't relevant anymore by the time she was an old lady?'

'You might well conclude that,' said Mr K. 'I am not in a position to make further comment.'

'You're right then,' Kathi said. 'The deathbed note is forged.'

'Or she was confused,' said Todd. 'Because she was dying.'

Mr K drained his glass and polished off the last crumb of his shortbread. 'I *can* tell you one thing that has just occurred to me,' he said, taking out a folded handkerchief from his waistcoat pocket and dabbing his lips. 'You can double-check which signature is the forgery, because I seem to recall that Crispin offloaded some of the lesser paintings and whatnot along with the house when he sold it to your parents. Is that right, my dear? Are there paintings of the Hall in various seasons still hanging in the bedroom corridor? Insipid watercolours, mind you. You might not have noticed them.'

'They're still there,' said Kathi. 'Views of the yard in spring, summer, fall and winter. I tried to make Hiro understand when I was carrying her past them, but she didn't get it. She liked the robin in the snow scene. She said "BIDDIE" and my ear was ringing the rest of the night.'

'What about them?' I said.

'Verity did them,' said Mr K. 'And, as far as I remember, she signed them too.'

'Jeez Louise,' said Todd. 'You mean her signature was right there in the house and we didn't have to drive all this way and bug you on Christmas Eve?'

Mr K's face clouded and I thought I knew why. In fact, I thought I knew something it hurt to acknowledge. He had side-stepped the question about how he was spending Christmas Day.

'Mr K,' I said, trying not to sound too treacly. 'What *are* you doing tomorrow? Did you tell us?'

'Oh, I'm too old and ugly to mind much about Christmas these days,' he said. 'I'll go for a little walk and then settle down to watch the Quing's speech. Dear, dear. And *Doctor Who*.'

'Nope,' I said. 'Sorry. I can't allow that.' He gave me a look that broke my heart, starting quizzical and ending up in a kind of timid hopefulness. 'Sling a pair of boxers in a backpack,' I said. 'You're coming home with me.'

NINETEEN

'Well, it's certainly a surprise,' my mum said, when I scooted in ahead of the others to tell her we had an extra guest for Christmas. She was topping up the water in the Christmas tree bucket in the front hall. 'How is it for me, particularly?'

'Wha—? Oh.' I had forgotten telling her that. 'Well, Mum, the thing is, Mr K knows the Garmont family and this house like the back of his hand and I thought what better way to . . . exorcise the ghost of Billy Bone than by discovering all sorts of other interesting titbits?'

'For instance?' said my mum, not sure whether she believed me.

'For instance, did you know that the four watercolours of the garden hanging in the corridor bit near Della and the kids' rooms were painted by Nelson's mum when she was a girl here?'

'Really?' said my mum. 'That's actually quite interesting. Unless you think we should offer to hand them over? I quite like them. Makes me feel dead posh, having a painting of my house in my house.' She looked beyond me to where Mr K was ascending the steps on Todd's arm.

'I thought you said you were an only child, Lexy.' Mr K took my mum's free hand in both of his and bent over it briefly, rising with a wink. 'My dear lady, I cannot begin to tell you what an unexpected joy it is to be invited to your family celebrations. The weather in town has turned terribly dreich, but here you are in a veritable winter grotto.'

My mum simpered. There was no other word for it.

'You kept the piano, didn't you?' Mr K said next. 'I seem to remember an item in the inventory? Well, I know all the old carol tunes if you're in the habit of a Christmas singsong. And don't worry about a billet. I can tuck up on any old bunk at all.'

'I've decided you're going in our room,' Kathi said. 'We can cuddle in with Hiro and Diego.'

'And who, pray, are Hiro and Diego?' said Mr K. 'I didn't know it was that kind of party.'

'They're children!' said my mum. 'And you're an old devil, aren't you?'

'I shall be a Christmas angel for you, my dear.'

I might have gagged if it had been me, but my mum's from a different generation and she tittered like a schoolgirl. If she'd had a fan in her hand, she'd have swatted him. As it was, she just banged the watering can against his hip and then had to reach out and grab him to stop him falling over.

'Well, well, well,' he said, looking at her hand on his waist and dropping a wink that would have dislocated the eyelid of a lesser man.

'What's going on here?' said my dad, emerging from the library. 'Oh, you're back, Lexy. Come and help me make up charades.'

'Gladly,' I replied. That's how bad it was to watch my mum and Mr K flirting.

'But we just need to check something up here first,' said Kathi, who was already at the bend in the stairs with Mr K's little suitcase.

'Right!' I said. 'One minute, Dad.' I followed Kathi, with Todd on my heels, to the passage connecting Della and the kids' rooms to their bathroom – and there it was. There *they* were. Four times over. Watercolour views of the lawn and terrace side of the house with blossom from an imaginary – or at least dead now – apple tree, with an explosion of colour from non-existent herbaceous borders, with autumn leaves brighter than Vermont can muster, and finally with snow and ice that actually reflected what lay outside pretty faithfully. And in the corner of each was a black 'Verity Garmont' – V like an arrowhead and y with a tail like a spike.

'There it is, then,' said Todd. 'That proves . . . Wait, which one was which?'

Kathi checked the pictures on her phone and said, 'Huh. Spiky V was the deathbed letter. Bubble V was the letters home. I'd have bet the other way.'

'Me too,' was all I had to offer.

'But this is better,' said Todd. 'If the two old ones matched, we could have said her signature changed over the course of her life. But this way? We know it stayed the same from when she was a girl at home to when she was an old lady at the end. And we know the letters are fake! She didn't type those letters to her mom and dad.'

'We still don't know who did,' I pointed out. 'Or why. Or whether it's got anything to do with what's going on now. And Mr K said the mission was dead in the water by the time she wrote the note. But if you're happy, great.'

Todd deflated visibly as I spoke. It's not a great talent to be able to do that to your friends.

'It would have been easier to make sense of the deathbed letter being fake,' Kathi said. 'It would go along with Nelson turning up here and the body coming to light suddenly.'

'But it's not fake,' I said. 'It's genuine. So Nelson could well be as innocent as he's acting.' I groaned. 'Everyone's either truly innocent or at least acting innocent or dead.'

'Is Miley acting innocent?' said Todd.

'Either that or stupid beyond belief,' said Kathi. 'She got messy drunk and came to talk to us, remember? Who would do that if they had something to hide?'

'Actually, I don't think Wilma's acting all that innocent,' I said.

'Are you insane?' said Todd. 'Wilma's acting the most innocent of all. She let us loose on those boxes of stuff.'

'I know, I know,' I said. 'Don't ask me what it's based on, because it's just a feeling. But it's a strong one.'

'You're not getting away with that,' Todd said. 'Just a feeling? Don't know what it's based on? Work it out, Lexy! Pin it down! We're standing on no legs here.'

'OK,' I said. 'Jeez, calm down. I'll go for a nice long soak in that lovely big bath and see if anything rises on the steam.'

'I don't reckon it will,' said Kathi. 'Wilma's antsy – I'll give you that. But she's the one whose first husband has turned up dead. She'd be a weirdo if she was OK.'

This was true but the thought of the bath had entered my soul and I wasn't going to give it up. 'In the absence of other ideas,' I said. 'And you know what? Now that I begin to focus on it, I'm almost sure there is something there that I could bring to mind.'

'Yeah, right,' said Todd. 'Of course, that's what's going on. You're going to dig deep and make the sacrifice of lying in a scented bubble bath all on your own with a glass of wine and box of chocolates while Kathi and I go downstairs and deal with your mom in a catering frenzy and two kids hopped up on frosting. You're a saint, Lexy.'

'I deeply resent that! The fact that it's true notwithstanding.'

'Wilma, Wilma, Wilma, Wilma,' I said to myself, as I scooted up and down searching for the perfect lean on the curved end of the big bathtub, not too low so my hair got damp and not too high so my shoulders got cold. When I was settled, I reached out one hand for my glass of champagne – it was Christmas Eve, after all – and grabbed a handful of crisps with the other.

There was a memory there somewhere of Wilma acting so skittish it was funny. I could almost hear her voice squawking. Or was it Crispin? But *what* were they squawking, whichever one of them it was? I couldn't remember. I would set it aside and come back to it later. What else about her had bothered me? She had left her long-lost sister-in-law's paintings behind. Sold them as part of the fixtures to my parents even. Was she hostile to Verity? Or just not sentimental? She was sentimental enough to cart a load of old family papers and photos away with her, some of which weren't even authentic if we were right about Verity's signature. But she had chucked out the Christmas stuff. And she'd bunged all the photos in the attic with the rest of it instead of displaying them. So was she full of family feeling or wasn't she?

Maybe it was more that she couldn't throw out anything from that time that might one day shed light on what had happened to Billy. She must have gone over and over it in her mind while he was missing, before she gave up on him. Only . . . something she had said, not to me but to Larg the policeman . . . didn't chime with that.

I took another gulp, belched salt and vinegar and gave a happy sigh. Solitude, where you can be disgusting and feel fine about it, is one of life's rarest treats. I stuffed another batch of crisps in and got munching. When I had swallowed, I rinsed the bubbles off one finger and dug all the stuck bits of crisps out of my molars. No wonder dentists hate them even more than popcorn—

Dentist! I sat up, making a wave that slapped against the tap end and then washed back, knocking me off balance. I steadied myself and examined the thought. Wilma, so Larg had said, couldn't remember the name of Billy's dentist. That struck me as very odd. If someone went missing from my life, I would go and tell everyone they ever dealt with – their doctor and their dentist, their hairdresser too if it was a woman – in case the absconder nipped back for a check-up or a fringe trim. Usual haunts, Kathi called it, and it was a legitimate PI tactic. A worried wife would probably keep checking her missing husband's usual haunts for months, to see if there had been contact. After that, you wouldn't forget. Would you?

Or maybe she had made a special effort to stop remembering everything all the time. To put it in the past and leave it there. She certainly hadn't jumped to the right conclusion when I said I'd found a body the day of the wassail. She thought it was my dad, because my mum was shouting his name the way she does and he was nowhere to be found.

The more I thought of that, though, the stranger it seemed.

'Lex?' The voice by my ear made me thrash so hard I slopped half the bath water over the side and got a big splat of the wrong kind of bubbles in my champagne.

'Taylor! I nearly jumped out my skin!'

'Well, you nearly jumped out of your water anyway. I thought I was going to have to scoop you back in off the floor like a goldfish.'

'Why did you creep up on me like that?'

'I didn't. You just couldn't hear me over the crunching.' He helped himself to the last of my crisps and started mopping the puddles up with my warm towel. But I couldn't be annoyed with him because it was useful to have a foil.

'Tay,' I said. 'If you went downstairs and saw my dad lying all crumpled and looking dead at the bottom of the cellar steps, what would you say?'

'Wow, festive. I'd say, "Keith, can you hear me?" Probably.'

'Not to him, you pillock. What would you say to the rest of us when you ran for help?'

'I'd say, "Your dad's had an accident. Call an ambulance".'

'Right. Exactly. You wouldn't say, "I've found a body", would you?'

'No one would.'

'That's what I thought.'

'What's this about?'

'Oh, the case. We keep sort of getting one stumbling step further on and then stopping dead again. It won't give, you know? We thought we'd worked out that Nelson had to be involved, because he's suddenly come over here and he forged a letter, and there was no way berry thieves would choose to nick that particular mistletoe instead of easier stuff, so we reckoned he did the tree thing to make the secret chamber come to light . . .'

'Berry . . .? *What?* What letter?'

'Oh my God,' I said. 'If it's not a bloody bird, you don't listen, do you? Anyway, never mind. Because the letter's real. And so it did give him a reason to be here. Anyway, it's probably irrelevant that he was in the country, because he stayed with Miley in Edinburgh the night the branch came down.'

'Can I say something?' Taylor said. He waited. He's annoying like that. I nodded. 'I do care. I came in here to say hello to you before I even looked at the nest. So.' He waited again.

'Are you expecting me to thank you? How many times did you check in on the egg cam while you were out today?'

'A few.'

'When was the last time?'

'On my way up the stairs. Can I say something else?' I sighed. 'It's about the nest.'

'No, then.'

'OK. Can I say this? There's no need to start worrying about your dad falling down steps yet. It'll come. I panicked every time my phone rang when my mom was getting frail and wouldn't stop doing stuff. But Keith's only sixty.'

'Fifty!'

'Well, fifty-nine. I wouldn't round up in front of his face, but it's nearer sixty.'

'No!' I said. 'That's what Wilma freaked out about. Or maybe it was Crispin. We said the skeleton had been there for fifty years and someone shrieked, "Sixty!"'

'It is sixty.'

'No but they said like *"Sixty!"* and that must mean something.'

'Yeah, it means her daughter is in her fifties and she got married more than fifty years ago and so her first husband has to have been missing longer than that or – Slut! Slapper!'

'But I think it *was* Crispin.'

'Scandal! Bigamy! See? I do listen sometimes.'

'Get me another glass of champagne with no soap in it and I'll forgive you.'

'How about if I bring two and get in at the other end?'

I thought it over and nodded. There are other nice things in the world besides solitude, and I'd finished the crisps anyway.

It would have been a wonderful evening even without the chummy bath, the two big drinks and relief of working out what had been bugging me about Wilma. It was Christmas Eve, after all – lamps lit, fires crackling, Mr K playing carols on the piano and my mum serving so many trays of wee sausages and vol-au-vents – literal mushroom vol-au-vents – that it didn't seem likely we'd ever eat our actual dinner.

'I always liked this room,' Mr K said, while he was giving his fingers and his neck a rest. 'I remember coming here as a very young man and Old Mr Garmont, Crispin's father, standing at the open window shooting rabbits on the lawn.'

'Lovely,' Della said, checking to see if the children were listening. They were not. The drawing room didn't have a fitted carpet and they had just discovered they could slide up and down the polished floorboards at the edge of the rug in their socks.

'Oh my dear, I know!' he went on. 'That's what I mean. I turned away and concentrated on the plasterwork because I couldn't bear to watch. It was then I discovered that those things that look like frogs are actually gargoyles. Up in the corners there, see?'

'Hmm,' said Roger. 'I'm choosing to believe that. But they might be representations of workers from the sugar plantation that built this place. That's what I'd say if someone asked me.'

'Ewww,' said Kathi.

'That expression seems to have a very non-specific utility,' said Mr K. 'A word for all seasons.'

Diego, who was skating past, stopped to give Mr K the benefit of his eight-year-old wisdom. 'You talk funny,' he said. 'But we don't mind.' Then he carried on to catch up with Hiro.

'Blimey,' said my dad, who had stood up and gone to stand directly under one of the cornices. 'We might fill them in with a bit of plain coving, eh Judith?'

'Right you are,' said my mum, sitting down with an entire platter of bacon-wrapped something or others on her knee and tucking in. 'I can't get upset about anything else we find in this house – sorry, Roger – after the big one.'

Roger shrugged. 'I'd lean in,' he said. 'Put an information card in here for your guests to read.'

'And don't take repeat bookings from anyone who's an arse about it,' I said, which probably wasn't practical, but then that was why I couldn't run a B & B. I'd be throwing people out at midnight in their dressing gowns because I couldn't stand them. Either that or I'd end up like Noleen, gritting my teeth hard enough to break my own collarbone. I gave her a friendly grin; I'd never really thought about why she was so cantankerous before now.

'What?' she said, with a scowl that turned her face into a boxing glove.

'*Is* there anything else though?' my mum said, hauling herself to her feet and offering Mr K the bacon things.

'Not that I recall,' he said. 'There's some fruity graffiti in the attics, I believe, carved into the joists by apprentice carpenters who didn't care for their boss, but other than that . . .' He looked around himself for something to wipe his greasy fingers on. 'What's remarkable is that it's even bigger than I remember. It usually goes the other way.'

'Mum? Are there any napkins handy?' But Mr K dressed for the world he wished he still lived in, and he had his cloth hankie to go with the cufflinks and tie. The rest of us were one step up from pyjamas – a lot of slipper socks and stretchy fabric going on. I started to say to Todd that he in particular looked like Williams-Sonoma made flesh, but something made me stop. Something made me will my brain back to where it had just been. I'd almost remembered. I'd had a useful thought lined up in my subconscious, ready to go, but I'd drifted on and left it behind. What was it? Nothing to do with Wilma this time. Sugar cane? No, it was after that. Leisurewear? No, that came later.

'Lexy! Lexy!' My mum was trying to tell me something. I turned my blank gaze her way. 'There's a festive kitchen roll on top of the microwave – elves and sprouts. Will that do?'

'I'll get it,' I said. Todd was telling Mr K that Miley, who'd lived here, *did* think the place had shrunk since she was a child playing Dorothy in the basement. Was that it? Was that the thing that had snagged on me? Could be.

So, hoping to shake something loose, I didn't go straight to the kitchen for my mother's idea of a cocktail napkin. I wandered along to the unsealed room and looked once again at the threadbare couch, the piles of broken bricks, the stain on the floor and the dim view of the trap doors beyond.

There was nothing here, I decided, playing the beam of my torch app around the walls. Nothing except a job to be taken care of. Whoever came to fill in the horrible cornice could finish removing these walls too. Then we'd get rid of the couch and paint the floor and try to think of what to put in here. I went over to the couch, set my phone down on one of the seat cushions and grabbed the thing by its carved arm, seeing how much it weighed.

That's the thing about real antiques: it felt like trying to lift a hatchback. I gave up and retrieved my phone, the sight of the picked-off flocking on the inside of the arm making me smile. Naughty little Miley, shredding away like a hamster, same as me with my beer-bottle labels and book-club stickers and price tags.

I turned to go.

Then I turned back.

Naughty little Miley couldn't have shredded the flock on this thing. It was an armchair, somewhere else in the house, that she'd laid into. This must have been Crispin or Verity. Maybe it ran in their family.

TWENTY

Sunday 25 December

We missed by one day. I opened my eyes at ten to eight in the morning to hear the familiar – nay, life-long – sound of determined Christmas rain outwitting stuffed gutters and splattering torrentially down the walls of the house. The light had changed from that magical hall-of-mirrors white, endlessly reflecting and refracting so that you couldn't help but think of angels, to a solid murky grey, dampening everything – the pages of my bedside paperback were starting to curl – and making my bedroom feel much chillier than it had done when Taylor was at the window with the sash thrown up because he couldn't see the nest through the ice on the glass.

He was at the window again today, of course, but was making do with rubbing away condensation with his dressing-gown sleeve.

'Merry Christmas,' I croaked.

'Happy Holidays,' he said back. 'I think it's cracking.'

'You sound like a Derry Girl.'

'That's "cracker". I meant the egg.'

'I know. I was giving you a chance to reconsider starting off today with a conversation about it.'

'Right.' He pulled the curtains closed and came back to the bed, getting in at the other end and leaning back against the footboard. 'About that though. When *would* be a good time to talk about something regarding the egg? Well, the nest.'

'Oh, I think during Christmas dinner, don't you?' I said. 'When Speccy and Zippy are here too.' His eyes flashed. 'My God, Taylor, I was *kidding*. Are they coming? Seriously?'

'They're both divorced.'

'Shocker.'

'And your mom invited them. She's all over Christmas, isn't she?' He sighed. 'I remember my mom making latkes for the whole block at Hanukkah. Blind as a bat but she was like a short-order cook when she got going. You never tasted her latkes, did you?'

I had, however, been barked at by her while I tried to make them instead. That had been fun. 'I'm sorry she's not here,' I said. 'She'd make mincemeat of Mr K.'

'At least she wouldn't have sneaked into our bedroom in the middle of the night,' said Taylor. His voice creaked as he stretched backwards over the foot posts to haul up two lumpy stockings that were hanging there.

'She didn't!' I said. 'Oh my God. Look, I'm going to have to believe that was Santa. I can't face knowing my mum was in here while we were sleeping. Well, at least we were tucked up like two bookends from the indigestion and not lying in a sweaty tangle with some ropes still attached.'

'Knock knock,' said Todd, backing into the room with two coffees. 'Your mom did that to us too. Roger woke up with the sheets at his thighs and now he can't stop wondering where they were when she came in.'

'Pyjamas?' I said, in vain hope.

'Puh-lease. We're married, not dead.' He arched an eyebrow at my nightie and cardigan. 'No offence. I run hot.' So he kept telling us. 'Now I gotta dash because I'm in charge of breakfast. No "eggs over-indestructible" today! Cranberry and hazelnut French toast and mimosas. Forty minutes tops, OK?'

'That sounds disgusting,' I said, when he'd gone. 'Let's have chocolate instead.' I tipped my stocking out on the bedclothes and started rootling.

He didn't mean cranberry and hazelnut, we discovered when we got down there. He meant cranberry *or* hazelnut and it had been delicious and we had missed the lot.

'And now I am going to go to my room and make myself beautiful,' he said.

'We'll send up lunch on a tray,' said Noleen. 'Will you be back in time for supper?'

The real adults were dressed already. My mum was in the outfit legally mandated for British women over fifty who were making an effort: comfortable dark trousers and a sparkly top. My dad had on his usual clobber with a slightly brighter jumper.

They both wore slippers with light-up red noses and 3D antlers.
Mr K was the real revelation. He had packed so quickly yesterday
that I hadn't expected a new look, but there he was in green-
and-orange hairy tweeds with a yellow-moleskin waistcoat, a red
bow tie and hanky, and bright red socks above his conker-brown
brogues. He made a point of switching on his cufflinks for me
to see. They flashed and played 'Santa Baby'.

'You look like a million dollars,' Taylor said, who himself
looked absolutely fine in dark denim and cashmere. I think he
must have asked Todd for a suggestion.

'Well,' said Mr K, polishing the buttons on his waistcoat with
his breakfast napkin – a real napkin, I noticed; not more of the
kitchen roll – 'if you can't make an effort for Christmas Day,
when can you?' He shot his cuff and looked at his watch. 'We're
going to church, aren't we Judith? Will you join us?'

'Me?' I said. I was thinking up an excuse when my mum
saved me.

'You can't, Lexy,' she said. 'Noleen and Kathi want to come.
So you've got to stay here and either do the spuds and veg or
set the table. Lexy? Lexy!'

I had found myself staring at Mr K, not sure why. At his
waistcoat and cufflinks, his bow tie and pocket hanky.

'Right, right,' I said. 'I'll do the spuds and the veg – as long
as it really is sprouts and carrots and you're boiling them.'

'What else?' said my mum as if she'd never read the December
issue of a women's magazine in her life. 'Here they come!' she
added, as we all heard a great clattering on the stone steps.

'I BOOTYFOOL,' said Hiro, halfway along the corridor,
testing the acoustics and once again finding them outstanding. 'I
PITTY KISMISS PINSISS.'

'Good Lord,' said Mr K. 'Is that that tiny child making all
that din?'

Right enough, Hiro had been busy skating the night before,
with a lollipop permanently in her gob until bedtime and, while
the sound of her protests at an extra-meticulous teeth-brushing
had drifted down the stairs, this was a very solid house.

She had a point though. She was already dressed, in a stiff
pink frock bristling with tinselly frills, and she had a tiara on.
Diego's hair was slicked down from a side parting and he wore

a little burgundy corduroy two-piece of trousers and waistcoat, with a white shirt underneath and a bow tie that matched Mr K's cufflinks.

'Ah, it fits!' said the old man. 'Splendid. Splendid.' Diego gave him a look up and down and nodded his approval. Again, that nagging question pulled on a bit of my brain, but the sight of Devin swept it away. He had shaved off every bit of Shaggy stubble and put on a shirt with buttons for the first time since his wedding. There was a knife-edge crease down the front of his non-denim trousers and his shoes had laces. He looked almost as grown-up as Diego. And Della, of course, was a knock-out in high-heeled long boots, a white coat with a fake-fur collar and a red dress sparklier than the ruby slippers. Mr K was speechless.

'Mama said presents after church,' Diego told us. 'I'm being brave but Hiro is struggling.'

I looked to my mum for a ruling. It was her house and when I was a kid presents came before everything except the kettle being boiled for my mum's tea and my dad's coffee. Then I'd dive in. And I'd still be in my jammies at noon, surfing around in a sea of paper on the living-room floor in case I'd missed one. I had no idea where this clothes/shoes/church nonsense had come from.

Still, it made for a peaceful morning with them all out of the house and only Roger, Taylor and me to wash dishes, peel mountains of veg and check on the nest seventeen times. Not respectively. Todd texted from upstairs now and then to show selfies of his emerging look, but nothing else disturbed the sweet burble of Radio 4 and the first waves of roasting turkey from the big oven.

Until the back door banged open and footsteps pounded along the corridor, accompanied by a cacophony of excited voices.

'You should have been there!' Noleen said, making it into the kitchen first.

'Oh my God, Lexy,' said Kathi, on her heels. 'Seriously. You should have been there!'

'It was very exciting,' my mum said, marching into the kitchen and managing to take her coat off, put her apron on and slide her hands into oven gloves without breaking stride.

'A Christmas Day family service in a Church of Scotland?' I said.

'Not the service,' said Kathi.

'There was an incident,' Noleen added.

'What happened?' I said.

'If this is what every case is like,' said my mum, 'I think I'll start agitating for "take your mother to work" day. Did anyone baste?'

'I didn't want to open the door and lower the temperature,' I said. 'And it's a bit of a commute from where you live to where I live, Mum.'

'That's cakes,' she said and turned away.

'I can't lie,' said my dad, headed for the wine store, still in his bobble hat, although he'd lost his coat somewhere too. 'I thought you were havering, all of you. But it was very suspicious. It was very revealing.'

'What *happened*?' I said. 'Mr K? What are they talking about? And where are the Ds?'

'Upstairs by the tree, waiting to open presents,' my mum said.

'Yeah, but what happened at the church?' said Roger, the most laid-back man in the world.

'I promised them we'd be three minutes,' my mum said, ladling juices over the turkey. 'Hiro's fit to burst and Diego's going to punch someone if he has to wait any longer.'

'Mum!' I said. 'What the hell happened?'

'There's no time for a big discussion. Keith? Sherry! Let's go.'

So it was that we finally got down to cracking the case, like the true professionals we were, sitting around drinking sherry and opening presents, with Della filming the kids and Diego's fart gun going off metronomically in the background.

'What happened?' I pleaded as soon as I'd arrived in the room and found a seat. But then Todd arrived in white leather and midnight-blue angora, to a chorus of . . . absolutely nothing. No one even glanced at him.

'What's up?' he said, mystified.

'Oh Todd, wait till you hear!' said my mum.

'You're kidding,' I said. '*Now* you can speak?'

'I'll take it from here, if you like, Judith,' said Mr K. 'Since

I am, after all, the cat that was dropped among the pigeons.' He paused dramatically. 'The Garmonts were there.'

'All of them,' said my dad.

'In a row along the front, like they were some kind of muckitty mucks,' said Noleen.

'Then Della caused a bit of a stir, kneeling and crossing herself before she sat down,' said my dad. 'Fine by me, sweetheart, I'm not saying anything. Just filling in the background for Lexy.'

'The whispering was like the wind in the trees,' said Kathi. '"Who is that?" "Someone should say something!" "Since when is this what passes for Presbyterianism?" – you know.'

'Get lost,' said Taylor.

'OK no, no one said that but there were a lot of shushy sounds and it fit.'

'Anyway,' said Noleen. 'This caused craning. Including from the VIP seats. That's when Wilma got a good look at us, snapped her head back round to face the front and started saying something to Crispin. Pretty urgently too.'

'I thought her tummy was playing up,' said my mum. 'Remember that time at Lake Como, Keith? After the fish stew? It's the most awful feeling and there's nothing you can do.'

'But it wasn't that,' said Kathi. 'It was us. Because Crispin turned round and gave our row a good hard stare. Then he kind of patted Wilma on her shoulder; we think he probably told her she was wrong and to chill out.'

'Wrong about what?' Todd said.

'At this point we don't know,' Noleen said. 'But fast-forward through a ton of church stuff—'

'Someone needs to have a word with that minister,' said my mum.

'What's wrong with him?' I asked.

'Her. Holier than thou, if you ask me. We had "Joy to the World" and "It Came Upon a Midnight Clear", for God's sake. No "Little Donkey", no "Hark the Herald". The weans were bored rigid. But eventually . . .'

'Eventually,' said Mr K, 'the service ended and we waited to leave. Kathi was right: Wilma *had* seen something alarming, had told Crispin, and Crispin had checked and disagreed about there being cause for concern. That lasted until they were passing our pew, too close for aging eyesight to allow denial.'

'What did they see?' I said.

'Moi!' said Mr K with a flourish. 'Wilma looked straight at me and turned as white as that rather comely minister's festive vestments. She stopped dead. For one awful moment I thought she was going to *drop* dead.'

'She just stood there,' said my dad. 'Causing a total back-up behind her, completely oblivious.' He was always very big on crowd control and traffic calming.

'Clutching Crispin's arm with one hand,' Noleen said, 'and pointing with the other, like the ghost of whatsit in thingumabob.'

'Christmas Yet to Come in *A Christmas Carol*,' said Todd. 'Half of that was already done for you.'

'So she's pointing a wavering, bony finger,' said Noleen, ignoring him, 'and she says, "You!"'

'What did you say back, Mr K?' I asked.

'He was awesome!' said Kathi. 'He said, "Oh, sweetie, it's been soooo long. How are you? Good to see you and Happy Holidays". You know? Cool as a cuke.'

'*Very* rough translation,' said Mr K. 'But you captured the gist.'

'Meanwhile,' said my mum, 'Crispin's standing there like a pillar of salt too.'

'And everyone's still trying to get out, remember,' my dad chipped in. 'Everyone's needing to get home to see to the dinner.'

'And then your mom killed it!' said Noleen. 'Judith shuffled out of the booth and said' – she cleared her throat and broke into a falsetto – '"Oh, Wilma and Crispin! So happy we ran into you! We're having drinks at noon for a few friends! Do pop off!"'

'Pop in,' I said.

'I don't talk like that, do I?' said my mum.

'No one talks like that, Judith,' said Roger. 'Outside of *Monty Python*.'

'But anyway, that blew their minds, you see?' Kathi said. 'Because whatever it is that they knew, or thought, or feared, when they saw Mr K, Judith asking them to a party without a care in the world made them think none of us were wise to it. Genius!'

'Well, to be fair,' I pointed out, 'we're not.'

'But we're close!' said Todd. 'We must be.'

'And even closer now,' said Kathi, 'because now we know for sure that it's them – Crispin and Wilma. Not Nelson, because he didn't know anything was going on. He was checking his texts and missed the whole thing. And it's not Miley either, because she was oblivious. She saw something was wrong with Wilma, but she was scratching her head as much as we were. So.'

'Ahem.' It was Diego. He was standing up behind a big, wrapped box, staring at us all with his hands on his hips. 'Can you stop going on and on, please? I'm trying to shake this to guess what's inside and I can't hear it over the noise.'

'No seas descarado!' said Della. 'Chico malo!'

'He's got a point, Dells,' I said. 'Just because you dress him up in a suit, he's still eight. Sorry, baby.'

'Half a suit!' said Diego. 'I wanted a top hat and one of those sticks too.'

'A wand?' said Todd.

'For dancing,' Diego said.

'Oh, a cane!'

'TOP HAT!' said Hiro, coming up for air between parcels.

'You're a funny old soul, Diego,' I said. 'Not even Mr K's got a hat and a cane.'

'OH MY GOD!' said Todd. He reached out both hands and clutched Roger and Kathi by an arm each. 'Oh my goggle-eyed goldfish!'

'What?' I said. 'What?'

'What's missing?' said Todd. 'Hankie, cufflinks, vest, top hat, walking cane!'

'Tell me!' I said. 'It's been on the tip of my brain all day and I can't bear it!'

'Vest?' said my dad. 'Oh, you mean waistcoat?'

'Todd,' I said. 'I'm going to have an aneurism.'

'A watch chain!' said Todd.

'YES!' I said. 'Oh yes, yes, yes!' I had never sounded so much like Meg Ryan in that diner in all my born days, but I couldn't help it. 'I kept looking at your waistcoat, Mr K, and it kept bothering me.'

'I don't wear a pocket watch these days,' he said. 'I've had my watch on my wrist since the seventies.'

'Exactly!' I said.

'Oh God, we missed it,' said Kathi. 'Idiots!'

'Is someone going to explain?' my mum said. 'What *about* Mr K's watch? Surely Wilma couldn't have seen it from all the way up in the front pew of the church? Not if it was on your wrist.'

'Not Mr K's watch, Mum,' I said. 'Billy Bone's watch. The watch that let Wilma identify his body after all those years had gone by.'

'What about it?' said my dad.

'The story was that Wilma and Billy were relaxing at home after work one random evening,' I said.

'And Crispin knocked at the door and said there was trouble at the big house,' said Todd.

'And when Billy heard what kind of trouble it was – his secret girlfriend getting hell from her dad—' said Kathi.

'He barged off there to stop it,' I finished up, 'and was never seen again.'

'And?' said my mum.

'Oh!' said my dad. 'You're saying he wouldn't have been wearing a watch on a chain on a normal working day?'

'Exactly!'

'But maybe he did. Maybe that was his style.'

'Except it wasn't,' said Kathi. 'We saw photographs of him and he was always wearing overalls, not a waistcoat with a watch pocket. The watch was planted to identify him.'

'So it's not Billy Bone?' my mum said.

'Oh no, it definitely is,' said Kathi.

'So why . . .?' said my dad.

'Wrong question,' said Kathi. 'The point is *when*, and then when tells us *why*.'

I stared at her and then, to stop the thoughts fizzing round my brain like party poppers, I put my head in my hands and squeezed my eyes shut. When told us why? What did she mean?

'But, Kathi,' said Todd, 'we know when he died because of the coins in his pocket.'

'That's not unlikely,' my dad said. 'I have coins in my pockets right now and there aren't even any shops open today.' He jingled them to prove his point.

Todd and I stared at each other. He looked constipated. I probably did too. We were so close, but we couldn't get there. Todd gave up first. 'Unh. It's no use,' he said. 'Kathi, you'll have to tell us.'

'Think about the coins in *Keith's* pocket,' she said. 'If he – no offence, Keith – but if he died today and his body was found sixty years later, we'd be able to date his death from the dates on the coins. I mean, we'd know he couldn't have died with a future-coin on him, and we'd guess that he probably didn't die with a pocketful of vintage coins either.'

My dad had his coins out in his cupped hands and was turning them over. 'Last year,' he said. 'This year. That's an old one. Two years back. What does this say? Pennies get so mucky.'

'So if we wanted to make people fifty years in the future believe that Keith had been dead *sixty* years,' said Kathi, 'what would we do?'

'You're getting a bit morbid,' said my mum. 'For Christmas Day.'

'Go and watch the wee ones open their presents, Mum,' I said. 'This is important. If we wanted to make people get the date of death wrong by ten years . . .'

'Oh come on, Lexy!' said Taylor. 'You haven't had that much Prosecco. You'd fill his pockets with coins that were more than ten years old, wouldn't you? Make sure he didn't have any new ones.'

I slumped. Of course you would. It was so obvious, once you knew.

'So it really *was* fifty years,' said Todd. 'And that's why Crispin lost his shi— lost it, when someone *said* "fifty years"?' He paused to think it over and then nodded. 'But, Kathi, you said if we worked out when, that would tell us why.'

'And it does,' Kathi said. 'The coins push the date back and the watch chain proves it's Billy, therefore . . . everybody believed that Billy died on the early date, that Billy died the night he came barging in here, that Billy died at the hands of Verity's angry parents, when both Crispin and Wilma were alibi-ing each other over at the lodge. Except he didn't. He died ten years later, when the parents were dead and Crispin and Wilma were in charge here.'

'Good Lord,' said my dad.

'But if he didn't die, where was he?' My mum was completely engrossed again.

'It's all so clear now,' Mr K said.

'Speak for yourself, mate,' said my dad.

'I always thought it remarkable that a girl as young and as sheltered as Verity would take off all on her own, get herself to Barbados and stay there, unprotected.'

'Of course!' I said. 'She didn't. She wasn't alone and she wasn't unprotected. They went together. They went together and stayed together!'

'So Nelson knew him?' said Todd.

'Nelson knew him!' I said. 'He never had three dads. He had two. One that loved him and his mum, and was loved in return, until he left them. After that, he was sometimes "a scumbag" who deserted them, and sometimes the love of her life that she still reminisced about.'

'That tracks,' said Kathi. 'A little kid wouldn't understand how the same man could be both.'

'Oh, that poor woman,' I said. 'The letter she wrote on her deathbed was so full of pain about him "abandoning" her! It seemed a bit much when she was the one that ran off. But he really did abandon her, didn't he? He came back here and they killed him.'

'Crispin and Wilma did?' said my mum, her voice nearly as high as Noleen's impersonation of her.

'Of course,' said Todd. 'Wilma and Crispin killed him, bricked him up in the cellar and started putting together a record of fake letters from Verity, in the real envelopes for extra authenticity. Fake confessional diaries by Verity's mother, too, in case he was ever found.'

'But then why oh why oh why did they sell the *house*?' said my dad.

'I don't know,' I told him. 'But it explains why they took all that guff to the cottage with them, even though they chucked out Christmas decorations and left paintings behind – which always seemed very dodgy, didn't it? They must have been sure he'd be found, now they've sold up. That's why they shoved all that mouldering old crap at us and paid us to look at it. It was their masterstroke, and they didn't want it to go to waste.'

'Or maybe it's more like they've been waiting for the boot to drop so long that they wanted it over and done with,' said Kathi.

'It nearly worked too,' I said. 'If they'd made a better job of Verity's signature, we'd have swallowed it. We'd have eaten it up.'

'You know what else?' said Todd. 'If it wasn't guilt and remorse that killed the old couple so conveniently early on in their lives, I wonder what it was.'

'Oh God,' said my mum. 'Mr K, can you remember if they were buried or cremated?'

'Dear, dear, dear,' said Mr K. 'That's a grisly thought for a day like today. But yes, they're in the kirkyard. I was there. I suppose I'll be there if they make a reappearance too.'

'Who are you texting, Todd?' said Kathi.

'Nelson. To tell him to get out of the house. He's got Verity's letter with the true signature on it.' His phone pinged. 'It's OK,' he said. 'Wilma's gone out for a walk. Crispin too.'

'This is all just so very hard to believe,' my mum said. 'How could you brick up a body and then bring a baby into the house. How could you let a tiny little child live here with that thing?'

'They didn't, Mum,' I said. 'That's the whole point. She was . . . Well, I don't know exactly but . . . getting on for ten, or something? Oh!' I clapped my hands together. 'She said it herself – Miley did. She said the cellar seemed smaller. And of course it did, because when she played Dorothy down there, the whole place was still open from end to end. And it *was* that couch – right there where it still is – that she sat on and picked the flocking off of.'

'Miley, still Camilla at the time, went to boarding school when she was quite a small girl,' said Mr K. 'I know because the trust was used for the school fees. I couldn't say how old she was exactly, but I would put a decent wedge on its being 1968, or thereabouts. And I'd put my *shirt* on it being about then that Billy came back. Because I think I know why.'

We all held our breath waiting for him to speak. So we all heard it.

'What's that?' said my dad. 'Judith? Is that a house noise? It's taken us a long time to start to learn all the sounds in this old place, but I don't think I recognize that one.'

'Oh no!' said Todd. 'Nelson told us they'd "gone out"!'

'I was wondering about that,' said my mum. 'Who goes out for a walk between church and dinner on Christmas Day?'

'People who've been invited for drinks,' said my dad.

The drawing-room door swung open to show Crispin silhouetted and dazzling a bit against the fairy lights on the hall Christmas tree. Wilma was at his elbow, peeping round the arm that was bent and shaking slightly as he pointed the gun.

TWENTY-ONE

'There are two children and two adults in this room who have nothing to do with any bit of what you've come here for. Let the rest of us all go downstairs and have a discussion.'

I had never heard my dad sound so . . . I couldn't even think the word I needed to think because I had never thought it in connection with my dad, Keith Campbell. He sounded like Liam Neeson calamitously miscast in a Barack Obama biopic.

'Phones out of pockets and leave them behind,' said Crispin. I dug my phone out and watched the others do the same. Flicking a glance at the Muelenbelts, I saw Della making notes about who gave what, all set to stand over Diego writing his thank-you letters. Devin was half watching his children and half checking that his video was properly catching his children, all with a soppy grin on his face.

'BOOK!' said Hiro.

'I'll read it to you,' said Diego, lordly as ever.

'We're nipping downstairs for a bit, Della,' I said. 'Won't be long.'

She nodded absently but didn't even look up as we all filed out of the room.

I had never seen my parents holding hands before. My mum would sometimes take my dad's arm if it was slippy or she was drunk, but they marched across the hall at the head of our little crocodile with fingers laced and shoulders squared. It wasn't only me who noticed either, because Noleen grabbed Kathi's hand and Roger took Todd's. So I reached for Taylor's as we fell in behind them, but he kept his in his pocket, staring straight ahead with a look of intense concentration on his face.

'You OK?' I said.

'No talking,' said Crispin, behind me.

'Me? Peachy,' said Taylor. 'After all the sneering and scolding you've done about America, I come to safe-as-sandwiches Scotland and get held up at gunpoint by a murderer.'

'I said, "No talking"!'

'Give it a rest, Crispin,' said my dad. 'You've got us dancing to your tune. Don't milk it.'

'Uh, Keith?' said Roger. 'I know it's the national sport and all that, but maybe now is not the time to play it cool. What do you say?'

Morgan Freeman beats Liam Neeson every time, so it was in silence that we trooped downstairs and arranged ourselves in the fake kitchen.

'You were right to worry when you saw me, Wilma my dear,' said Mr K. 'Excuse me! Force of habit. I should have said, Wilma you bitch.'

'Jesus,' muttered Roger.

'I worked out why Billy came back, you see,' he went on.

'Billy? He didn't come back. He never came back. He never left. They killed him.' Wilma doled out these short bursts of speech like puffs from a steam train.

'I see,' said Mr K. 'In that case, what's the gun for?'

It was, in my opinion, a very good question.

'But, for entertainment's sake,' said Crispin, 'what nonsense have you concocted with that addled old brain of yours?'

Mr K took his sweet time. He cleared his throat. He adjusted the crease of his trousers over his top knee. He even steepled his fingers. 'In essence,' he said at last, when I could feel the beginnings of a tension headache in my temples, 'this case hinges on the meanings of two words. Well, three. But two that concern us today. "Legitimate" and "pure".' He grinned. 'How am I doing so far?'

Crispin only scowled.

'Your father wished to leave his fortune to grandchildren born in wedlock to a pure woman. He thought that would cut out Wilma here and would certainly cut out the baby that Verity was already expecting when she left his house. However, in 1968, the law of this land changed. As you well know.'

'Ohhhh,' I said. 'Wait, which one was that?'

'The Act to amend and codify the law of Scotland relating to the legitimation of illegitimate persons by the subsequent marriage of their parents. *The subsequent marriage of their parents.* In other words, if Billy and Verity had married at the end of the sixties, their child, Nelson, would have become rightful heir to half of the fortune you were living off quite happily.'

'Nonsense,' said Crispin. 'Legitimation after the fact and "born in wedlock" are two different things.'

'Possibly, possibly,' said Mr K. 'But I'm glad that you've given up the pretence that this is hypothetical. Much less tiresome.' Crispin scowled again but did not deny it.

'I would have relished the chance to mount the argument,' Mr K went on. 'But I admit it could have gone either way.'

'And didn't you say it wasn't retrospective?' said Kathi. 'Mrs Fitzgerald and all that?'

'Retro*active*,' said Mr K. 'Mrs Fitzherbert. I did, young lady. Well remembered. But you will also recall that Alex Garmont's will gave a life interest to Crispin who was then – is now – still alive. No retroaction at all, you see. So let us turn to the other salient word: "pure". A pure woman. And let us ask ourselves this: out of the two women whose purity was relevant, which one would have come out closer to the angels if Billy hadn't died in 1968? The woman whose child had been legitimated, and who only wanted some of the fortune to come to her son so that he could give it away – nay, give it *back* – to the descendants of those whose toil produced it? Or the twice-married woman who worked to declare her first husband dead so she could enjoy that fortune for the rest of her life and pass it on to her daughter to keep? If I were a judge, I shouldn't have taken long to decide. And if I were offered the chance to argue such a case, I should grab it.'

'Penge bungalow again?' I asked.

'A whole street of Penge bungalows, my dear,' said Mr K. 'Of course, even that becomes moot if you murdered your parents, doesn't it?'

'Murdered?' said Crispin. 'That is monstrous!'

'Oh, *that's* monstrous, is it?' said my dad. 'That's where you draw your line? You're fine finishing off her husband with a shovel and living beside his rotting corpse, but killing your mother and father— Actually, you know what? That is worse, isn't it? Sorry.' My dad wasn't cut out for this.

'Is that true then?' said Noleen. 'You can't benefit from your crime? I thought that was just Poirot.'

'Oh no, my dear,' said Mr K. 'It's true. Agatha was always quite sound on the law. Legalities and poisons.'

'This is all very interesting,' said Crispin. 'But you've no proof of a single bit of it. We did you the courtesy of coming along here today to ask you not to keep gossiping about my family. That's all.'

'Thing is,' I said, 'Nelson's got proof. He's got Verity's signature and it's nothing like the one you put on those fake letters she's supposed to have sent.'

'That's not proof,' said Wilma.

'And Miley remembers the basement before the wall,' said Todd.

'Childhood memories are notoriously fickle,' said Wilma. 'Unless she's got a picture or a diary, that's nothing too.'

'Oh yes,' I said. 'The diaries. All those diaries your mother-in-law kept until she died. That didn't mention Billy being in Barbados and hinted at a terrible deed that filled her with regret.'

'We burned them yesterday,' said Wilma. 'It was cathartic, wasn't it Crisp?' She grinned at us all. 'Like we said, you've got nothing.'

But that wasn't quite true. They might have burned the letters and journals and even the photographs, after making them and keeping them and being so bold as to let us see them. But they were banking on us not having taken anything away.

'Did you count them?' I said. 'Before you burned them? Are you sure they were all there?'

'Nice try,' Wilma said. 'Yes, we did. We checked them very carefully.'

'But not quite carefully enough,' I said. My heart was hammering but I managed to hide it. 'I've got a bad habit of picking off stickers. Beer-bottle labels, book-club screamers, price tags . . .'

'You don't still do that, Lexy, do you?' said my mum. 'I told you till I was blue in the face. All those little mouse nests of paper wherever you'd been.'

'What's a screamer?' said my dad.

'I *don't* still do that, Mum,' I said. 'I've completely stopped leaving mouse nests behind me.' Then I paused to see if Wilma would make the connection and realize what I was saying. Because what had always bothered me, ever since we'd been in the cottage looking at the boxes of documents and I'd peeled that little sticker off, was why exactly – if she was going to black it out, like she had – she hadn't just peeled it off. It came away easily enough for me. I cast my mind back and tried to relive the moment when the gummy edge of the price tag let go of the journal cover beneath and rolled back. What was under there, I asked myself. And I was pretty sure of the answer: it was black-and-white stripes. The journal was pale lavender, no pattern, but under the price tag was black-and-white stripes. A barcode.

'You covered the barcodes on the journals you bought,' I said. 'Because your mother-in-law, who was supposed to have written in them, died before barcodes came in.'

Wilma looked uncertain for the first time. And for a moment, I wondered why. Then it came to me.

'Wait though,' I said. 'If you'd done that, you would have covered it with something innocent,' I said. 'Not with something you had to black out. And it *was* blacked out. So . . . the sticker was on the journal when you bought it and you blacked it out because . . .?'

I dug into my pocket, right in the corner, and found the little ball of sticky paper. Thank God, though, light dawned before I got it out of there. She could have taken it and swallowed it and I couldn't have stopped her. Not with a gun trained on me.

'Because you bought it sometime in the seventies!' I said. 'And so it wasn't a price tag for two shillings or elevenpence ha'penny. It was a price tag for thirty-eight pee or something, wasn't it? Post-decimalization. Which didn't happen until Mrs Garmont was in her grave.'

'A blacked-out price tag?' said Wilma, with a wobbly attempt at a sneer.

'To the naked eye,' I said. 'Not to a forensic expert, I wouldn't have said.'

She glanced at Crispin, whose gun hand was starting to waver.

'Give it up,' I said. 'You're not going to get away with it. If you shoot one of us today, it'll only make it worse. You must know it's over now.'

They said nothing, but they both looked exhausted.

'Wilma,' said my mum, kindly under the circumstances, 'why didn't you just stay in the house? You're over eighty. You could have ended your life with no one any the wiser.'

'It was Miley's fault,' Wilma said. 'The way she is. That flat like a laboratory. Never wanting any of our treasures. If we'd died here, Miley would have had a clearance firm in without checking anything. Then Billy would have been found, and people might have thought we'd killed him.'

'You did kill him,' said my dad.

'But we worked so hard to get away with it,' Crispin said.

That was when it struck me that the pair of them were just a little bit off their rockers. He sounded as if he genuinely expected sympathy.

'And besides,' said Wilma, 'we do love Miley. We didn't want her to have to deal with a skeleton.'

'So you decided we should have to deal with it instead?' my mum said.

'Eventually!' Crispin said. 'You turned out to be extremely off-hand custodians of our beautiful house. It's been months!'

'I can't—' my mum said. 'I can't—' If we all survived this, I was going to teach her the phrase "I can't even", because that's what she was scrabbling for. In the meantime, she shook it off and tried another tack. 'And why did you even care?' she said. 'No one else would have. By the time Billy came back. Divorce, annulment, legitimate or whatever. So what? 1970? It was David Bowie and the Rolling Stones.'

'Money, Judith,' said my dad. 'Not everyone is as decent as you.'

'But if no one inherited under that mad will,' I said, 'then you'd have split the Garmont money in two and had half. You'd hardly have been on the breadline. Or even if Verity got it, she'd have seen you right, wouldn't she?'

'You haven't been listening,' said Crispin, piping up at last in a reedy voice. 'Mr Kilquhanity just said it. Nelson said it. Verity never shut up about it. And Billy said it too when he came back. Reparations, beneficence, largesse, philanthropy. They wanted to take *our* family money and give it away to a bunch of lazy n—'

'Watch it,' said Roger, standing up.

'Oh, of course you'd be on their side,' said Crispin. 'All the bloody same. Work-shy scroungers.'

Roger opened his mouth to speak but, before anything came out, we all heard a sound. A blessed sound. A sound not normally more melodious and delightful than the song of a nightingale, but at that moment the best sound in the world. It was the crackle and buzz of a police radio and, as far as I could tell, it was halfway down the stairs.

Crispin froze. Wilma grabbed him by the arm. The gun went off, so loud in that vaulted kitchen with the stone floor, that it brought him right back to life. Together they fled, running faster than two people their age could possibly have run for years. When the deafening ring of the shot started to fade, we could all hear Larg shouting and pounding along the corridor. He swung round the door, crashing into Roger who was headed out.

'They've gone!' Roger said. 'They're hiding!'

But they weren't. They knew this house and they had made for the passageway lying there newly opened up again, scrambling through the jagged holes and over the piles of bricks, making for the ladder. All I saw by the time I got there was the cuffs of Crispin's twill trousers and the hand-stitched soles of his shoes.

But I could hear something going on, up in the garden. There were muffled shouts and grunts and someone was crying. I took the next shot of the ladder after Larg had attacked it with his massive, booted feet and disappeared into the square of daylight.

'Careful, Lexy,' my mum said. 'It's not meant to bear that kind of w—'

I popped out and staggered to get my balance. Miley was holding her mum by the arm. Larg had Crispin in a tight grip, and Nelson was holding the gun at arm's length with one finger and one thumb, hating touching it but scared to drop it too. Beth was there, brandishing a rake, although she couldn't make up her mind whether it was Wilma or Crispin she was gunning for, so actually she was waving a rake in *everyone's* face. Not helpful, really. Speccy and Zippy, who I'd completely forgot were coming, stood side by side under the owl tree with arms spread wide, making sure no one bumped into it and disturbed the egg.

'Is everyone OK?' Miley said. 'We didn't know! We didn't

know! It wasn't till after they went out we suddenly realized. It's going to sound so stupid. But we were talking about memories, and Nelson showed me the picture of his dad that Todd gave him, and I recognized him. I met him. In this house. I saw him.'

'But she couldn't have,' said Nelson. 'But she did.'

'And so we worked it out,' Miley said. 'Only we were so late. We heard the shot. Is everyone OK?'

'I'm not,' said Nelson.

Roger, who had just got out of the hatch, walked over, took the gun, opened it up and let the bullets fall to the ground. 'Not to be a cliché,' he said.

'Everyone's fine,' I said. 'Our ears are ringing. That's all.'

'And my turkey's missed a baste!' My mum's voice came up through the hatch.

'Thank you for phoning the police,' I said.

'We didn't,' said Miley.

'You wouldn't do that to your own mother,' Wilma said, trying to nuzzle in to her daughter's neck.

'We totally would have, Mum,' said Miley. 'We just never thought of it.'

'That was me,' said Taylor. 'I pocket-dialled. Everything that pair said is on the nine-nine-nine tape.'

'But we took your phones!' said Crispin.

'You took my personal phone,' said Taylor. 'I kept my owl phone.'

'Of course you did,' I said, and threw my arms around him as three more police appeared at the corner of the house and, between the lot of them and Larg, got the Garmonts cuffed and cautioned before leading them away.

TWENTY-TWO

S peccy and Zippy decided to go to the pub with Beth – and who can blame them? – but Miley and Nelson stayed on for dinner. Apart from anything else, by the time the CID had finished the interviews, it was too late to save theirs back at the cottage. Even my mum's turkey had been rubbed with extra butter, soaked in gravy and rested for so long you could carve it with a spoon. And the Brussels sprouts were baby food, rejected by everyone except Hiro.

'That's not going to be good later,' said Devin, watching her wolf them down. No one but me heard him because, just at that moment, someone else bit into a roast potato and the sound of shattering crust drowned him out.

'You know what I don't understand,' Nelson said, when we were all slumped in our seats sipping fizzy water and waiting for the main course to settle before we started in on the puddings, 'why did Muma think she had a crack at reversing the will? Not early on – I get that – the 1968 Act.' He tipped his glass at Mr K. 'But just before she died. Why was she so convinced she had a case then?'

'Poor woman,' said my mum. 'She thought he'd run off and left her. Run off and left both of you.'

'RUN OFF AND WEFF HURRRRRR,' said Hiro.

'But it's nice to think that the man you remember really was your dad,' my mum said. 'Isn't it? I wouldn't know. We're so Neapolitan, the Campbells.'

I was baffled but Taylor, despite spending most of his time gazing at a nest, had obviously cracked my family code. 'You might mean vanilla, Judith.'

Mr K had been blinking patiently and wiping his mouth with his napkin for a while, waiting for us to settle. Clearly, he meant to take the floor. 'Ahem,' he said, when he finally had silence. 'I've been thinking about that, as you can imagine. You are right, Nelson; it's nothing to do with the 1968 Act, or the 1976

Legitimacy Act, the 1977 Presumption of Death Act, or even the 1982 Act that swept all before it, sans adoption, which, as you will recall, took until 2006.'

'Just as well he's got the accent,' Noleen said, in an undertone. 'Because boy howdy.'

'No,' said Mr K, 'I suggest that we need to go all the way back to the Scots Law of . . . well, the precise date escapes me, which doesn't matter, I daresay.'

'Please do. Please dare,' said Noleen, a bit louder. Then she jumped as if someone had kicked her. I wasn't sure who but I was glad.

'If you recall, I told you that under our law, the bairn's part is a third and the widow's is another third, leaving a third for the dead man to do with what he may, when it comes to portable property, but that fixed assets – houses and land – are in his gift.'

'Like a vicarage,' said Kathi. 'In Jane Austen.'

'That would require rather a tangent into defunct Anglican ecclesiastical practice,' said Mr K, for all the world like he wasn't taking the scenic route to wherever *he* was headed, 'but if it helps you understand, then by all means.' He paused and held up a finger. 'But!'

'BUTT BUTT POOPY B—' Hiro managed to get out before Devin plugged her mouth with a sausage.

'Forgive my sister,' said Diego. 'She is too small to be polite.' If I wasn't mistaken, he was trying to sound like Mr K, which was all we needed.

'But!' said Mr K again. 'If you remember the preamble to that . . . *Does* anyone recall what I said? Hmm?'

'You've got us there, Mr K,' I said. 'I mean, what would be the point of all the studying if hearing it once over lunch did the same job?'

'Indeed, indeed,' said the old man, not immune to a bit of sucking up. Who is? 'What I said, although you don't recall, was *all debts once discharged*. The terms of the will apply, the arguments over the will begin, the great grinding might of our beloved Scots Law creaks to life . . . all debts once discharged.'

If he was expecting a big response, he was sorely disappointed. No one said anything. Todd took a drink from his wine glass, obviously beginning to digest the meal.

Mr K tried again. 'Think of who cherished these hopes. Your mother, Nelson. Your dear mother. Your sadly unknown aunt, Camilla. It was she who saw the hope at the end of her life.'

'Oh!' said Kathi, getting several syllables out of it. 'I see. Was she right?'

'I would have loved to pit my wits against any solicitor arguing that she wasn't,' said Mr K. 'I would have filled the whole town of Penge with nothing but bungalows.'

'What. Are. You. Talking. About?' said Noleen.

'I see it,' said Roger. 'And I'm going to be kind and give the rest of you a clue. I see, but then I would.'

'Oh! I love a parlour game after dinner on Christmas Day,' said my mum. 'Roger sees, but then Roger would. So . . . something to do with medicine?'

Roger grinned. 'Good for you,' he said. 'No!' he added when my mum clapped her hands. 'You're wrong, but good for you for looking at me and thinking "doctor" first.'

'Ohhhhh!' said Todd.

My mum had gone pink. 'Right,' she said. 'So it's something to do with your . . . I know it's not lifestyle but I don't know what to call it.'

'Homosexuality?' said my dad.

'No,' said Roger.

'Sorry,' my dad said. 'I try to keep up but, honest to God, son.'

'Oh!' said Roger. 'Yes to the terminology, but no to the guess. That's not why I would. But this is all very reassuring. For anyone like me thinking of moving to a country like this. It's extremely reassuring, I can tell you.'

'Ohhhhhhh!' I said. But I was faking. Like Todd had been, I reckon.

'Kathi?' said Mr K. 'Enlighten us, won't you?'

'Verity believed that there were unpaid Garmont debts in Barbados that would have to be taken care of before anyone in the family saw a cent of the fortune.'

'Precisely,' said Mr K.

'Ohhhhhh,' said my mum. 'Because you're *Black*.'

'Her heart's in the right place,' I said.

'And connected to her mouth as far as I'm concerned,' said

Roger. 'I'll take doctor, gay, Black in that order all day every day.'

'Doctor, gay, gorgeous,' said Todd. 'I like this game.'

'Can *I* ask a question?' said my dad. 'Nothing to do with the Garmonts but it's been eating at me. Devin? Della? How come you didn't react to a gun going off? Lexy always told us we didn't have to worry about her over there, but . . .'

'Lexy's always *telling* you that you *don't* have to worry,' I said, fixing his tenses for him.

'We thought it was something to do with dinner,' Della said.

'Well, thanks a bunch,' said my mum. 'I'm not the best cook in the world, I know.'

'No, just that there are those gunpowder tubes we all pulled and you said you were going to set fire to the dessert?'

'Actually, I must go and check it hasn't boiled dry,' my mum said. 'If you hear a gunshot while I'm out of the room, it's a gun and you should come and save me.' She rolled her eyes and hurried off.

'Also,' said Devin, 'Hiro might have been singing.'

'She certainly does . . . um . . .' said Nelson. 'Doesn't she?'

'She sure does,' Della said, gazing adoringly at her daughter who was still noshing on that chipolata, just the end of it sticking out of the side of her mouth like a fat cigar.

'So do I,' said Diego. 'And I started first.'

'Might *I* ask a question?' said Mr K. My dad gestured for him to go on. 'Did you insist that your gardener work on Christmas Day or did she volunteer? Is she all alone in the world?'

'Eh?' said my dad.

'No matter,' said Mr K. 'I could persuade her to leave either penury or solitude behind, I hope.'

'Eh?'

'The striking young lady with the rake.'

'She's not a gardener,' I said. 'She's a pub landlady.'

'Is she, by Jove?' said Mr K.

Poor Beth, I thought. Then, reflecting on how far past seventy she had looked out in the cold with no make-up on, and considering what thin ice age differences were for me, I found myself smiling.

I had been watching Miley on and off throughout the meal.

'You OK?' I took the chance to ask her while everyone else was laughing at the kids.

'Can't stop thinking about them,' she said. 'Where they are. In cells, probably, eh? On Christmas Day. At their age. I know I should harden my heart, but it's not that easy.'

'I'm sorry,' Nelson said. 'But I can stay on a bit. Or you can come back with me. We need to stick together, the two of us. Six of us, counting my wife and kids, seven with my daughter's boyfriend. You won't be alone.'

'That was really nice of Nelson,' I said to Taylor much later when we had gone to bed.

He lowered himself on to the eiderdown and lay back carefully. 'I am so full,' he said. 'I can't believe you ever scoffed at Thanksgiving. At least we don't try to feed anyone supper an hour after dinner.'

'Dinner was late, to be fair,' I said, but I shuddered. I had managed a small slice of Christmas cake, hidden the marzipan and icing in the couch cushions, and told my mum to use a damp tea towel to wrap the sandwiches. Sandwiches!

'Yeah, it was,' Taylor said. 'I'm really glad it wasn't him. I didn't understand why you ever thought he was guilty.'

'How many times!' I said. 'Because the tree branch came down and revealed the skeleton as soon as he came to Scotland, after it had lain hidden for sixty years.'

'Fifty,' Taylor reminded me. 'But the tree branch—' He stopped talking.

'What? It wasn't a berry heist. Larg worked that out on day one.'

'No, it wasn't. If I say something, do you promise you won't bite my head off.'

'Of course.'

Taylor snorted, then groaned. 'Everything in my stomach just moved,' he said. 'OK, since you promised not to bite my head off: the tree branch broke because someone was trying to raid the nest and steal the owl egg.'

I said nothing. I heard the scrape of Taylor's stubble on the eiderdown as he turned to face me. 'Did you hear me?'

'How long have you known that?' I tried to speak neutrally but, even to my own ears, I sounded cold.

'All the time,' he said. 'Why did you think we set up the cam and the live feed?'

'Because you're unhinged about birds,' I said. 'Taylor, if you had told us that, we would have stopped wasting our time trying to work out why Nelson might have done it!'

'I tried,' he said. 'You told me to shut up.'

'Sorry,' I said. Then I did something I don't often do. I applied work stuff to home life. I said, 'What can I do to make it up to you?'

Taylor grinned. 'Come and look at the nest,' he said, leaping up and dragging me upright too. He put his hands in the small of my back and shoved me to the window where the video camera was poking out through a gap in the curtains. 'Look,' he said. 'You won't see anything with your naked eye but look through the night vision lens.'

I squeezed one eye shut and applied the other to the viewer. In the familiar grey shades of every bear, badger and fox cam I'd ever watched Janey Godley apply a Glasgow voiceover to, I could see a pale dent of lined nest, one massive talon belonging to the babysitting parent owl and a puny, slightly damp-looking little alien with bulging closed eyes and a gaping beak.

'Aww,' I said. 'It's lovely.' Because he deserved it, not because of loveliness, believe me. 'And you saved its life. Speccy and Zippy and you.'

'We could do great things together, Kev and Trev and me,' he said, putting an arm round my shoulders and squeezing gently.

'Are you really serious?' I said. 'About staying? About living here?'

'I mean, obviously we need to talk, but I thought you would rejoice.'

'You know it might rain till May? Is Noleen serious? Is Roger? Is Della?'

'A lot of people have to have a lot of conversations,' Taylor said. 'But, apart from anything else, don't you want your baby to be British?'

'What baby?' I said. 'I'm not pregnant. I've been hammered every night and starting on the sherry before lunchtime.'

'I know. But you didn't bring your birth control pills with you.

I saw them when I was checking the bathroom at home in case I forgot to pack anything.'

'I was going to mention that,' I said. 'I mean, it's very unlikely to happen the minute I stop. After all these years. I'm sorry I bottled it over telling you. I'll take a test and get a morning aft—'

'Do you hear me complaining?' Taylor said. 'I was just surprised that you would think of having an American pregnancy, with doulas and yoga and all. And an American kid, with all the orthodontistry and after-school activities. You'd have to go to playdates with all the other moms.'

'It's not the law.'

'And watch football every weekend and call it soccer.'

'Not if we don't feed it enough to make it sporty.'

'And start thinking about colleges . . . well, tomorrow.'

'It might be too thick for college. It'll be yours, too, remember.'

'Or,' he said, 'you could have it at a dingy NHS hospital where you can swear at the nurses and they'll swear back, and your mum can babysit and spoil it, and we can all go on vacation to Paris in our car.'

It did sound lovely. 'Let's see where the rest of them have got to,' I said. 'Let's ask in the morning.'

'I owe Roger twenty bucks. Quid, I mean. He said you wouldn't stay unless everyone else stayed too. I didn't believe him.'

'The thing is, Tay,' I said. 'I love my mum and my dad. I'd forgotten how much I loved them and they're not nearly as annoying as they used to be now they've got this place occupying them. And you must know how much I love you. I pretended that clump of drain hair out there was cute because I love you so much. And, if one of my wizened old eggs does manage to pop out some human drain hair of our very own, that'll be great. But I'm an only child. And these last few years, with Todd and Kathi and Della and all their people too . . . for the first time in my life, I've been . . . I don't want to lose that now I've found it.'

'You'll never lose them,' Taylor said. 'Even if *you* went back to Cuento, Todd moved to Australia and Kathi decided to run the first laundormat in . . . Tanzania, and you'd still be as close as you are today.'

'Todd would never move to Australia.' I said. 'Because of the spiders. And Kathi couldn't survive a week in Tanzania.'

'Why?'

'Squat toilets.'

'But New Zealand is a possibility,' came Todd's voice, as he swept in through the bathroom door. 'It's mostly sheep and Scottish people, same as here.'

'Why are you still up?' I said, meaning why was he in my bedroom. *Again*.

'Roger's asleep - surprise, surprise - and I was bored. Kathi's here too, but she's hiding.'

Kathi sidled round the door. 'Diego's sleeping horizontally,' she said. 'No space for me. And, actually, I dont mind squat toilets because you dont have to touch anything.'

'Glad we cleared that up,' said Taylor.

'Go to bed, Taylor,' Todd said. 'We don't need you for this, do we?' Kathi shook her head but I was lost.

'For . . . ?' I said.

'There's no point in the *three* of us talking to the three of *them*,' he said. 'We need to talk to each other. Decide what we're going to do.'

And so, even as the house chilled down once the heating went off, I spent the last hours of that action-packed Christmas basking in the kind of warmth you don't get from radiators anyway.

FACTS AND FICTIONS

The real-world geography of Edinburgh and Midlothian is pretty much as you find it here but the village of Yule, though it bears a passing resemblance to Temple, is fictional. All the characters are fictional, as ever, although the real Gloria Naify and Beth Mullen donated generously to the Sacramento Literacy Foundation to have their names adorn the flight attendant and pub landlady in the book. Thank you, both. Finally, you really can get an ox cheek on the Christmas menu at the Dome.

ACKNOWLEDGEMENTS

I would like to thank: Lisa Moylett, Zoe Apostolides, Elena Langtry and Jamie Maclean at the agency; Sara Porter, Jo Grant, Rachel Slatter, Martin Brown, Jem Butcher and all at Severn House; my friends and family in the US and UK, cheerfully accepting the teasing they get in six books now; the NaNoWriMo community, who were right there as I pounded out the first draft last winter; Sisters in Crime, always. And Neil.